The People
vs
Cashmere

The People
vs
Cashmere

Karen Williams

www.urbanbooks.net

Urban Books, LLC
78 East Industry Court
Deer Park, NY 11729

ISBN 13: 978-1-60162-506-9
ISBN 10: 1-60162-506-5

First Mass Market Printing December 2011
First Trade Paperback Printing March 2009
Printed in the United States of America

10 9 8 7 6 5 4 3

*This is a work of fiction. Any references or similarities
to actual events, real people, living, or dead, or to real
locales are intended to give the novel a sense of reality.
Any similarity in other names, characters, places, and
incidents is entirely coincidental.*

Distributed by Kensington Publishing Corp.
Submit Wholesale Orders to:
Kensington Publishing Corp.
C/O Penguin Group (USA) Inc.
Attention: Order Processing
405 Murray Hill Parkway
East Rutherford, NJ 07073-2316
Phone: 1-800-526-0275
Fax: 1-800-227-9604

Acknowledgments

Here I go again y'all . . . book number two! God is good to me. So many amazing things have been happening in my life and I owe it to prayer and Him. Of course I have to praise my family, my mom who is still crazy but supports me so much. I even got you to get your butt on the freeway for my book signings. I love you Banna. To my sister Crystal, I love you big sis even when you're bossy because I know you'd give your arm, leg and hair on your head if I needed it. Thanks Adara for being the special girl you are. We're a team and I'm so proud of the young woman you are becoming. Thanks for letting your mommy shine. Shouts of love to my adorable nieces Mikayla, the diva, and Madison, the little hellion. My nephew Omari. My cousins Donnie, Devin, Mu-Mu, Jabrez, keep in mind I am officially a deputy probation officer now and you guys are not too young to be arrested. Thanks to Michael. Hey to my little god-daughter Lanaya, miss you.

Love you Auntie Tammy, Uncle Noonie. Thanks Faye. And to my extended family, Addie Graham, Patricia, Bobby, Antoinette, The Perdomos and Kevin.

I once again thank my friends with the utmost sincerity. Lenzie, you still haven't helped me and you still haven't bought *Harlem On Lock*! But, you still got me laughing. Cheryl, Christina W for always listening. Christina T, for your wisdom, Linda, Ronisha RIP, Misty, Sewiaa, Janel Carla, Roxetta, Gina, Tina, Valerie Hoyt, Valeen, Valerie Sweet, Tara, Pearlean, Maxine, Jennifer, Barbara, Chanin Paige, Lexus, Candis, VI, Phillipo, Latonya, Shannon, Tymisha, Kimberly, thanks for always paying homage girl, Shanni thanks for everything. Vanilla thanks for teaching me the power of prayer!

Thanks to Los Padrinos Juvenile Hall staff who made an impact on my life, Salazar, Yates, Tate, Rodriguez, Rona Rogers, Reyes, Sampson, Tara Suttle, love you Ms. Suttle, Lydia Oates, Abadanca, Regalado, Mr. Taylor, you were a father figure to me and never even knew your impact. Thanks! Pickney, it's a blessing to know the blessed, that's you, Marcet, little Mrs. Davis, Wright, Placencia, Cassas, Tolliver, Rushing, Calcote, Mama Bush, Love, Ms. Harris, Long, Mr. Walker, thanks for the shoulder that day, Gaeta, Dickerson, Washington, Westcott. Thanks for believing in me!

Thanks to all the bookstores who supported me. Extra special thanks to Smiley's Books. Candace and Lori, you really pumped my book. Thanks for all the love you showed. Thanks Chardine from Zarahas Book and Things, James and Eso Won Books, Marcus and James from Borders. Thanks to Divas of Literature, some funny and sophisticated ladies. Hey, Ki Ki! Hey Lady Scorpio! And also thanks to Dr. Mulligan, Yasmin Coleman, Apooo Books, Urban Reviews and Rhonda. Thanks to all the beauty salons and barbershops who supported me. Special thanks to Studio Six and to all the women who purchased my book. Shout out to Tiffany and Robin! Hey, Robin, what's the secret to your banana pudding? Thank you for your belief in me Heads Up Hair Salon!

To Tysha, you have helped me in so many ways. I can't wait to come out to Ohio and hang girl! And to Joylynn, did I tell you how incredibly flattered I am to be included in *Even Sinners Still Have Souls Too*? Thanks again.

To my fans, I just wanted to reserve a spot in my acknowledgment for you guys, my fans . . . Is it all right to say that? I know I'm little ole me but still . . . to say I have fans sounds so freakin' good! And it's true! So . . . to my fans (clearing my throat): You bought my book, you read my book, and you passed it on to someone else. To know I have your support means the world to me. Thank you again and again! Your kind words inspire me to keep on writing. And to my #1 fan Danika. See I told you I wasn't going to forget about you.

To my man, Terry Graham. I never had a man believe in the power of me as you do. When I say I love you baby it's an understatement. I love you to the highest capacity. I feel incredibly lucky to have you in my life. With you it seems as though there is nothing I can't do. You're my rock, my king. I love you baby.

To anyone out there with aspirations never let anyone break you down, laugh at your dreams or allow their fears of inadequacy to become yours. Use the haters as fuel to keep on going. And in the end, thank them like I'm doing here (clearing my throat): To all the haters out there from the bottom of my heart I thank you, I pray for you, you made me stronger, better . . . and as you can see I'm still shining.

Mama, I made it!

Dedications

This book is dedicated to my little woman, Adara, thanks for letting me shine. My mom for your support and love.
My sister always willing to give even when you don't have. And, Terry, the absolute love of my life, my Sugar Bear.

Chapter 1

I was cold, but it didn't mean shit. And, most importantly, after the shit that just went down, I was mad and hurt at the same time. But it didn't matter. Black had already warned me on what I had to do. I had to numb myself, and I didn't want to be dumb like my sister Desiree, who was always getting blown on that coke, didn't know what the niggas cut it with. Give me some Grey Goose and X, and I'm good. The problem was, despite how tight my clothes were, or how much makeup I piled on my face, my ass didn't look no more than the age I really was. I'll tell you more about that later.

"Aye, yo! Yo, buy me some Goose, nigga." I strutted up to a nigga I saw smoking outside the liquor store on my block. The polish was chipped off my fingers, and two of my nails were cracked and bleeding from me trying to fight Black off of me. I had a busted lip, a bloody nose, and my side was killing me. I ran my finger through my wild hair and tossed a ten at him.

"All right, but, bitch, I'm keeping the change."

"Go ahead." I stood for a moment waiting.

"Cash? Bitch, what the fuck you doing?"

I didn't bother responding to my sister Desiree as she ran down the block toward me.

She stepped in my face. "Bitch, you hear me talking to you?" She smelled like cum, dick, and balls.

"Yeah, bitch, I hear you."

"No, I don't think you do. You want Daddy to fuck you up again?"

My eyes traced the letters on her neck, pretty cursive writing. I knew I would be next, or it was another ass-whipping.

I pierced her with a look. It was her fault I was in the mess that I was in.

"Look, I said I heard you. I'm getting some drank then I'll be there, damn. Hell, I just might fuck the nigga buying me the drink."

"Whatever. But when you get fucked up this time, don't say I didn't tell your dumb ass. You'll never be a 'bottom bitch' if you don't get your shit together."

"In case you didn't know, bitch, I don't want to be a bottom ho. Fuck this shit, fuck these hoes, this track, and fuck—"

"Say it, ho. Disrespect Daddy." She balled her left fist and held it inches from my face.

I bit off my last words, anger searing from my eyes. He ain't *Daddy*. I knew where the fuck my daddy was. And since I was too weak to fight her ass, I kept quiet.

"Here."

I turned my attention to the man behind me. I grabbed the bag from his hands, and with the quickness, slipped it from the bag, uncorked the top, and downed it like it was fucking Gatorade and I was on a bike trail.

My sister stalked off, yelling, "You a stupid bitch!"

I waited for her to make her turn before I followed to my stroll.

"You too pretty a ho for this bullshit, girl. I gives a fuck about you grinding all day. Get the fuck out there and make my money. And I don't care if you have to be out there all night. Don't come back till you do." Black stomped me in the back of my head, making my ponytail slip from my head. It was all because I refused to sleep with a trick.

All the other hoes laughed, including my bitch-ass sister.

As I walked, I was getting dizzy with each step. My stomach was also churning. Which was probably due to the fact that I hadn't eaten shit that whole day, and downed the Goose way too fast.

I paused, feeling my stomach doing flip-flops on my corner with the regular hoes. I heard them whispering, "Black fucked her up."

I gripped my stomach just as the vomit flew from my mouth. When I heard siren and squad cars swoop up on us, I was too weak to even move as hoes flew everywhere. I continued to heave on the ground. When I heard the shuffle of feet and felt hands on me, and the cold steel of the cuffs on my wrist, I knew they were taking me to juvenile hall, and in that moment I didn't give a shit.

I was lifted to my feet and assisted to the squad car. Once there, I stared at the cracker officer who was looking at me like I was a piece of shit. Like he wasn't a piece of shit.

He shook his head at me in disgust. "Look at that nappy-headed nigger. She's like a wild animal."

"Fuck you!" I yelled.

"Fuck me? You nigger bitch!" he snarled, his pasty face turning red.

Despite the pain in my side and head, and the handcuffs chafing my skin, I managed a mock smile at his ass. "Naw, I take that back. Ain't that the problem, Officer? I wouldn't fuck you last week, and I still won't fuck you this week. Don't hate the player, punk bitch! Hate the muthafuckin' game. I may be a ho, but this ho got standards. And this pussy you will never get, so take me to jail. I gives a fuck!"

The pepper spray he used on my ass hurt like hell. I felt like I was having a seizure as snot flew from my nose and I was drooling. I screamed like a wild woman, my eyes cooking, "Muthafucka! You didn't have to do that shit. I wasn't resisting arrest! That's illegal use of force."

He gripped the back of my hair. "Yeah? Well, I hope your black ass can prove it."

I continued to whimper as pain pumped through me. The burning wouldn't stop and there was no air from the window because he closed both doors of his squad car.

I was determined not to beg him, but damn, I sure wanted him to wash this shit out of my eyes. But he didn't. And since I'd been in more pain when sprayed with pepper spray, I disregarded it, thinking it would go away. But the pain wouldn't stop, and truth be told, I didn't need to be arrested. I had never been. So I swallowed my pride and begged him.

"Okay, Officer, you want this pussy, come and get it." I breathed deeply as snot slid down my face and everything was a blur.

He chuckled then got in the car, turned on the ignition, and drove down an alley. He stopped the car, jumped out, and pulled me out the back seat. The burning in my eyes was easing now, until it was nothing but a tiny sting and I could see . . . see this smirk on his pasty, white-ass face.

"A deal's a deal. I want some of that black pudding. Been wanting some for a long time." He grasped my hand and rubbed it against his dick.

I sighed, raised my dress, and bent over against the car, and let him have his way with me.

And I'll bet you think I was a nasty bitch. Hell, I was, but it wasn't always that way.

Chapter 2

The good old days three years earlier

"Desiree, hurry up. Mama and Daddy will be here soon." I ran around the house making sure everything was tidy for the dinner that I'd slaved over to celebrate Daddy's promotion.

"I'm coming, shit. I don't know why you had to do this shit today of all days."

I followed my sister's yelling and found her puffing on a joint in the bathroom in her underwear. "Put that out. You know Daddy would have a fit, Desiree." When she continued to puff, I yelled, "Desiree!"

"Cash!" she retorted back, after taking one last puff and grinding it out on the windowsill.

I was so happy for Daddy. He was such a hardworking man. He had been working for the trucking company for the past fifteen years. He worked sixteen-hour shifts four, sometimes five, times a week, so we had everything we needed, and to supplement the one-income household, 'cause our mom didn't work. Mama had been home for as long as I could remember.

I felt so bad for Daddy sometimes because he worked some long-ass hours, so I made sure I always packed him a big lunch—a big jug of coffee with thick ham, bacon, tomato, lettuce, chicken salad or tuna sandwiches, fresh fruit, and his favorite snacks, like beef jerky and salty peanuts. He always gave me a big kiss before he smacked Mama in her mouth.

Sometimes they would be so into their kiss, they'd forget I was standing there. Then he'd whisper something to Mama, and they'd rush back upstairs. When he came back down, I'd say, "Oouuu, Daddy, you know you just nasty," and he'd wink at me and be out the door.

Well, now Daddy would be promoted to supervisor, which meant he wouldn't have to drive any big-ass trucks out of town. He would be home in bed at nights, which I hoped would make Mama happy—and she would keep her ass in the house now.

See, Daddy worked straight through Friday-Monday shifts, which was cool for my mom, because she never had to worry about Daddy finding about her ass backing that thang up in the club. And during the week, she would stay home and take care of all of us.

They had been married for over sixteen years. We lived in a spacious two-bedroom house in a nice neighborhood. But, don't get it twisted, it wasn't always so safe. When we'd moved here, it was so bad, prostitutes fucked in our backyard, drug addicts got high in our laundry room, and illegal immigrants slept in our garage.

Daddy tried to be nice about it at first. Then he went to the police station to get them to clean up the neighborhood, something they told him had to be a combined effort. So, shit, Daddy combined the effort by doing what the hell he knew. He would throw firecrackers in the garage and lock their asses inside, so they got popped by the firecrackers. If he caught a crackhead getting high in the laundry room, he would sneak to the door, and as soon as he got ready to step out, he hosed his ass like cops did, yelling, "Get the hell off my property!" When he saw prostitutes in our backyard, he shot them in the leg, arm, and ass with his BB gun, and they would hobble away screaming.

When they saw Daddy wasn't playing with them, they thought he was crazy as hell and stayed the fuck away from our house. A few other neighbors took notice of Daddy's actions and banded together with him 'til all the addicts, gangstas, and immigrants were gone. Then it got so safe, you could sleep with the windows open. Hell, Daddy was a legend on our street.

Mama decked our house the hell out. Every six months she would get bored with the way the house looked. Then she would go whining to Daddy, throw some pussy his way, and he would feed her hands dollars so she could go out and buy new furniture. And although I appreciated everything my parents had done for me, I wished me and my sister had separate rooms.

Truth be told, although we looked a lot alike, we were different, like night and day. We both had Mama's mahogany-colored skin, and thanks to Daddy's Creole ancestry, shiny, silky, black hair that hung to our shoulders. Lots of girls hated on us for that, which was fucking stupid to me, because we wore the same hairstyles they did. Besides, it was easier to grip coarse hair, and you could do more with it. In our case, you couldn't put too much heat and shit, so to me it was more of a nuisance than a good thing. Desiree was named after our dad. I don't know who I was named after.

Desiree inherited thin lips from who the hell knows, while I inherited Mama's pout. We both had Mama's nice nose, medium-sized and slightly pointed, and the shape of our faces had the same symmetry as Daddy's. Blessed with high cheekbones, we both had straight pearly whites. I had Mama's big ass, but Desiree got her big-ass titties.

Then the other thing that set us apart from other females was our chinky eyes, which Mama had too. She would brag and say she had Japanese in her family. But we knew her black ass was lying. We just had tight eyes, that's all. But dudes said it made us look exotic, and my sister ate that shit right up.

We were almost the same height. I was five foot seven, and my sister was five foot nine. While I was a big-time square, Desiree was a party machine. She would sneak out and go to parties, dragging me with her sometimes. And when she was tired of leaving the house, she was sneaking guys in the house to her room and fucking the shit out of them, leaving me no choice but to place my pillow over my head.

"Get dressed!" I yelled.

Desiree pointed her free hand in my face. "No. You seem to forget who the big sister is."

"Well, if you act like you are, then maybe—"

"What? Go ahead, bitch. How am I supposed to act—like you? Please . . . you a fucking peon. You ain't got shit going on."

"What you got going on, but a loose pussy?"

The smack my sister gave me sent me falling backwards into the laundry hamper. She got like that when she was high.

I stood to my feet and flew with my fists at her. "Bitch, don't ever put your fucking hands on me!"

Desiree swung back and missed.

I swiped underneath her feet with one leg, making her fall backwards. Then I dragged her by her hair. From the hallway to the bedroom, with the intent to fuck her up.

Then she kicked me sideways and tripped me over. Then we went after each other again, throwing blows.

"You high-ass bitch!" I yelled.

"No-titties-having bitch!"

"But, bitch, I got ass and you don't. And I ain't got to give my pussy to get no dudes to like me either!"

"Fuck you!"

After the punch connected with the side of her face, Desiree shoved her finger in my eye, a bitch move.

I screamed and blinked rapidly. "Bitch, you couldn't take your ass-whipping like a woman. You had to take the punk way out."

Desiree took my temporary blindness as an opportunity to leap on me and hold me down. "Talk shit now, bitch!"

My eye was burning like crazy, but I still struggled against her.

"What in the world are you girls doing?" Mama, was standing in the doorway.

Pearla Pierce was a petite, dark woman with a big, dazzling smile, full lips, a sassy, big behind, and small waist that drove Daddy wild. At least once a day Desiree and I caught Daddy playing in our mother's behind. Whether he was smacking it and saying, "Damn! Them video wenches ain't got shit on you!" or caressing it, or just plain out bending over and kissing it, he worshipped our mother's ass. And he seemed to worship her too. And, best believe, Mama had Daddy wrapped around her finger. His ass wasn't going nowhere Mama wasn't going.

Desiree looked up, and I struggled to look up at Mama, who had her hands on her lips, her eyes narrowed. Desiree shoved me one last time and adjusted her robe.

I fixed my outfit as well. "Nothing, Mama. We was just playing around, you know us girls." I waited for Desiree to corroborate my lie. I didn't want to jack up Daddy's dinner.

"Yeah, Mama, we were just playing."

"Well, girl, put some clothes on your naked tail, please. You going to drive one of them boys around here crazy. Next thing you know, they gonna be leaping through you girls' window."

The look Desiree gave me dared me to drop a dime on her ass. Instead, I smirked and wiped my burning eye.

Mama switched over to the mirror of our room and inspected her appearance. She eyed her curves and rubbed her hands down her hips, licking her lips. "Y'all little bitches betta be happy y'all came out my pussy and got my genes. All this body and this good-ass pussy!"

"Mama!" I yelled.

Desiree just smiled." Uh huh! I know that's right, Mama."

Mama looked Desiree up and down. "Too bad you ain't got no ass, Desiree, damn!" She shook her head at Desiree sadly.

"Well, Cashmere ain't got no titties, and I do!" she yelled, gesturing toward her big-ass chest.

"With that ass, she don't need none! And as soon as a nigga get to sucking on them, trust, they gonna sprout. But, as for your ass, I don't know what to say about you, boo."

Desiree glared at me angrily, like it was my fault she didn't have no ass and I did.

"Baby? Girls?"

Daddy was walking down the hallway toward our room. As Mama sashayed away, he swatted her ass.

I hugged him.

Daddy tilted my face up and looked at it. "Your eye okay, baby?"

Desmond Pierce—people called him "Deuddi P"—was born in Louisiana and was brought out here when he was five. He was a tall man, six foot four, had a handsome face, and was cream-colored with piercing, brown eyes, and a set of dimples, which I also had, and which made Desiree jealous.

Many girls around the way always wanted to get their clutches into Daddy, but over the years, he only seemed to have eyes for our mother. Although sometimes Desiree and I had heard rumors about our Mama fucking around on Daddy, we knew it was bullshit. The last time we'd heard a comment like that, we ended up beating a girl's ass.

"Fuck you, bitch!" Desiree yelled, stomping the girl with her boots.

I clocked the girl in the face. "What the fuck you know about our mommy?"

We beat that girl so damn bad that we both were suspended. Daddy was pissed and whipped both our asses; while he did it, mama looked at us sternly and said, "That's right!"

Later, behind Daddy's back, she gave us both an extra five dollars on our allowance, a high-five, and made us crab legs, our favorite dinner.

But, see, we weren't really that bad. Well, Desiree was. She didn't go to school, fucked anything that was walking, cursed, drank, and smoked weed. But, see, me and Desiree, we shared one thing in common. We had bad-ass tempers.

My butt was still rearing from the incident in my art class. I had managed to get an A on my test, but the teacher accused me of cheating. So on my test my A was crossed out with a red pen and "failed due to copying neighbor's answers" was scribbled across the top. If anything, the bitch next to me was the one who was looking on my paper. But I wasn't a snitch, so I kept quiet. But because she was white and we had the same answers, I was automatically the one who was wrong. I got the F.

Bitch, please, you got me twisted.

Anger pumped through me when I saw the white bitch relieved she didn't fail. Instead there was an A. I slid out of my seat and slowly walked up to my teacher, seated behind her desk drinking coffee.

I leaned over her desk so our faces were inches from each other, our noses damn near touching. "You mean to tell me that after all the time and hard work I put into studying for this test that you gonna give me an F? Bitch, I'm gonna kill you, your husband, your kids, and your fucking dog!"

Her eyes widened.

I snatched the coffee mug from her hand and threw it into the wall, shattering the glass, and coffee flew all over the place.

Boy, did Daddy whip my ass.

"Baby, I asked if your eye was okay."

I blinked and smiled at Daddy. "Yeah, Daddy, you know I'm okay. It takes more than this to get to Cash Money!"

Desiree sucked her teeth, and Daddy chuckled.

"Congratulations on your promotion, Daddy!"

He hugged me close again.

"Congrats, Daddy," Desiree said, hugging him stiffly.

I don't know why she had to act so damn stupid.

"Girl, put some clothes on your tail!"

"I am."

"Well, your mother already in the kitchen nibbling on tidbits, with her greedy rump. Y'all come out this room, so we can eat this food y'all prepared." Daddy walked out.

As Desiree threw a dress on, I whispered, "Aye, you did a bitch move, but reality is, you, just as usual, got your ass kicked."

"Fuck you!"

"HA!" I teased then ran from the room shouting, "I'm coming Deuddi P!" Once I hit the living room, I shouted, "You in for a treat, Daddy!"

He was flicking through the channels on the television before settling on a game. That was pretty much Daddy. He worked hard all day, came home, kissed us, spent a little time with his wife, ate, and watched television. Even though he was a handsome man, he felt no need to be out in the streets. In fact our mother did way more partying than he ever did. Every Friday she was at Tobos in Long Beach, a club where there was a dance floor, bar, and pool tables.

"So what did you cook, baby?" Pearla asked, pulling the foil off the platters on the table.

"My special, chili spaghetti, Mama, with some shredded cheese on top, you know, a little salad with romaine lettuce. You know we doing it up, because we got the romaine."

Daddy chuckled and shook his head at me. "Baby, you know you silly."

Me and Mama laughed too.

"We also got some buttered rolls, and for dessert, Daddy, I made your favorite."

Mama screeched as if the dinner was prepared for her.

"Damn, Mama! Why you gotta be so loud?" Desiree snapped, emerging from the bedroom and sitting down.

"Watch your mouth!" Daddy had an angry look in his eyes, rising from the couch and coming to sit at the dinner table.

Desiree sucked her teeth.

"Like I was saying, Daddy, I made your favorite, peach cobbler. And I even went to the market and got some vanilla ice cream to go on top of it."

"Well, hell, let's sit on down and eat," Daddy drawled. He smacked Mama on her ass.

We all sat down and passed the food around.

"So, Miss Desiree," Mama joked, "what did you cook, or did your ass stay on the phone like you usually do, Negro?"

Desiree ignored Mama and kept eating.

I felt generous and helped her out. I took a sip of my soda. "She made the salad, Mama."

"It's a good salad, and you put your foot in this spaghetti, baby!" Daddy leaned over, grabbed the platter, and spooned some more into his plate.

That shit just made it worse. I didn't even bother to look up or say thank you. That would've made Desiree angrier. "So, Daddy, you excited?" I asked.

"Yeah, baby. Monday thru Friday, nine to five, I got my own office. Shit mileage—Can't get no better than that."

"I know that's right, baby!" Mama sashayed to the fridge and grabbed a beer. She flicked the top off and took a long sip of it.

"And if I need to do overtime, I can, baby, as much as I want. And since Christmas and birthdays are coming up, I know my ass gonna be back on that road killing that overtime." Daddy winked at Mama, who walked back over and sat on his lap.

"Yeah, Deuddi," she said, "'cause there's this real pretty bracelet I been real partial too, baby. I saw it when I was at the mall shopping."

Daddy moaned, but his hands tightened around Mama's waist.

I hopped up. This was a celebration, so I turned on Daddy's favorite song. "Hey now, Daddy check this out!" It was Marvin Gaye's "Got To Give It Up."

Once the music wafted around the room, Mama stood up and began her wiggling, enticing Daddy.

I started twisting also and booty-bumped Desiree, and she stood to her feet as well and joined us. Then I pulled Daddy to his feet and danced with him as well. "Shake it, Daddy!" I yelled.

"Man, my girls growing up!" Daddy twirled me around in circles then joined me in the two-step, while Mama twisted and shook like they did when they were in their twenties, dances that neither Desiree nor I did.

"Y'all gotta do some new shit—stuff," Desiree yelled. "Come on, Cash Money, let's show them how it's done."

"All right."

We crouched down, placed our hands on our knees, and popped our booties back and forth.

Daddy fell back on the couch, just messing around, and screamed, "Lord, no!"

Meanwhile Mama tried to copy what we were doing. And, yeah, she had enough ass, but she just couldn't get it.

Me and my sister high-fived each other, the fucked-up words and the blows we threw that morning disregarded. Yeah, that night we had a blast.

Chapter 3

Things were cool for a minute. With Daddy being home on the weekends, we did more things as a family. But I knew two people that weren't too pleased—Mama, 'cause she couldn't go out like she wanted to, and Desiree, who had to be extra careful when she snuck guys in the house, with her dumb ass. I mean, I loved the hell out of Mama and my sister, and Daddy was such a good man. That should have been enough for Mama to keep her ass in the house and Desiree to keep her legs closed. One night I stayed up with him and watched a horror flick while Mama was out clubbing. Desiree was in the room getting fucked, and Daddy had no idea. When I could no longer keep my eyes open, I gave Daddy a hug and went to bed.

As I was getting in bed, Desiree was on her bed, scrubbing her pussy. I shook my head at her. Daddy would be in for a surprise to see Desiree's trampy ass. Sure as hell can't wear any damn white at her wedding, but she'd probably fake the funk, and her husband would be cool, 'cause he wouldn't know Miss Desiree really ain't so damn innocent.

"What?" she asked, rubbing herself with a washcloth, her legs in the air.

"You a nasty bitch, that's what."

She threw the washcloth at me.

I threw it back. "Mark my words, dumb ass, one day Daddy gonna find out."

"Stop hatin'."

"Whatever." I turned over and pulled the covers over my head. She had the whole room smelling like *budussy*—butt, dick, and pussy—for sure.

And, true enough, a couple nights later, the shit hit the muthafuckin' fan.

I was awakened out of my sleep by the sound of moaning and rocking, and the smell of butt, dick, and pussy was in the air again, stronger than I had ever smelled before. I froze when I heard more than two voices in the room. Maybe I was still half-'sleep. I rubbed my eyes as quietly as I could.

"Ouuu, yes! Right there!"

Pretending I was still 'sleep, I took a deep breath and flipped my body over, so I could get a good view. I moved slowly, sliding my legs and moving on my stomach. I even faked a couple of snores. But, shit, I wanted to know what the fuck was going on in here. I saw clothes scattered on the floor, shoes, drawers, shirts, pants, belts, my sister's nightgown, but there was nobody on the bed.

My eyes scanned the room, and I saw her. Them. Desiree was on all fours on her knees, like a dog, a nigga behind her bucking like he was a disc jockey, and a nigga in front of her, his dick in her mouth.

But that wasn't the biggest shock, if you could imagine. The biggest shock was seeing Daddy standing in the doorway. The small light the hallway cast in our room showed the horrified look on his face.

"Suck my dick right, bitch!"

That was it. Daddy's look changed to anger. In the next millisecond, he tore through the room and rushed them both, knocking them both off Desiree. They groaned and scurried around like mice.

"Get the fuck out of my house!" he yelled. Then he hauled off and knocked Desiree in her mouth.

She fell on the floor, screaming, "Daddy!"

Daddy didn't stop there either. He took off his house shoe, snatched her up by one arm, and began beating her naked ass with it. She was crying hysterically and begging him to stop. The dudes took the opportunity to rush out the room and, safe to assume, out the house.

Mama rushed in the room, and it took both of us to get Daddy off Desiree.

"Daddy, please stop," I pleaded.

"Des, baby, stop before you hurt her!" Mama shouted, grabbing his arm.

Daddy jerked away from Mama and flung Desiree on her bed, where she continued to cry loudly. He pulled away from me too and stalked out of the room, and Mama chased after him.

I followed her into the hallway but didn't enter the living room and just listened.

His voice was angry and hoarse. "I done worked too gotdamn hard all these years to see my flesh and blood ho'ing in my own house."

I took some more steps, hid in the corner, watched and listened.

Daddy turned to Mama. "Woman, you betta put a stop to this, and you betta do it now!"

I had never seen him shout at Mama, unless they were doing their love sessions. But that would be more like, "Pearla, damn! Give me my pussy!"

Mama rubbed her hands up and down his back. "I will, baby."

He pulled away and sat down on the couch.

Mama held her neck in both her hands. "I'll go talk to her right now, Des."

I heard her house shoes slide on the carpet. When she saw me standing in the hallway, she said, "Cash, go calm your father down."

I nodded and offered a smile, and she brushed past me.

I approached Daddy slowly and sat down next to him. He was leaning over, his face in his hands. He didn't acknowledge my presence. I leaned forward too and tugged at both of his hands, damp because of the crying. Poor Daddy, his eyes were shiny with fresh tears.

I made a cross-eyed face that I did to make him laugh when I was a kid, and he gave a small chuckle.

"Daddy, you can't sit up all night. This the night you gotta do your overtime for Mama."

"I know, baby." He grabbed my face in his hands, caressed it, then kissed both my cheeks.

"She won't do it again, Daddy."

The scene from earlier must have flashed before his eyes. They watered again.

"Y'all girls mean the world to me. Y'all always been my angels. I never cared about busting my ass day in and day out, working those double shifts, 'cause I wanted you girls to have a mom at home to raise y'all properly. This shit is not what I wanted for y'all. I'd rather die than see what I just saw—you girls being treated like tramps. I want the best for y'all—college, marriage, healthy children, a man that's gonna court you, treat y'all right. The best the world has to offer, baby, that's what I want for you girls."

"I know, Daddy. And we want that stuff too. I'm gonna give you that. And, Desiree, she gonna give you it too. She just messed up this once," I lied, "but she won't pull that stunt again."

He pulled me up by curving an arm around my waist till I was in his lap, like he used to do when I was little. To tell the truth, he never stopped doing it, letting me know, no matter how old I got, I would always be his baby, his little girl. He kissed me all over my face and said, "Darling, I love you so much. If I could, I'd have your behind cloned, so we'd have a dozen Cashmeres walking around."

"I love you too. And I'd want them all to have you as their daddy."

He told me this at least once a week. He used to tell Desiree too, but somewhere along the way, with her getting suspended from school, caught smoking and drinking, and failing all her classes, and all her promises to him that she never kept, somewhere in there, he stopped saying it to her. And I understood why.

"I ain't gonna let you down."

I hugged him close.

"I don't think you can, bay. I don't think you can."

I hoped he was right. I didn't think I was half-way near as perfect as he thought me and Desiree were. And now he saw she didn't belong on that pedestal he'd put her on.

I hoped Daddy wouldn't leave the house upset, and maybe he didn't, but he sure left tired as hell. I stayed up with him and, despite my nursing, he wouldn't fall asleep. Daddy was like that when he was awakened out of his sleep. It took him a while to fall back. So we stayed up and watched reruns of Martin's crazy ass. It was the episode where Martin's stereo was missing. Me and my dad were busting up when Brotha Man came through the window of Martin's house. By the time the episode went off, he was dozing.

Then Mama came with his lunch and uniform. "Baby here!"

Daddy's eyes fluttered open quickly.

"Remember you signed up for that overtime?"

"Mama, maybe Daddy should—"

She pierced me with a look telling me to shut up.

Daddy groaned and rose to go in the bathroom with his uniform.

"Cash Money, you know it's only one income coming up through this house. And, plus, Christmas is coming up. Girl, you betta let Daddy make that extra money."

My jawline twitched, 'cause I itched to suck my teeth. Instead, I shook my head and got up from the couch to go in my bedroom to go back to sleep, wishing Daddy would just tell Mama no and go to sleep too. He needed some rest after everything that had just went down.

When I got there, Desiree was sitting on her bed, her knees curled up to her chest. "Is Daddy mad, Cash?"

"Naw. Just don't do that stupid shit no more," I snapped, laying in my bed and pulling the covers over myself.

"You enjoying this shit, ain't you? You want him to hate me and think I ain't shit except a ho, so you can be his favorite."

I ignored her, but she continued with her silly ass. I saved her, and she still was talking shit. *What's wrong with this girl? God, strike her down next time we go to church, please.*

"Yeah, well, you damn sure ain't no betta than me, bitch. Your inner ho just ain't came out yet. But, mark my words, it will, and you gonna do worse shit than what I eva done. I'm going to make sure of that. Make sure Daddy look at you and have the same expression in his eyes that he has when he looks at me. Not like you no damn angel, but a slut."

The only reply I gave her was my middle finger.

Chapter 4

A loud crash woke me out of my sleep. *Lord, what is it now?* First, I thought I was dreaming. Then I heard the sound of glass shattering, so I didn't have time to try to figure it out. I needed to be up and ready for whatever was going down, or about to go down. I pressed the button on my alarm clock, which sounded in that moment, and jumped from my bed to see where the noise was coming from. I heard the scream again. My heart pounding, I picked up the flat iron on our dresser, just in case someone was hurting Mama. Since Daddy wasn't here to defend her, I would have to.

I couldn't wait for Desiree, but still I quickly tried to wake her. "Desiree, get up," I whispered as I slipped out the door and charged into the living room, yelling as I ran, "Muthafucka!"

But there was no one hurting Mama. She was the only one in the room. I paused my run and looked at the broken glass scattered all over the floor near her feet. Her shoulders were shaking, and her back was to me. She had the phone to her ear.

A weird pain came into my chest. "Mama," I said quietly. I sidestepped some of the glass and tapped her gently on her shoulder.

She didn't budge. "I'll be there!" she yelled into the phone. Then she turned around to face me, her face streaked with tears and snot. She was breathing hard and sniffing. She looked at me and slammed the phone into the wall.

"Mama! What is it?"

"Cashmere, Desmond was in an accident, and he's in the hospital. And it's serious."

Mama's crying was fucking driving me crazy and putting my nerves on edge as we drove to the hospital. I was crying too, but not like her. My crying was silent. And it was pissing me off too. So each time I felt a tear drop, I scratched it off my face. My sister pissed me off too, 'cause she was way too calm about the situation. She wasn't doing shit, except snoring on the back seat. *The nerve of that bitch.*

But then again I think I was just trying to make myself angry, just build up anger so there was no room anywhere in me for pain, 'cause, truth be told, we didn't know what to expect as we made our way to the Kaiser Hospital.

"Cashmere," Mama said in a hoarse voice and parked the car. "Wake your sister up."

"Desiree, get up." When she didn't budge, I reached over and punched her in the arm. "Wake up!"

She woke with a start. "Bitch!"

I ignored her and jumped out the front seat and closed the door behind me. I glanced at Mama. Her hands were shaking as she puffed on a cigarette. She ground it out with her shoe.

Desiree hopped out of the backseat and followed behind us as we walked to the hospital entrance and went directly to the lobby to the reception area. The farther we walked in the hospital, the more fearful I got. I was biting on my lip so hard, it started bleeding.

We stood at the reception booth waiting for the receptionist to acknowledge us. When she didn't, Mama said quietly, "I'm here to see my husband."

She looked at Mama before staring at a list. "Well, let's see. There's no *husband* on my list of patients on the pop sheet," she replied sarcastically.

"Bitch!" I fired, "you betta check yourself, talking to my mom like that!"

"Excuse me?"

"My sister said *bitch*, 'cause that's what you are," Desiree said, calmly rolling her neck in a half-circle. "Now read that chart, fat ass, and tell us what fucking room he's in or get fucked up!"

We stepped to her, both our fists were balled up.

She turned red and took a step back.

Mama grabbed our shirts gently and pulled us back. "Move, girls. His name is Desmond Pierce," she said softly.

"Room 113," the receptionist said stiffly, as Desiree and I continued to glare at her.

"You lucky my husband is sick, else I'd mop this muthafucka with your shiny-ass face. Come on, girls."

Wasn't shit could prepare us for what we saw, or that shit the doctor told us about Daddy when we stepped into his room.

He shook Mama's hand. "I'm Doctor Polanski. Ma'am, there's really no easy way to say this. Desmond fell asleep at the wheel of his truck, and it flipped over on the ramp. Right now all I can say is, your husband is paralyzed in every sense of the word. He can't move or talk, ma'am. I believe he is also in shock."

"Oh dear Lord, no!"

My hands went numb, a sob stuck in my throat, and my head was clammy and sweaty. I had no strength in me to cry when he said that shit. Mama couldn't stop moaning, and Desiree couldn't stop cursing. With each step to Daddy's room, my heart was slowing down. I thought I was going to pass out.

Then suddenly Mama did, and me and Desiree had to catch her before she hit the floor.

"Mama, wake up," I sobbed. "Wake up!"

Desiree had a cold washcloth on Mama's head. Her eyelids fluttered the way Daddy's did earlier when Mama woke him up on the couch. Then they came into focus, and she started crying again, as did me and Desiree.

I cleared my throat. "Ma, we gotta go see him. We got to go see Daddy."

Desiree reached for our mother's arm and helped her to her feet in the lobby just outside Desmond's room.

"I can't see him like that."

Desiree snapped, "Come on, Mama, we have to. And he might not be as fucking bad as they saying."

I rubbed Mama's back and suppressed a new sob that wanted to break loose.

Daddy looked like a vegetable, plain and simple, like he was on somebody's damn plate. It was hard as hell to look at him like that in that bed, attached to all those damn tubes. Yeah, it was hard to stomach. Was he better off this way or dead?

Mama took steps back and covered her face with her hand, shouting in a muffled voice, "Dear Lord, no! No!"

I wrapped my arms around her, and we both cried again. I tried to reach out to Desiree, but she shrugged my hand off her shoulders, ran to a corner, and bawled. Then my anger got the best of me. Mama's hug wasn't helping, so I pulled myself away, ran to the window, and punched out the glass till my hand was cut and wouldn't stop bleeding. Yep, this was the start of the end of things.

Daddy never made any progress. Oh, he could see and hear us, but he couldn't do shit else. No talking, moving, responding, nothing. Just seeing and hearing. Poor Daddy. Poor Daddy. Of all people, why did this shit have to happen to him?

Despite all the visits nurses made to our home to show us how to work the equipment, Mama had a hard-ass time when he finally came home. Her cigarette intake had increased from half a pack a day to one and a half packs a day. Every time you turned around, she had a cigarette in her fucking hand. Shit, we'd probably all die of cancer, thanks to her.

A lot of things changed after Daddy's accident. For starters, Mama stopped wearing makeup,

and getting her nails and feet done. She wore
house robes all day and looked sleepy all of the
time. She stopped doing the house chores, leaving me to do them, since Desiree's lazy punk-ass,
sure as hell wasn't going to do any of them. All
she did was run the street.

Mama stopped cooking the meals that made
Daddy fall in love with her and stay his ass home
all the time. Instead of pot roast, red potatoes,
string beans, lasagna, salad, grilled salmon and
rice pilaf, it was now frozen burritos, cup of
noodles and shit. Or I broke down and cooked
something. But that was usually a waste of food
and time, because Mama didn't bother eating,
and Desiree would get home late and crash.

Sometimes I had to stay home from school to
care for Daddy because Mama wouldn't make it
out their bed. Before I left for school, I always
checked with her to see if she was gonna get up
and tend to him. Usually, she wouldn't budge,
making me throw my backpack down and tend
to Daddy.

Today was no different. She was lying across
her bed in the same gown she'd worn the day
before. I cleared my throat as I stood in the doorway, but she didn't respond. I knocked softly on
the door. Nothing.

"Mama."

"Humph?" She rolled over and squinted her eyes at me.

"Do you need me to stay home with Daddy, or do you got it?"

"Ahh. Shit." She rubbed the sleep out of her eyes and gave me a sad smile.

I twisted my lips to the side and waited.

"Every time I go to sleep, I wake up just knowing this shit is a nightmare. Then it takes something like what you just said to remind me that it ain't."

I sat down next to her on the bed and glanced at Daddy, whose eyes were closed.

"We are gonna get through this, Mama, if we can't get through anything."

She gave me a weird look. "Shit! Cash, ain't nothing to get through. This is it. This is our life now, baby."

"Naw, the doctor said there is always a chance that Daddy will fully recover."

She chuckled. "You sweet. But I ain't gonna waste time in hope. Such a hopeless, bottomless thought. But you go ahead, sweetheart. Hold on to your hope, since I'm taking all your strength from you."

I massaged the inside of my right hand with my thumb. "Daddy gonna . . ." I stopped myself, before she could say more, and her negative thoughts rub off on me.

"Thank you for all your help, Cashmere. Why the fuck can't Desiree be like you? Huh? Why? Damn! The Lord can be so cruel." Mama stood up and scratched her dry, flaky scalp.

"But I'll tell you what—if that bitch think she's gonna sleep all gotdamn day just 'cause she was doing the devil knows what, she got me fucked up."

I rose from the bed too. "All right, Mama, I'll see you later this afternoon."

I stopped by me and Desiree's room on my way to school to check on her. She was snoring loudly, her mouth open. She didn't bother to change her clothes or wipe the makeup off her face.

"Desiree." I raised my voice and kicked at her leg. "Wake up!"

"What? Damn?" She rolled her body the other way.

"School, dumb ass. Whatchu think?"

"Fuck school. They can't school a boss like me."

I pierced her with a look. "Dig a hole."

"What?"

"Bury yourself. Mama gonna get in that ass, best believe."

She sucked her teeth at me, and I shook my head and headed out for school.

I heard the shouting even before I made it to my front door. I rushed up the steps to my house and entered it quickly to find Mama and Desiree going at it, arguing. I watched silently.

"You don't run me. I do what I want to do."

"Really, muthafucka? I run everything in this bitch, got it?"

"Shit. All you ever ran was Daddy."

Mama rushed up to Desiree so their faces were inches apart. "What the fuck you say, little girl?"

Desiree swallowed like she was forcing herself to shut up.

Mama smirked. "Yeah, bitch, you bad, but you ain't bad like me. And you think 'cause you passing your pussy around that you a big girl. Shiiit! You ain't. And don't bring up shit about your father, unless you ready for the truth."

Desiree's cheeks popped out with air. First she turned to walk away, which made me sigh with relief, but then she stopped and faced Mama again. "And what's the truth, Mama?"

"Mama, don't—"

Mama tossed her hand to me. "Shut up, Cash."

"Just say what you gotta say, Mama," Desiree whispered, her eyes narrowed.

I held my face in my hands, and Mama said nothing.

"The truth is, Mama, if Daddy ain't had to make that extra dough to buy all that dumb shit for you, this shit wouldn't have happened."

Mama's eyes watered. "Bitch!" She tapped Desiree in the forehead. "If it's anybody's fault, then know that it's yours. He was stressed about finding out his princess ain't shit but a ho that can take it up the pussy and mouth at the same time, so if it's anybody's fault—"

"Move your fingers, Ma—"

"It's yours."

I yelled, "Desiree! Don't do it."

Before I could step between them Desiree swung at Mama and struck her in the face, snapping her head back.

"Oh, hell no." Mama said.

Then they went toe to toe. While Desiree could scrap for sure, Mama was fucking her ass up, drilling her in the face with her fist. Mama dragged her by her hair and slammed her into the wall. When Desiree fell to the floor, Mama was on her again.

I rushed over and tried to pull her off.

"Get off of me, Cash. I'm your mother and you do as I say."

I obeyed and stepped back.

Mama rose to her feet and told Desiree, who was moaning, as she lay on the floor. "Next time, step up or step off. I ain't one of these bitches in the street—I'm your Mama and I'll fuck your shit all up! Now that we got that understood, clean up this mess."

Damn shit was really falling apart by the seams. I tried to help Desiree up. Mama had whipped her ass, for real.

"Don't touch me, shit!"

I pulled my hands back and walked away toward my parents' room to see my daddy.

"Hey, Daddy." I leaned over and kissed him. His skin felt so cold and lifeless against my lips. "Man, Daddy, I wish you would get your butt out of this bed so you can come in here and watch the game with me. You know what teams are playing tonight? I'll give you a little hint—I hope Kobe's behind passes that ball, but he probably won't. Guess who the Lakers playing, Daddy? The Heat. I know it's crazy, huh? After the way Kobe burnt up Shaq's spot, now he playing against him. I'll bet Shaq gonna let him have it. And Dwayne Wade playing too. Sound like a dream team to me."

Daddy blinked.

"Awww, don't get mad at me 'cause your boys might not make it to the championship and get that ring. There's always next year."

I heard the toilet flush. Mama opened the door and yelled out, "Don't bother. He can't, and he ain't gonna say shit!"

I rolled my eyes and ignored her. "Yeah, so, Daddy, don't get mad when they lose." I used my hand to rub his legs and arms while I talked.

The doctor had said to give him constant stimulation. I placed a small ball in one of his hands, hoping he would grip it. I knew Mama wasn't doing this with him, and Desiree wouldn't spend more than five minutes with him. But I chalked it up to her hating seeing him this way. But, then again, I didn't like seeing him this way either. But we had to do what we had to do. It shouldn't be no different for her ass. But I was done arguing with her dumb ass.

Thirty minutes later Mama emerged from the bathroom all dressed up in a tight-fitting black top, a short white skirt that, if she bent over, all her ass would fall out, and a tight-fitted belt around her waist. She completed her outfit with the skinny stilettos. She made up her face and, for once, styled her hair.

"Where you going?" I demanded.

She gave a curt, "Out."

Chapter 5

The next day wasn't no different, only a little worse. When I came home from school, I noted that the kitchen was dirty. Fuck, the whole house was. I puffed out air impatiently. The laundry hadn't been done, and all the meat in the freezer was going bad.

After throwing down my backpack, I washed the dishes and waited for the load of clothes in the washer to finish, while I cooked pork chops in one pan, and chicken and hot links in two other pans, so they wouldn't go bad. At least we'd have some cooked food.

Desiree was missing in gotdamn action, and I hadn't caught a peek of Mama.

Once I had got the house together, I went in Mama's room. She was guzzling down some Grey Goose, her eyes glued to the TV screen. The longer I stood in the doorway, the more I started to notice something wasn't right. The room didn't smell like the cinnamon potpourri she kept in there, it smelled like shit. And it could only be for one reason.

"Mama?"

Her silly ass ignored me.

I marched over and stood in front of the TV, trying my fucking hardest not to sass her. "Why hasn't Daddy's diaper been changed?"

She offered no reply.

I raised my voice slightly. "Mama!"

She tossed the bottle on the carpet, causing it to spill, jumped up and ran into the bathroom. "Gotdamnit! You got a problem with how I do things then you do the fucking shit." She slammed the door behind her.

I took a deep breath, grabbed the gloves, wipes, and extra diaper, and turned to Daddy. "Shit," I mumbled. Since the shit had obviously been on Daddy for a while, it was smeared all over his butt, boxers, and pants.

"Okay, Daddy, I'm gonna get you all cleaned up."

I strained to lift the plastic pad underneath him, to not soil the bed. "Just give me a second and you'll be all clean. I'll even put some of your favorite cologne on you."

I wiped him down with the damp towels, wiping around his penis and testicles, then his ass. Then I tossed the soiled wipes on the floor, hoping Mama would step on them, so she knew what it felt like to have shit on her.

Even if Daddy was paralyzed, that didn't give her the right to fucking neglect him. Damn, I wished I could be like Desiree sometimes and speak exactly what's on my mind.

Once I had him squeaky-clean, I struggled with his legs, pulling some clean boxers and pajama pants on him. I sprayed some of his cologne on him, like I'd promised. I then greased his scalp, and brushed his hair like he liked it, until his pretty hair waved up.

After I went back into the kitchen to cook the other meats, Mama made another appearance. She slipped behind me and hugged me, but I pulled away from her and kept my focus on the meat sizzling in the pan.

"Don't be mad at me. I just have a lot of shit on my mind, Cashmere. Baby, I'm so tired of being cooped up in this damn house. I can't go nowhere, do shit, but care for Desmond. He won't move, won't say shit—"

"'Cause he can't."

"I know. But on a woman it's hard."

"It's hard on all of us."

Mama wrapped her arms around me and had her head on my shoulders. As she talked, I felt the vibrations of her voice on my skin. "I got to worry about bills and shit," she said. "It's a lot you don't know, and a whole lot you don't understand."

I finally turned and noticed she had on another one of her getups.

I shook my head and asked dryly, "Going out?"

She gave a nervous laugh. "Baby, I just wanna go get a drink. That's it, Cashmere . . . dance a couple of songs." She swayed and snapped her fingers. "Ease a little tension out. Then I'm gonna come back home and be a rejuvenated woman. I'll clean, cook those bomb-ass meals I used to make, and take good care of Daddy. I promise, boo. Just give me tonight."

I stared at her for a long time then turned back to the bacon in the frying pan in front of me. My tone was acidy. "Do what you gotta do, Mama."

She squealed, "Thank you, baby." Then she gave me a quick peck and dashed out of the house.

I wondered if she knew that Desiree had been gone for the past two days.

Chapter 6

Man was Christmas a fucked-up day. We opened our gifts in silence, like they didn't mean shit, when they had such a value on them. And, boy, was it some really nice stuff.

Daddy truly was the sweetest. He bought me a portable DVD player, an iPod, a new pair of Jordan's, and a Rocawear sweatsuit. He got Desiree a camera cell phone to replace the one her dumb ass lost, portable Nintendo DS, 'cause even though her ass was almost grown, she was a big-ass kid, and some shoes like mine, with a matching sweatsuit.

He bought Mama a bad-ass Michael Kors bag, a flat-screen TV, and a beautiful tennis bracelet, but she didn't even bother to open up her gifts. We did it for her. She just sat on the couch with this far-off expression in her eyes and sipped on her wine. I knew exactly how she felt . . . well, minus the guilt.

The gifts were really nice, but they didn't really bring joy or excitement out of us. The gifts represented all the hours of overtime, and sleep Daddy had sacrificed because he cared about making us happy, but he couldn't move, nor feel his damn toes, or even wiggle them. That made the day fucking bitter.

Mama threw her glass down. "Naw! Fuck this shit! I can't take this no more," she said, and started running toward the hallway.

Me and my sister looked at each other before chasing after her to her bedroom.

Before we even made it her bedroom door, we heard her shout, "Muthafucka, say something!"

When we got there, we found her on top of Daddy, straddling him and shaking his shoulders. "Speak, Desmond. I'm sick of this shit!"

"Get off of him!" Desiree yelled.

Mama gave Desiree a dirty look. "Fuck you, Desiree!" Then she turned her attention back on Daddy. "Talk, damn you!"

I rushed forward and grabbed Mama's hand as it was in midair. She was about to slap Daddy's face. "Get off him!"

Her eyes challenged mine, but I wasn't backing down. I held my breath and my gaze, and slowly the power in hers disappeared.

She slid off Daddy and then snatched her hand out of mine. "Fuck this shit!" She marched up to her closet, yanked it open, and pulled out a skimpy dress, before disappearing in the bathroom.

I pasted a smile on my face and turned to Daddy. "Mama was just playing, Dad."

Desiree stayed planted in the doorway and shook her head so hard, I thought she was gonna get a crook in it.

Five minutes later Mama emerged in a more slutty dress than the one she wore the night before. Her face painted, she had on enough damn perfume for me, Desiree, Daddy, and her ass. She walked out, clickety-clacking her heels. "I'm going out," she snapped. "Don't bother waiting up."

I kept my head down and didn't acknowledge her, and Desiree tossed a hand at her.

"Come on, Daddy. Let's get you a bath, so you can get a good night of sleep."

"Man, this is starting to be a bit too much. I'm going to bed." Desiree stormed out the room, much like Mama did.

I was able to give Daddy a sponge bath, feed him, and send him to bed. Desiree's punk-ass was knocked out, 'sleep, so I knew I had to do the cleaning up. The damn turkey I had slaved over went to fucking waste, so I stuffed it in the fridge, along with the dressing, greens, macaroni, peach cobbler, and pound cake I'd made. Then I took a long shower and took my tired ass to bed.

When I heard moaning that was loud as fuck, I almost thought it was Desiree, but it wasn't. She was knocked out and snoring.

A surge of hope hit me. Maybe Daddy was moving again and fucking the shit out of Mama. I tiptoed out of my room down the hallway, passed the bathroom, and slipped over to my parents' room.

I was horrified to see Mama not only fucking a man in Daddy's house, but she was fucking him in the same room she shared with Daddy.

"Ouu, baby, fuck me!" she moaned, her titties jiggling in the air as she rode on top of some clown.

I glanced at Daddy, hoping his eyes were closed and he couldn't see the shit. I didn't say nothing, just ran back into my room and closed the door.

I felt like smoking some weed, maybe taking a swig from one of Mama's bottles of "feel-good," which she had a lot of nowadays. I was stressed and mad. Mad, 'cause I was too damn young to be stressed. I should've been hanging out with my friends at the movies, the mall, the beach, or in some boy's room getting my titties or pussy licked for the first time, but instead I was playing the role of a wife, nurse, housekeeper, and damn cook. And Mama wasn't doing nothing, except clubbing and fucking—Desiree and her, both.

Mama interrupted the little bit of free time I had as I sat on the porch collecting my shitty-ass thoughts. It had been two months since the accident, and I now had to face the fact that Daddy would stay the way he was. The hope I had before didn't do shit but hurt me more. All I was doing by having that hope was prolonging the pain by running away from reality. Hope wasn't just a bottomless thought, it will kill your ass. Morgan Freeman had said that shit well in *The Shawshank Redemption*.

I rubbed my sleepy eyes and took a sip of water. I had just cleaned, cooked, and got Daddy straight. Now I was sitting on the porch staring out at kids coming home from school. I ended up not going today 'cause Mama wouldn't get herself up yet again. And who in the hell knew where Desiree's worthless ass was?

"Hey, Cash."

I didn't bother looking when I heard her voice and the shuffle of feet behind me. I continued staring off, even though my focus mentally wasn't on what was taking place in front of me.

"Mama fucked up, huh?"

I glanced her way finally as she rubbed her arms like she was cold. I was cold too. Inside.

She sat down next to me so close, our thighs were touching, so I scooted over slightly and felt her stiffen when I did. But then she pretended she didn't feel it and it didn't bother her, when I knew it did. Oh, well.

"Boy, yo Daddy sure loved me. I say he loved me, 'cause I don't know if he still do." She smiled, her eyes glazed with tears. "But I sure do love him. Hell, I don't know if anything is gonna ever change that shit. That's what worries me."

I bit my lip as she pulled out a cigarette, lit it, and took a long drag. I was tempted to ask her for one, but when she continued to talk, it cancelled the want. *Thank God. Addictions in people is something ugly.*

"Remember how much fun we used to have. Your Daddy, boy, was so silly . . . a straight fool. But he has always been the kindest, sweetest man I've ever known my whole life." She licked her dry lips. "He's been a friend, protector, lover, provider, and he did it all without ever making me feel neglected in any of those areas, Cash."

"Then why can't you do the same for him?" I spat out angrily.

She smiled. "'Cause it ain't in me. It just ain't. Some people equipped with the right stuff, some ain't. That's why God put people in the position in life they in. He looks out less for some and more for others. You ain't nothing like me. That's why we ain't never had no drama all these years. But your sister"—she blew out a circle of smoke—"shit, Desiree is a reincarnation of me. Her downward spiral started when she was ten years old, soon as them titties started sprouting out. She ain't gonna be shit."

"Does that mean you ain't shit?"

"Naw. See, that's the twist. I wouldn't have been shit if it wasn't for yo Daddy."

I shook my head at her fucked-up logic. "You ain't making a bit of sense."

She ground out her cigarette. "Oh, it will one day. Like I said, some people built with the good stuff, and some ain't. God looks out more for those who ain't got it and less for those who do."

"What does this have to do with me?"

"In other words, baby girl, life is gonna be hard as hell on you, so figure it out." Mama pointed her finger at me. "But there is one more catch. Those people He looks out for more tend to find a way to fuck up, so they end up in the same fucking barrel as the ones made of the good stuff."

I hung on to every word, but just as quickly dismissed the shit as babble. Maybe later on I'd have the time to decipher her words and determine if something there made sense, or if it was all pure butt shit. *Mama's moment of deepness.*

"You would take good care of Daddy, wouldn't you?"

I pierced Mama with an evil look, at what she was implying with her question.

She just stared down at her bare toes. "Shit, yo Daddy loves the hell out of you. Things gonna always be cool 'cause, as long as he got Cash Money, he's going to be okay."

I looked at her for as long as I could before my face crumbled. I covered it with both my open palms and cried into them. She pulled them away, kissed both my tear-stained cheeks, my mouth, then both my hands, and then she walked away.

That was the last time I saw or heard from Mama.

Chapter 7

"Now check this shit out. Y'all bitches have to pay me this month, and I don't care if y'all have to sell your ass to do it."

Me and my sister sat on our Aunt Ruby's beat-up couch as her fat, bubble-shaped ass paced back and forth in front of us, slapping one of her flabby hands into the other. So much for family. Our mom had ran off, and because me and my sister were still minors, my aunt collected us. And after all that we'd been through, the fat bitch was demanding money from us.

Aunt Ruby was dark-skinned like our mom, but nothing else like her. I guess Mama took all the looks, 'cause she didn't have none. For real. She had a smashed-down nose and beadie-ass eyes. And her ass was so big, you could put a *wide load* bumper sticker on it, and no one would question it.

My aunt was dressed in a old-ass muu-muu, which clung to her. Imagine that shit—a muu-muu clinging to a fat ass—not an appealing sight in the muthafucking least.

There was a hole on one side, so all you saw was an old, tired, wrinkled-up nipple, and splits all in the bottom, showing mounds of cellulite. She looked like a tar-colored Beanie Baby. A chocolate popsicle. No damn curves, just fat.

The only positive attribute she had was that the fat bitch could cook. But, shit, I'm sure you'd assume that. I'll bet the first thing people probably said to her after first meeting her was, "I'll bet you fry up a mean-ass chicken," or "How much gumbo filé do you put in your gumbo, girl?"

She had a double fridge in her kitchen, and a lock and bolt on that bitch, not to mention a small fridge in her room, and a fridge and a meat freezer in her garage. Can you say, *Gluttonous to the muthafuckin' extreme*? And she kept them all under surveillance. If you walked anywhere near one of her fridges, she would yell, "You betta stay the hell out of my refrigerator!"

She continued in her deep voice, sounding like Darth Vader from *Star Wars*. "If y'all don't cough up three hundred apiece, y'all going in the muthafuckin' system, 'cause I don't want no kind of they support. I'm still on Section Eight, and it would raise my rent. And, on top of that, I got to be assured this gonna work. If I tell the courts your mama gone and I take full responsibility of y'all, then I'm stuck." She studied us and shook her head. "And I'm not so sure if I wanna be stuck." She twisted her lips to one side. "Plus, y'all mammy may come to her senses, what little she has." She started coughing.

Desiree whispered, "There she blows."

I cleared my throat to cover my laugh.

"And, girls, let's face the facts. Your mammy, despite how fine and sexy she thought she was, is a self-centered bitch. And she fucked y'all off."

When my sister made a growling sound, I elbowed her quickly.

"Now first things first—yo Daddy can't stay here."

Me and Desiree both said in unison, "What?"

"He can't. Ain't no one to care for him. He already gone anyway. I hauled his ass off to Pine Meadows. And there ain't shit y'all can do about it." Aunt Ruby placed both her hands on her fleshy hips.

I sighed loudly and slapped myself in the forehead at what this bitch was telling me.

Desiree mumbled, "This is bullshit."

"Y'all got a problem with it, then run up on me. I guarantee, if you do, y'all asses will be out on the street." She made a fist with one of her hands.

I held Desiree down. There was fury in both our eyes.

"Why didn't you tell us?" I asked as calmly as I could.

"I ain't got to tell y'all shit. I owe y'all no explanation for anything I choose to do. He don't belong here. He better off there anyway. He'll get the help that he needs."

I sighed again, and Desiree grunted.

"It's a nice place too. Y'all welcome to visit if y'all like. Matter of fact, y'all need to go down to the social security office and get that money transferred over to them."

"How we gonna do that if the money is in Mama name?"

"Exactly. Desiree, you look the oldest and look more like your mom—worn-out—so y'all going to take y'all ass down there, and Desiree, you act like you Pearla Pierce and figure out why they ain't sent a check this month. And, like I just stated, make the recipient of the money over to Pine Meadows."

"I wanna see Daddy," I said defiantly.

"Honey, you can see him whenever you want to. You can live there if you like. But I'll tell you this once and one time only—take your ass down to the social security office, or be on the street."

Me and Desiree huffed and puffed as we slid off the couch to leave.

"Oh, and when you get back, I want my hair braided." Aunt Ruby looked pointedly at me, as if I had no choice.

My only question for her was, "What do you want braided? The little hair you have on your head, your beard, or the hair on your chest?"

After her fucking sermon about what we could do and couldn't do, could eat and couldn't eat, me and Desiree left the tiny-ass bedroom that used to belong to her eighteen-year-old son, who was locked the fuck up. And her oldest daughter who was on crack, and she didn't know where she was.

"Hey, ladies."

We brushed past our uncle by law. My aunt's husband, Byron the bastard, was a tall, lanky, light-skinned dude with an Afro. And though the nigga was lanky, he had a big-ass beer belly. He was regular-looking, except the nigga was cock-eyed. And that shit is worse than trying to figure out whether or not a cross-eyed person is looking at you. With a cockeyed person, you couldn't tell when they weren't. But the other fucked-up part about him was, where we normal people had two front teeth, that nigga had three. He said it was because he was born a twin and he got one of his teeth.

I said, "Naw, you just one ugly muthafucka."

The nigga didn't work either. He spent all his time picking up broads and hanging in titty bars.

"Looking good, Cashmere. You got a man yet, or do you need to be broke in?"

"Go beat your little shit," Desiree told him.

I laughed loudly.

"You betta watch your mouth, Desiree, before I tell Ruby on your ass."

"Tell her, ugly muthafucka."

He ignored Desiree, knowing he couldn't win an argument with her.

"And get your eyes off of my sister's ass. She wouldn't piss on you, bastard, if you was on fire."

"Let her tell me that," he shouted as we walked out the house.

"Fuck you, R. Kelly!"

"Man, his ass is a fucking pervert," I yelled as we jumped down the porch steps. We hadn't been there long, and he had already rubbed up against me and jiggled his dick and balls at me.

"I know, girl." Desiree said, studying the pamphlet with the location of Pine Meadows.

"Man, I can't believe she just shipped him out like that, like he ain't shit," I said as we waited at a light.

"Well, Cash, I mean, maybe it's better off this way. I mean, neither of us can take care of him. I'm seventeen and you only fourteen. We got school and shit."

"I was doing a good job without you or Mama."

The light changed to green, and we crossed.

"I know you did. I was being selfish. But I'm just saying that now we can't do it twenty-four hours a day. And when we not at home, are you comfortable with Ruby's evil ass caring for him? She probably wouldn't feed him or bathe him or do the therapy with him in the way he's supposed to be taken care of."

She was right. I nodded.

We turned a corner and walked slowly.

"Desiree, I'm so stressed. I wish—"

She stopped me in mid-sentence. "I do too, but wishing ain't gonna change the state of things. Let's just check this place out to make sure he straight, and if he is, we'll go to this social security office to get things straight."

I smiled and nodded, happy I could lean on Desiree for once.

"Look up, little sister. Here it is."

Still I hesitated at the door. Why? Because I felt like I was legitimizing Daddy being abandoned if I were to leave this place without leaving with him.

"Come on, little sister, go on inside," Desiree coaxed. "It don't look too bad out here, so it can't be too bad inside."

"Yeah, it does look nice."

And it was. Daddy was in a nice place in a nice-ass room equipped with everything that he needed. They had nurses around the clock who looked and acted real professional. Every time they tended to Daddy, they washed their hands and put on a fresh set of gloves. They did therapy with him too. Just being there gave me my hope back, hope that Daddy would get better.

"This place is perfect, Desiree," I told her.

"I know, girl."

"And everybody so nice."

I nodded my head over and over again. They even had a swimming pool. *That would make Daddy happy*, I thought. But then I remembered that he couldn't feel anything. But maybe they knew what to do and would figure out a way.

"Come on, it's getting late. And the visiting hours are up in a few minutes."

As we walked to the exit, the lady at the front desk stopped us. "Are you young ladies related to Desmond Pierce?" she asked.

"No."

I pinched Desiree's arm. "Yes, we are."

"Okay. Well, according to his ledger, we still have not received the deposit. We offered a Ruby Malone an extension because of the circumstances, but we really do need the deposit to continue his stay here. If we don't get it in another two weeks, we are going to have to release him."

I bit my bottom lip, stress building back up into me just as I was feeling good. And even though we didn't have a quarter of that money, I asked, "How much is the deposit?"

"Nine hundred and seventy-five dollars."

I gritted my teeth. *Shit!*

"Thanks. We'll have it to you real soon," Desiree assured her, and the perky blonde-haired lady smiled.

I nodded as well. "Please take care of our Daddy," I pleaded, and she smiled at me in a soothing way.

After we walked out, I asked," Why did you say no, dumb ass?"

"'Cause, shit, never ever volunteer info to anybody. Mama—"

"Fuck Mama."

"Looks like she fucked us and Daddy," she said dryly.

"Desiree, you know what this means—we gotta go to that office and you gotta act like Mama to a T. Shit, we need that money transferred over."

We didn't really do much. Desiree just changed her getup, fixed her hair like Mama fixed her hair, and put on makeup as well.

"How does it look, Cash?"

"Cool, Desiree."

Shit! How the fuck can they remember Mama to a T?

And, plus, I remembered she mailed that paperwork into them. I don't think her lazy ass ever stepped foot in that office. Long lines just weren't her style. And since Daddy catered to her, she never had to wait in any of them. If it was time to do the taxes, get the clothes from the cleaners, or get the car registered, Daddy, despite being tired from work and having red eyes from lack of sleep, always went while she sat her ass on the couch and sipped Alizé.

And being here, I know how Daddy must have felt. The shit was getting on my last fucking nerves, all the damn people coughing, bumping into me, bad-ass kids stepping on my feet and not bothering to say sorry or excuse me. Man, if me and Desiree were to ever do that in public, Daddy would wax our ass.

"How long we been here?" Desiree asked me, sucking her teeth and patting her hair.

"Long enough," I said. "It's been an hour and a half."

"That bitch said fifteen minutes."

"This is some bullshit, for sure," I mumbled, leaning against a counter.

"Fuck this! They gotta call us next."

Our eyes desperately scanned the monitor. We were number fifty-one. We had to be next.

"Fifty-three."

"Hell no." Desiree snatched away from the counter and marched to the information desk, and I followed her.

"Excuse me."

The old, white, funny-looking, four-eyed lady raised her brows at Desiree.

"We're number fifty-one, and we were skipped."

She took a deep breath as if we were hassling her. Like it was an aggravation for her to have to do her own damn job. *Weird-looking ass.* I wanted to yell, "Crow face!"

She walked toward us and said, "Have a seat. There are only two people working in the back. That's why there's been a delay. She'll be right out."

"Thank you," Desiree said stiffly, tilting her head to one side as she said it.

Desiree was freaking me out, acting just like Mama.

Another woman, who was black and appeared to have an even worse attitude than the previous woman, came from behind a door and called our number. She held the door open impatiently, her eyes staring at the ceiling until we reached her. The dainty-looking chick, light-skin, weave-*alicious*-looking, with some wavy weave on her head, had on a navy business suit, some matching heels, and was doing a little too much, if you ask me.

As soon as we reached her, she backed up a bit to let us pass her. Then as we stood there, she locked back the door without acknowledging us by saying hello, and began switching away, making a clackety-clack sound with her cheap-ass-looking stilettos. I knew some quality stilettos when I saw them, 'cause Mama had tons of them. Them weren't it. It looked like she got them muthafuckas from Payless, and the strap was going to give out on her ass any second. And I'm not knocking Payless, but don't wear Payless and fake the funk.

We followed behind her till we got to a set of cubicles. There was only one other lady seated across from her, a fat, older, white woman on the phone talking about her grandson walking for the first time.

Me and Desiree both shook our heads. She was getting paid to do shit, while we were waiting to be seen.

I then focused my attention on this woman in front of me and tried my hardest not to laugh at her. She still had not mouthed a word to us. Instead, she had cleaned the dirt out of every damn finger on her hands, traced her brows with her fingers, straightened her suit, and then added some more lip gloss to her lips.

After all of this, she turned to us and said in a bored and distracted voice, "How can I help you, ladies?"

"Well, the thing is, I need my husband's social security to be transferred over to the—"

"Name?" She hit a key on her computer, cutting my sister off.

My eyes narrowed.

"His name is Desmond Pierce, and my name is—"

"Didn't ask for yours. Give me a second to verify that the information you gave me is correct," she snapped, drilling away on her keyboard.

Desiree and me locked eyes. She told me to stay calm, but I couldn't help but feel that this bitch was being hella rude for no damn reason. But, shit, this was for Daddy, so I had to keep my cool. Hell, if Desiree could, then I could.

"Birth date?"

"I was born—"

"Once again, I don't need *your* information, I need *his*, since the claim is in *his* name."

"Two, thirteen, sixty-three," I replied in an icy voice.

Her eyes locked with mine, and she twisted her lips to one side of her mouth. "Is that correct, ma'am?" she asked Desiree, while continuing to look at me.

Desiree took a deep breath and nodded.

She drilled her keys some more. "I see here there's a note attached. Let me read it." Her eyes scanned the screen. She shook her head. "According to this note, his benefits were terminated, effective December fifteen, two thousand and six."

"Naw, that can't be right," Desiree cried.

She smirked. "Oh, it can't? Our records show you were given a termination letter on December first, two thousand and six, warning you that you had two weeks to submit paperwork to verify eligibility that he was still in the home and still incapacitated."

I closed my eyes and shook my head. Mama didn't turn in those forms like she was supposed to. *Fuck!* "Well, can't we turn in the forms now?" I asked.

"Nope. You would have to re-apply, and in order to do that, you have to wait at least ninety days after the date you were terminated. That's the rules."

We didn't have ninety fucking days to wait for the money. We needed the shit now. Desiree rubbed her forehead and asked, "Can you make an exception? My fa—husband doesn't have that—"

She gave us a cold look and held her tongue in front of her teeth. "That's . . . the . . . rules—same for everybody,"

"But we have no—"

She took out her nail file and began on her nails, as if we were dismissed. "Not my problem. You should have kept up with our paperwork. Start being responsible instead of asking for a handout."

Desiree jumped out the chair and leaned over the desk. "Who the fuck you think you talking to, huh? Ugly, unsympathetic bitch!"

"You a bitch!" she fired.

I jumped up too and slapped all the papers off her desk, and they flew in different directions, making a scattered heap on the floor. "Who the fuck you calling a bitch? You don't know us. We'll kick your ass right here, right now and don't give a fuck who sees. Then we'll call customer service on your ass."

The lady in the cubicle opposite of her got up and slipped away. "I'll get help, Monique," she said over her shoulder.

Monique tried to stand up, but when she saw me and Desiree take a fighting stance, ready to fuck her shit up, she sat right back down and yelled, "Ron!"

"Fuck Ron! You think you hard, then step the fuck up . . . please." I wanted to ease some of this tension off. "You'll get a bone stomped out of your ass."

Before we could get a lick in, a man rushed toward us. He was tall, handsome, and light-skin, with a goatee and a low fade. "Ladies, is there something I can assist you with?" He was calm, despite the tension in the room, and how heated we all looked. Slyly, he stood in front of her ass as she was now on her feet.

Desiree yelled, "Yeah, hold her trick ass, so we can roll her up."

He hid his smile, pursing his lips. "Ladies, I can't let you do that. But, whatever the issue is, I'm sure that I could be of some assistance to you. Why don't you ladies step into my office. Monique, go take a break."

She huffed and puffed as she rushed past us. Once she was gone, he escorted us to his office.

Based on the size of it, and all the plaques he had on his wall, I knew he had to be somebody important, and maybe, just maybe, he could offer some type of assistance to us. So I checked my attitude and gave him a tight smile. It was the best I could do.

"Have a seat, ladies, and tell me what the problem is." He sat behind his desk.

Me and Desiree both sat down in the chairs across from his.

Desiree took a deep breath. "My husband's benefits have been stopped, and that bit—lady is saying we have to wait three months before reapplying. We need that money now. We can't wait that long. I ain't never heard about no rule like that."

Truth was, we didn't know shit about any of this, but still I thought Desiree was doing real good, so I continued to play along, nodding my head.

"I apologize for not following up with the paperwork. I must have forgotten to turn in the claim form last month, but that didn't give her the right to talk to us the way she did, like we got shit on us."

He leaned back in the chair, his hands clasped together. He looked from Desiree, who was biting her lip, to me. When he wouldn't stop looking at me, I looked down at the carpet.

"If you don't mind me asking, where is your husband now?"

"He is at Pine Meadows, and his payment is past due. They gave us two weeks to pay. That's all we came for, sir, was to get the money transferred over to the home so he can stay there, sir. That's all."

His phone rang before he could offer a reply. "Excuse me." He scooted over to it, and answered, "Ron speaking. Yes . . . Yes . . . Fine." He hung up and stood quickly. "Ladies, I have a meeting to attend that can't wait, but I'm sure if you come back to the office, say about six, I should be done, and I can assist you with your dilemma. I may even be able to cut you ladies a check today for your troubles. I just need you ladies to do three things for me."

We both leaned forward and listened intently.

"The first thing I need you to do, ma'am, is to keep up-to-date with the paperwork. The second thing I need you ladies to do is meet me back here at?"

"Six," we both answered. He chuckled. "Good. And the last thing I need you two do is smile. Ron is going to take care of you, promise." And we did.

As we walked back up to the social security office, Desiree said, "Cash, I don't know about this fool. What if he just said that shit to calm us down so we wouldn't whip weave-alicious ass, and when we get there his ass won't be there?"

"It's possible he could be lying, but we at least gotta see. And he was hella cool."

"Yeah, he was cool, not like that bitch. Man, I wanted to whip that ass."

I laughed as we turned the corner. The office was now only half a block away.

Desiree said, "Hell, we might catch her on the street one day."

I was silent. I knew we needed to put our focus into getting that money for Daddy.

We climbed the steps and entered the office. "Is it closed?" I asked as we went inside.

"If it was, would the door be open, Cash?"

I bit the inside of my mouth. Hell, the door was open, but wasn't a muthafucka up in there. The lights was off and shit.

"Ladies, I'm in my office. Come on in," a voice yelled.

Desiree gave me a shove. "Go."

I quickened my steps and walked through the door, past the cubicles, ignoring the urge to fuck up Monique's desk. It looked so neat and tidy. But I shook the thought out.

We both stepped inside to find him at his desk sipping some shit from a glass. He looked relaxed too. His jacket was off, and his tie was loosened around his neck.

The paperwork made a crumpling sound in Desiree's hands as we both paused at the door.

"Come in, ladies, and have a seat."

Why, oh, why was the muthafucka playing music?

Some type of jazz, the kind Daddy used to play on his days off from work. Wasn't shit relaxing about this.

"Would you ladies like a drink?"

I remained standing, and so did Desiree.

"Naw. We can't stay too long," she said. "We just came to drop the papers off and see about the check you said you could get."

He sat the drink down, rose from behind his desk, and sat on the edge of his desk. He licked his lips and smiled. "Ahh, yes, the check and the paperwork. I'll take care of this issue, if you take care of me, *Desiree* and *Cashmere*."

My eyes widened.

Desiree kept her cool. She cleared her throat and said, "No, I'm Pearla and—"

"No, you're not. I've met her before personally."

Desiree's eyes now matched mine.

"You ladies are beautiful, especially you." He winked at me.

Desiree stammered, "B-b-but—"

He continued smoothly and calmly. "No buts, ladies—unless they are yours." He chuckled at his own dumb-ass humor.

We didn't.

He continued, "Now here are the stipulations. If y'all take care of me like she did, I'll handle this right here and now. But before I do . . ."

We watched in silence as he unzipped his pants, pulled out his dick, and stroked the shit right in front of us like he was in the privacy of his own damn home.

Ain't this a bitch! You nasty bastard.

With the reflex of a jackrabbit, Desiree grabbed the drink on his desk and flung it in his face. "You piece of shit! We trying to help Daddy, and you trying to fuck us?"

While he was temporally blinded, I lunged at him and slapped him across his face with an open palm so hard, my hand stung. "You a nasty, perverted muthafucka! You old as our damn daddy!"

Desiree grabbed his phone off his desk and bashed him in the head with it, and he screamed and doubled over in pain.

Then we tag-teamed his ass, throwing blows all over his ass, kicking him in his dick and nuts, and shoving him all around his office.

"We ain't no fucking prostitutes, punk-ass!" I screamed.

"Bitches!"

"Yo mama!" I yelled.

"Bastard!" Desiree yelled.

I grabbed Desiree before she could go after him again, crouched in the corner of his office like a chump, and we ran out of the office like some runaway slaves.

We didn't stop running until we were five blocks free of that place. We stopped in front of a liquor store to catch our breath.

"Just what the fuck we gonna do now?"

Desiree took a deep breath, which didn't slow her breathing. "Shit," she panted, "you know we can't go back there, now that we beat the supervisor's ass."

"Desiree, you think he was telling the truth about what he said about Mama?"

"Who gives a fuck! Wait, I'm sorry, Cashmere—no, naw, fuck this! I'm not gonna sugarcoat this no more. Wake the fuck up! You fourteen now—she ain't shit. Yes, I believe him. He only one of many. You know damn well she was fucking around on Daddy. And I'll tell you this too—she knew about all the guys I was fucking. And in case you ain't realized, she ain't comin' back, so it's gonna be up to us to get that money for Daddy and pay that fat bitch her share to get her off of our backs. Then when I'm eighteen, we can split."

"But we ain't gonna go back there now. How we gonna get the money in a couple weeks?"

"Shit, you really wanna know, little sister? Hustling—that's what we gonna have to do. We ain't got no other choice. Let's go. I already got a plan."

Chapter 8

Stripping didn't bother me. In fact, for some crazy reason, I enjoyed the shit. I just didn't like niggas thinking they could touch on me, but niggas admiring me and giving me money, that was cool, since the last person that admired me was Daddy. The only problem was, since we were both under the age of eighteen, we ended up stripping at underground spots.

Since we were in the rinky-dink stripping, which was usually at somebody's house or some shit like that or at a private party, the money wasn't much of shit. So at night we took to doing something really horrible—selling dope for some dude name Keefee.

"We ain't gonna do this shit forever, so stop your fucking whining!" Desiree yelled one night when we were on the corner slinging some rocks.

We even had to cook the shit, using some jar to boil it in, then, after we let it set, we had to cut it up in cubes of different sizes. And I'll be damned if I wanted my hands in that shit. We was contributing to the whole drug epidemic, people getting robbed, people dying, crack babies being born, mothers and fathers neglecting or abusing their kids. I hated doing the shit.

But one day turned to several, and we really did have to look out for ourselves, since our aunt didn't supply us with shit and she always had her greasy, fat-ass hands out.

Once we gave her her dough, she'd shake her head at us. "I don't even need to know how y'all got this shit. Y'all ain't going to be shit, you know."

And we'd nod in agreement and watch her fat ass waddle on, like she shitted out some kids that were so damn perfect.

"Desiree. You said we only had to do this shit until we got up enough money to pay that deposit."

"Well, shit! I thought so too. Hell, Cash, in two more weeks his monthly bill is due, and wide ass upped her price on us. So we need to at least get enough for his bill for next month then we can stop."

I sighed.

"I know it's hard to stomach, but at least you don't gotta touch the shit. I do that for us."

"You a damn lie. You made me cut the shit." I changed the subject. "We can get a regular job. We ain't gotta be out here."

"Bitch, you fourteen. That ain't old enough. Ain't nobody gonna hire you. And, yeah, I can get a job at McDonald's or Burger King and we can quit dealing, but that won't do shit for Daddy's bill. And it would only be part-time, 'cause of school. Shit, and I wouldn't bring enough home for nothing after taxes. But, like I said, we won't be doing this shit forever. But the stripping, little sister, we ain't giving that shit up."

"We ain't got to, but I don't like being out here. It ain't safe."

"One more week, that's it. We'll sell off this last zone then we'll put a fork in this shit, I promise."

I nodded as a dopey approached us and asked for a rock. "Ten," I said absently, the rock clutched in my fingers.

"Ten, damn!" the man said, his ashy-purple lips poked out.

"Ten, or step the fuck off!" Desiree yelled.

He tossed it her way, and I threw it at him. He rushed away, looking behind him.

"I wished we could do it at a classier spot, the stripping." I said.

"We ain't old enough, boo boo. But, before I forget, I heard the manager at the Velvet Fox is on vacation, so we can sneak in there and give lap dances tomorrow night. But we can't work the stage."

"Cool," I said. "And if we make enough to pay off the bill for next month, can we stop selling this bullshit?"

Desiree laughed. "Cashmere, you hold people to their word, don't you?"

I laughed too. "Hell yeah!"

"Well, you need to stop, 'cause they'll disappointment you time and time again."

Now the Velvet Fox was a cool little spot. Wished we could work the poles there. It was clean even in the bathrooms. The clientele was more upscale than the niggas I was used to who wanted you to stick bottles up your pussy and lick your own asshole. My sister and I had on our sexy getup. She wore her hair up, and I wore mine down, giving me an exotic look, like I was from Brazil. While my sister managed to captivate niggas with her pretty titties, it was my face that got their attention and my big ass that managed to keep it. We went to one man after the other, rubbing our titties in their face. I just pretended I was rubbing all over Omarion's fine ass and not men old enough to be my father.

They told me I was so fine, so innocent, young-looking, and how much they wanted to eat my pussy and fuck me, or whichever one I was willing to give their nasty ass; I just continued humping them and shit, getting twenty-five bucks for each one. Some gave me more. One nigga gave me twenty-five for the lap dance, a hundred as tip, and offered five hundred to fuck me. When I told him I was a virgin, his eyes widened, and he offered me a thousand. I got away from his ass real quick and moved on to another nigga.

I had done a total of four, and Desiree had done two. Her ass moved slow as hell.

I had just emerged from the lap dance when Desiree motioned for me to come over to where she was. I adjusted my tube top, smoothed down my booty shorts, and closed the distance between us.

She was standing near two men. One was in his early twenties, and the other looked like he was too young to be in there. And despite where my focus should have been, I noticed he was cute as hell. He was tall, with a caramel complexion, had full lips, a medium-straight nose, and some sexy-ass bedroom eyes. And he had some muscles too. *Um-um-um.*

"Hello? Cash!" Desiree looked at me, an annoyed look on her face.

"Yeah, what's up?"

"We got a birthday boy here. Caesar is celebrating his eighteenth birthday, and this is his friend Martin. She leaned over and slid an arm around Martin's waist, her way of letting me know she had dibs on him, probably assuming that since he was older, he would be a bigger tipper. But the whole time the brother was watching me.

And so was Caesar. I avoided gazing back. He was so fine. Then I almost hit myself, 'cause my hot ass was putting my focus in the wrong things.

"Well, hello, Caesar. My name is Cashmere, and I am going to give you a very special lap dance."

He scanned my body and licked his lips like he was nervous.

I led him by one of his hands to the room where lap dances were given. (They called it "the satin room.") I noticed as I walked that his hands shook the whole way.

Once we got there and I stepped inside, he stood in the doorway frozen. I turned around confused then laughed at him. I jerked my head toward him. When he still didn't step into the room, I laughed softly and said, "Come in, baby."

He still wouldn't budge.

I strolled over to him and pulled him by his hands all the way into the room. I shoved him gently on the couch, pushed the play button on the CD player, and E40's voice blared into the room.

In a seductive way I slid between his legs and pushed my body down, so my ass could rub up against his dick. When I did this, his dick sprang forward.

When I glanced back at him he looked embarrassed and tried to push me off of him. "Maybe." He tried to stand.

I shoved his ass back down. "No maybe, my ass. You came your ass in this room and you gonna get this lap dance. You took away from somebody else, so sit your ass there and enjoy it," I ordered. "I need the dough, bottom line."

He raised his hands in peace, and I continued what I was doing. I was on him backward and continued my grind as his dick continued to slap against me. "You like that puddin' pop?" Daddy used to call me that when I was little. *So don't get mad, Daddy. I'm doing this for you.*

He smiled finally and relaxed. "Yeah."

I chuckled. I turned and faced him, and trailed my fingertips down his head. I slid one finger in his mouth, while grinding on top of his dick and told him, "Suck."

He opened his mouth and sucked it like it was my nipple.

I smiled. "Can I have my finger back?"

He nodded and I slid it out.

"You know this song?" I asked him.

He nodded and smiled again. "Yeah."

"Then sing it to me."

"Naw."

I pushed my pussy into his crotch. "Please sing it to me. It gets me going."

"Girl, I been shaking, sticking and moving
Tryin'a get to you and that booty"

I twisted my body in the shape of a C, whipping my hair all up in his face. I knew he was aching to touch me, but he didn't.

I rose and pulled myself from his lap and put my booty all up in his face. "Now here's my part on the song:

"Yeah, I see you looking
But my ass in these jeans got you shook."

I bit my lip and eyed him from between my legs. Then I pulled off my top, so my titties were free. "Touch it," I commanded. As my booty jiggled in his face, his eyes were wide as golf balls. He didn't know what to do with all that ass in his face.

He used the tip of one of his fingers.

"Rub it."

He tried his best to, his fingers rippling across my behind as the song continued,

"Slap it!"

He tried, but he wasn't no suave type of dude.

I almost busted up laughing at him. I was used to smooth niggas, even though they wasn't getting shit.

But I found Caesar to be cute, maybe because he had the innocence I used to have. I mean, I was still innocent, to a certain extent. I mean, I hadn't had sex yet. But I was selling my body, so I was far from being a saint. I was doing dirt, selling a fantasy to these dudes, putting my pussy all up in their face. And half of them had wives and girlfriends. They could be spending that money on them. Or even their fucking kids. I was cold for using my body to seduce them into dropping what was in their pockets. And on top of that I was helping my sister sell crack. So some of my innocence—naw, a lot of it was gone. I just hoped it stopped there.

I shook those thoughts out of my head and tried to focus on the task at hand. "Don't be scared. Cash, taking good care of you, aren't I?" I crooned as I grinded my breast up in his face.

He nodded between his ragged breathing.

I scooted out of my shorts and wiggled my body in my thong. By the time I was done, his dick was poking straight through his pants. I gave my ass one last clap. "Okay, homie, that's a rap. I truly hope you enjoyed it as much as I did." I looked at his crotch.

He cracked another smile. He looked so cute, I wanted to kiss him, but that was a no-no. So I stopped. Instead, I winked at him and pulled on my clothes.

"Thank you." He handed me a fifty.

Humph, not bad for someone so young. I tucked it in my bra. "No problem." Then I hightailed it to the door before I did or said something I'd regret. Like, "Do you have a girl?" or "You wanna call me sometime?

I reached for the doorknob, and before I could turn it, another stripper named Spice was pulling in her date by his hand. I nodded at her and backed up against the wall to let them both pass.

I could have shrunk into the wall when I got a good look at the dude who she was pulling inside. Shit, it was my uncle, Aunt Ruby's husband.

His eyes widened when he recognized me. That was after he was done checking me out— my legs, thighs, pussy, waist, titties, and then he went to my face—his eyes stretched to the muthafuckin' ceiling.

I brushed past him, embarrassed as hell, hoping he wouldn't say shit to me or my aunt at home.

Did my aunt know that he was there? Whether he was here or not, it wouldn't hold no weight with her. Her fat ass wasn't leaving him no way, even if he turned her house into a strip club. And it wasn't so much about her knowing about me and Desiree stripping, it was more of her judgment if she found out, her feeling justified in saying that we wasn't shit.

Chapter 9

My only salvation from the shit me and Desiree were doing was my monthly visits to this café located down the street from my aunt's house. I always squeezed an extra twenty out of my stash that went to my aunt and to Daddy's rent at the home, to allow myself something sweet from there. Sweet Tooth Café had the best desserts I'd ever had, and they weren't cheap. I only stopped by there once a month, my time of the month, when I had some serious cravings for something sweet. Usually I got their strawberry shortcake or their chocolate pound cake.

I glanced inside the café. It was empty, except for an older woman sipping coffee. It was still early out, which explained why it was so empty in there. And now was as good a time as any to chew on something sweet to get my mind off my uncle.

I walked in and stared at all the desserts displayed in the glass. Even though my ass always got the same thing, I still looked at all the other desserts. There was cheesecake, strawberry and blueberry, lemon custard, something called soufflé, apple strudel, chocolate mousse, and some other shit I couldn't pronounce.

"I'll be with you in just a second."

I jumped and turned to catch the person behind the voice. When I did, I wanted to run the fuck out of the café, despite how much I wanted something sweet and knowing nothing could give me the fix Sweet Tooth Café could.

It was Caesar, the dude from the strip club, the one who came in for his birthday. He must have not seen me or recognized me at first, 'cause he was balancing two plastic bags along with a box. He rushed behind the counter to sit the stuff down, and when he finally looked up and got a good look at my face, he stuttered and bumped into the counter.

I laughed, my embarrassment gone, and shook my head. "You know what," I started, "I'll go somewhere else." I regretted the shit even as I said it. This was the only real fucking luxury I had in my life, and I didn't want to give it up. Come to think of it, I had never seen him there before anyway.

I turned to leave when his voice stopped me.

"No, don't," he said. "I don't want you to leave, and I'm okay with you being here, if you're okay with it."

I smiled, showing him that I definitely was, and he smiled back, making me wanna blush. He was so damn cute. Why couldn't I have met his ass under different circumstances? Like on my way from school, at a dance, the movies, maybe the park, anywhere but the fucking strip club.

"What would you like?"

I stared at all the yummy desserts then I laughed at myself.

Confused, he smiled at me again. "What are you laughing at?"

"I have the same problem every time I come here. I can't make up my mind between the strawberry shortcake or the chocolate pound cake."

He chuckled in a sexy way that rolled off his tongue.

I giggled happily when he made the choice for me. He handed me a slice of both on a tray and said, "The only catch is this—Cashmere, right?"

My smile dropped. *Catch*? I thought he was just going to be cool, just on GP. The last time a nigga had a "catch," he had his dick out in front of me and my sister. He didn't get shit, except an ass-whipping, and this nigga wasn't getting shit from me either.

I shoved the tray away. "Forget it."

He narrowed his eyes, confused, not quite knowing how to respond. I didn't wait for him to. I slid off the stool and rushed out of the café.

I was half a block from the café, when I heard him calling my name and chasing after me with a bag in his hand. I heard his feet hitting the pavement behind me. "Stop!" He reached for my shoulder.

I spun around with my fist. "Boy, you done lost your damn mind. When did I say you could touch me?"

Caesar held his hands up in surrender. "Sorry. I didn't mean to disrespect you."

I grimaced. "What do you want? I got shit to do."

"I just wanted to apologize for whatever I said to offend you, but, before I do, I want to know what I did wrong."

"What you did?" I got all up in his face. "Muth-afucka, I may be a damn stripper, but I'm not a ho. And you just treated me like one, a cheap one at that, trying to pimp me for some damn cake!"

His eyes widened, and his voice went up an octave. "How did I do that?"

I mimicked what he said about "catch."

"I didn't—" he shook his head. "Look, Cash-mere, all I was going to say was, if you sit and keep me company while I stock the shelves. I wasn't trying to get you to sleep with me."

I was considering what he was saying, but even as I did, I wouldn't stop frowning at him, even though silently I admitted to myself that I looked like a damn fool because what I was thinking wasn't what he meant at all. Still I wasn't just going to make it easy.

I crossed my arms underneath my chest. "Check this out, whatever your name is. I'm young but, homie, I'm not dumb. Why in the hell would you want me, the girl that just the other day had her young, damn-near-naked ass all up in your face, to sit and keep you company?"

He gripped his chin in his hand, trying not to blush at what I just said. "'Cause I never wanted you out of my face. I looked for you after you rushed out that night, and, Cashmere, it has nothing to do with sex, I swear."

I smiled at that but, just as quickly, put my game face back on by frowning. "How you know my name?" I couldn't think of anything else to say.

Caesar chuckled, keeping his eyes on mine. "Because you told me your name that night."

Humph.

Most niggas forgot my name the moment I dropped my clothes. I was called everything from bitch, ho, trick, wifey, baby, boo, even Glennisha, Shaquida, Diana, Maria, Kimberly, Becky, but never ever by my name. Even if I danced for a dude on more than one occasion, which I have, it never failed; they always forgot my damn name.

Since I had given this dude such a hard time, I cracked a small smile at him 'cause the look in his eyes was different when he looked at me. Why was his different? Maybe he didn't see me like I feared he would, like a cheap stripper, or worse, a ho. Maybe he saw me like I was just a regular person.

"So that's what you chased me down the street for? No. Thank you for chasing me down the street." My smile grew longer and seemed to make him smile too. My eyes locked with his, and I couldn't, for some reason, drop them.

"You're welcome. I also came to give you this, for the inconvenience, free of charge and obligation. I mean that." He handed me the bag he was carrying.

Inside it had a huge slice of strawberry shortcake and a piece of pound cake. I laughed. I turned to go but noticed he made no moves to walk away, so I paused and looked back at him.

"Can I walk you back home? I mean, if you feel comfortable with it, just to make sure you make it there safely."

"Are you propositioning me now?"

"No."

"You telling me the truth?" I kept my gaze on his, one hand on my hip.

He shoved his hands in the pockets of his baggy jeans. "Yes."

I nodded. "Then come on."

After a small moment of silence, he asked," Do you come to the restaurant a lot?"

"Not too often. Just when I have a sweet tooth. And, come to think of it, I never saw you there before."

"My parents just bought the place a couple weeks ago. It's a little project I'm taking on. I made a bet with my mom that if I can run the café successfully and stay within the budget, I could pick what college I attend."

"Damn! Y'all got money to burn like that?"

"It ain't mine, girl."

I laughed. He had a very proper voice and speech, like he wasn't from around here, and it sounded cute when slang slipped out of his mouth.

"How about you? What does your family do?"

I stiffened. "I don't live with my mom and dad. I stay with my aunt. I know my uncle don't do shit, and all my aunt does is cook."

"At a restaurant."

"No. So the bitch can eat."

He laughed hard as hell when I said that. Maybe he thought I was playing.

Chapter 10

The next day my Uncle Byron cornered me. So much for thinking that he would cut me some damn slack. I was in the kitchen making myself a bowl of cereal. I felt something hit me in my ass then heard it fall to the floor. I looked down and saw a crumpled dollar bill then some size ten Velcro tennis shoes. I turned my back on him like he wasn't shit and poured the milk in my bowl and sat the milk down on the counter.

"Shake it."

I spooned a spoonful in my mouth and chewed on my corn flakes but I had a hard time swallowing them when he stood behind me so close that his pot-gut and dick were rubbing up against me.

I took a deep breath and tried to slide past him. He wasn't having it. He blocked me between the sink and the fridge. Before I could protest he was sliding his finger up and down the crack of my ass.

"You like that, baby?" He had his hands on both sides of my face on the wall blocking me in. His tongue licked my ear lobe.

I sighed wanting to throw up. But I knew I was overpowered so I had to play it cool.

I yelled my sister's name as loud as I could, then my aunt's.

"They ain't here."

My heart started to beat faster.

He grabbed one of my titties. "You like this, huh? Ain't this what you was getting paid to do at the strip joint?"

"No, you ugly muthafucka!"

He placed a hand over my mouth, muffling my words, and continued talking while gripping both my hands in his free hand. "If wish I had known that this is all it would take to get that young, hot pussy of yours, *Cash Money*," he drawled.

I struggled against him and turned around to face him. He allowed me to and removed his hands from my mouth.

"Please get off of me."

"Hell no, I paid for this."

I spit the chewed-up corn flake in his face.

That pissed him off. He grabbed me and slammed my back into the fridge. I whimpered and felt tears shoot from my eyes at the pain, but I ignored it and struggled against him. He wouldn't budge. He pulled my tank top up and started licking on my nipples.

I started crying loudly and trying to free myself, but it didn't help.

He pulled down my shorts and jabbed a finger in my pussy then he licked it. "Sweet, like I thought. I usually don't eat pussy, but, Cashmere, I'll tell you what. I'll eat yours, if you suck on my dick."

"No, please, uncle."

He kneeled down to completely free me of my underwear. Once he was on his knees, he left his face all open to me, so with the quickness, I took one foot and stomped that nigga directly in his face so hard, he fell backwards. Then I took off running out that muthafucka half-naked. I slipped out the house, jumped off the porch steps, and kept on running and crying, screaming at what my uncle just tried to do to me, yet so happy I got away.

I stopped running and straightened my clothes. I wish I knew where Desiree was. I kept walking until I made it to the café. Now was as good a time as any to chew on something sweet. I glanced in the windows and saw Caesar behind the counter. It was still early out, which probably explained why there was nobody in there. I opened the door and slipped in.

Caesar smiled when he saw me, and I managed one also.

I took the rag that was next to some silverware on the counter and started shining a fork.

"What's got you up so early, Cashmere?"

That mess that went down with my uncle flashed before my eyes. My eyes watered, so I blinked rapidly to stop them. And my hand started shaking so much, I dropped the fork on a plate.

"You okay?"

I blinked my eyes again, looked up, and noticed that Caesar had abandoned the stuff he was putting away to sit next to me on a stool. He had a hand on my shoulder and another on my cheek. His eyes looked so damn concerned. I hadn't seen concern like that since Daddy. And without much thought, like a dumb ass, I buried my head in his shoulder and let out months of pent-up frustration and pain. And he just held me.

I didn't want to go home until I was sure that Desiree or Aunt Ruby was there, to be safe from my nasty-ass uncle, so I stayed at the café with Caesar.

I learned a lot more about him. He attended private school, which explained why I had never seen him prior to the club, and was getting ready to graduate high school and go out of state to a good college called Grambling. I told him my goal was to graduate from high school and go to cosmetology school. He really was a nice guy, the kind of guy I was sure Daddy would have loved for me to date. He was nothing like the trashy guys me and Desiree shook our ass for, not at all.

It wasn't long after that he asked me to be his girl, and I accepted.

My monthly visits to the Sweet Tooth Café turned into weekly, then, any chance I could spare, which with school, stripping, and dealing wasn't easy. The only thing I never negotiated my time with was my Sunday visits with Desiree to see Daddy. We always stayed there until midnight. It had been a tradition since he came to Pine Meadows.

When I was home I would find any excuse to go to the café and to see Caesar. Sometimes I would offer to get my auntie something sweet, and she would say, "Are you paying?"

And I would say, "Sure, no problem, Auntie. It's for everything you do around here."

She would look at me for a moment like, and it was almost as if her face was going to soften up and she was going to say something nice to me. But all she'd mumble was, "You ain't as bad as your sister, but I still don't like you."

I would always nod and race off to the café. Then I would spit in whatever I was giving her and watch her eat the shit with relish. She never said thank you either.

Caesar was cool. He would walk me home and hold my hand like a real boyfriend, the calm after the storm, I called it, after having to do the shit I did. He was my salvation, I guess. Daddy used that expression a lot to describe Mama. But, boy, was he off.

Chapter 11

"Fucking Cash! Your ass needs to focus." I sucked my teeth at Desiree. "I am."

"No, you not." She gestured toward the street. "Did you see that damn man make eye contact? No. We need to get rid of this shit."

I pursed my lips and rubbed my arms to ward off the night chills I had. "You said that crap last week," I told her. "I don't wanna sell this shit no more."

"Well, I don't neither, so there, dammit!"

"Whatever."

"You know stripping gigs been slow. What else we gonna do?"

I shrugged.

Caesar said he would talk to his dad about offering me a job at the café. It wouldn't be much, but it was something. And since I was under the legal age to work, he said he would pay me under the table. But the last time I brought it up to Desiree, she laughed.

"He lying. He just want your pussy, girl. If he want it that bad, then give it to him, but he ain't gonna give you, a stripper, a job in that damn café."

I started to believe her and didn't want to call his bluff and get my feelings hurt. And even if he was bullshitting about offering me a job, I still wanted to be around him 'cause it felt genuine, even if it wasn't. I didn't want to not have the café to go to, or Caesar to go to.

"And please don't bring up that fool you in love with. He full of shit. He ain't offering you shit, but some dick. You just too dumb to see it, Cash."

"Yeah, well, fuck you!" Tears started coming out of my eyes.

She laughed and tried to hug me. "Did I hurt your feelings?"

"Get off of me, trick!"

"Trick? She busted up laughing and released me. "Face it, we strippers. Ain't no decent man going to ever want us, and that's the bottom line."

"Caesar want me—"

"Oh Lord. You know what, Cash? Fuck Caesar! He ain't paying Daddy's rent or rent to our aunt, now is he?"

"But he offers me money all the time."

She stared at me for a long time before shaking her head and rubbing her hands together. "It comes at a price, Cashmere. Don't you get it?"

She kept babbling, but my eyes slipped away from her as three niggas came out of nowhere and were coming toward us, walking at a brisk pace, the tallest one fumbling in his pockets.

"Desiree, run!" I took off, and she trailed behind me, confused at first, but smart enough to follow my lead, and screaming like a damn fool.

"Stop, bitches, and give us your shit!"

I was too scared to look behind me, but I heard the slamming of their feet on the pavement. They were on our heels. As we turned the corner, I could hear popping sounds like a firecracker and I saw smoke.

Desiree yelled, "Oh my God, Cash, they shooting at us!"

That's when I felt it—something plunged into me, and a sharp ass pain in my shoulder. Then I fell to the ground, and blood squirted out of me. I closed my eyes, as an ache I had never felt before spread through me.

"Please don't kill me," Desiree pleaded, hovering her body over mine.

The three dudes surrounded us and bumrushed Desiree, knocking her to the ground beside me.

"Bitch, like we said, give us y'all shit," one of them demanded.

Another one said, "She the carrier, man, the one screaming."

The guy with the gun pointed it at Desiree. "Give it up!"

"Okay! Okay! Just don't kill me, in the name of Jesus." She fumbled in her pocket and tossed the paper bag their way.

One of them kicked us both. "Next time, don't play."

Then they ran off into the night.

"Muthafuckas, you didn't have to shoot my sister! Oh my God, my sister gone. You mutha-fuckas, why the fuck did you do this shit?"

I almost laughed when she tossed her fist at the air. I was in a whole lot of pain, but I damn sure wasn't dead. I thanked God for that. "De-siree."

She wasn't listening. Instead she pulled my up-per body on her and rocked me back and forth.

"Oh Lord, my sister dead. Why me? Why my sister, Lord, why?" She was breathing in pants through her nose as she talked.

Then it occurred to me that I still had some shit on me, and the commotion she was causing could alert the cops to us. "Desiree, will you shut the fuck up!" I whispered. "I'm not dead."

She froze, placed a hand over my heart, then hugged me tight and said, "Praise God."

"Shut up! Your ass falls asleep in church." I winced in pain as blood continued to ooze from my shoulder. "Now you calling on God."

"Come on, little sister. I thought I lost you there. Let's get you seen at the hospital."

It turned out that it was just a flesh wound, because the bullet grazed my ass, but it was more than enough for me to make plans to step out of the dope game for good.

Chapter 12

My retiring from the dope game pissed Desiree off, but hell, she had a lot of nerve. I could have been killed. I'd always have the bruise in my shoulder to remind me that wasn't shit good about fast money. Or maybe it was karma, plain and simple, because what we were doing was wrong.

I buried my pride and the doubts she put in my head as I walked to the café.

"You stupid," she yelled behind me. "He don't want you! Girl, he wants some ass, so be prepared to give that shit up."

I flipped her the bird and kept on going. Once I reached the café, I took a deep breath. Before Caesar could get out a hello, I said to him, "Look, I need a job. And since you suppose to be my man, and since a while back you offered I need you to offer to hire me again 'cause I don't like asking people for a damn thing."

I was holding my breath the whole time and didn't release it until he laughed, hugged me, and whispered in my ear, "Now I get to see my girl more. Cool."

And it was cool from there. I came in after school, and on the weekends when me and Desiree weren't doing stripping gigs. And I loved it, getting paid to spend time with my boyfriend. But don't get me wrong, Caesar worked the hell out of me. I worked the cash register, stocked the inventory, washed dishes, and cleaned the store up at closing time and all. And he always watched me hustle with a smile on his face and a wink at me. Sometimes he would pull me back in the storage for a kiss or pat my behind, and it would make me tingle inside.

I didn't make as much as I wanted, but I managed to pull almost even with what he paid me, my tips, and the extra dough Caesar gave me just because I was his girl. The shortage I did have, Desiree, talking a lot of shit, had to cover.

Caesar even showed me how to make some of the dishes. He said, "One at a time," so we started with the pound cake. It was early one Saturday morning, and we were in the kitchen. He held a spoon in his hand and asked me with his eyes wide. "Now are you sure I can trust you, Cash? 'Cause this is a family recipe, and my nana would kill me if she knew I was sharing it, even if I'm sharing it with my girl."

I laughed and shook my head.

"Aye, girl, this ain't a joke." He pointed the big spoon at me.

I pulled my lips in to keep from laughing and leaned against the countertop. "Sorry."

He tapped me on my butt with the spoon.

"Ouch." I whined, pretending it hurt.

"Oh. I'm sorry, baby."

He kissed the spot on my butt where he hit me, making me tingle, but I acted like it was nothing, like on a regular basis fine-ass men kissed me on my butt.

"It's okay, sweetie," I said.

He sat the spoon down. "Okay, now get that right hand up, girl." I sighed and raised my hand as he instructed. He crossed his arms over his sweater.

"Now repeat after me. I, Cashmere Pierce."

"I, Cashmere Pierce."

"Do solemnly swear."

"Do solemnly swear."

"That I will never ever ever ever ever ever."

"That I will never ever ever ever ever ever."

"Ever!"

"Ever."

I held in my laugh.

"Will repeat any recipe I learned in Sweet Tooth Café."

"Will repeat any recipe I learned in Sweet Tooth Café."

He turned serious. "You being honest with me, Cashmere?"

"I'm always honest with you, Caesar, just like you honest with me. Aren't you?"

"Yeah."

He bit his bottom lip. "But can you keep a promise?"

I nodded. "I'm taking this to the grave, I promise, Caesar. And I'm gonna always keep my promises to you."

He scooted closer to me and hugged me. Then he packed my face with kiss after kiss.

Even though I didn't want him to stop, I pushed him away. "Okay. Come on, Caesar, we gotta get this stuff baked."

"Right." He pulled himself away. "Two and a half cups of flour." I nodded, measured it off, and poured it into a bowl.

"Two teaspoons of baking soda, a teaspoon of salt." He cracked six eggs and mixed them in a bowl, while I mixed the dry ingredients.

"Cashmere, you know what I always wanted to ask you?"

I scratched the sides of the bowl with the spoon. "No. What?"

He added some vanilla to the eggs and continued to beat them. "Where is your real mother?"

I paused on the mixing for a moment. Then I shook my head and went back to mixing. "I don't know. Gone"

He gave me a weird look, poured three cups of white sugar in the bowl of eggs, and stirred slowly, so the sugar wouldn't splatter. "What do you mean, she's gone? Gone to where?"

I didn't respond.

He poured in some unsweetened chocolate cocoa. Then he poured a tub of sour cream into his bowl.

The silence was uncomfortable.

He studied me a moment. "You don't want to talk about it, do you?"

I smiled to let him know I wasn't mad that he was being nosy. But, still, I'm sure the hurt in my eyes showed. And my tight lip showed I just didn't want to discuss it with him.

"Now let me just mix the wet with the dry ingredients." He poured his bowl into mine. "Now just mix those together good, Cashmere."

I nodded.

See, the thing was, I was mad as hell at my mom. She did us wrong and had been doing us wrong for months. It had been a good seven months, and I still hadn't heard from her. And, deep down, despite the shit I talked about her to Desiree, part of me wanted her to come back. I wanted us to be a family like we used to be. I thought about the old days all of the time, and to be honest, I missed Mama. So my love and my desire to see her seemed to dominate all the anger I had, and the anger I tried to build up against loving and missing her. My damn heart won, I guess.

From the corner of my eye I watched Caesar walk over to the sink and wash his hands. He then stood behind me and wrapped his arms around my waist and kissed me on my cheek. "I didn't mean to make you sad, Cashmere."

I smiled to show him I was okay and that I wasn't mad at him.

Mama said never to show a man you were a broken woman. When I asked her what a "broken woman" was, she explained patiently, "A broken woman is someone who goes through shit. Maybe she was hurt at a young age. She could have been abused, raped, molested, felt abandoned, which would have made her bitter and angry, and therefore broken. 'Cause the world, including men, could see it and couldn't love her because of it. That's why they can't keep a man. Mable Curtis—broken and single." Mable was her friend. "Carolyn Porter—broken and single. Can't keep a man for shit." She was also a friend of Mama's. "But don't worry, Cash, none of those things are gonna happen to you, so you don't have to worry about ever being broken."

She sure predicted wrong, but I was determined not to let the shit I had already felt because of her break me. I wanted to be able to keep Caesar. *It would kill me to lose him.*

His arms tightened around my waist, pulling me from my thoughts and putting my attention back on him.

"The thing is, I was asking about your mom because, see, my parents are having a dinner party, and I wanted you to attend. It's only right that I ask your mother's permission."

I turned around and hugged him before he got the rest out, and he laughed and hugged me back.

See, Desiree, you don't know what the hell you talking about. Caesar cares about me. That shit Desiree was drilling in my head all this time was just bullshit. No man would bring a woman home to his parents that he didn't care about.

This had to mean he was sincere about being with me.

He patted my butt and said, "All right, let's finish up."

"Right."

After I unraveled myself out of his arms, he pulled me back into his arms and kissed me, but it was different from the usual kisses. He slipped his tongue in my mouth, and it made my heart rate speed up. I didn't know what to do, and I didn't want to look stupid. I was the girl who backed her damn near naked ass up in clubs and couldn't even French-kiss?

"Relax."

I tried to follow his lead in the kiss, but in all honesty, I didn't have experience to compare with. But my young intuition told me Caesar either wasn't the best teacher or the best kisser. Maybe he was bad at both, but I still liked him. I ended up with slobber all over my mouth, and his dick poking into my waist.

He pecked me one last time and slid his fingers down to my waist. "You gonna always be my girl."

I looked up at him with wide eyes and asked in a little girl voice I hated, "You mean that?"

He traced my bottom lip with one of his fingers. "Yeah, I mean that. I'm gonna always take good care of you, Cashmere. I'm not going to ever hurt you ever. And I'm gonna make sure no one else will as well."

My hold tightened on him, as he stroked up and down my arms.

"Okay," he said, "let's put that baby in the oven."

After a tiring day, Caesar drove me home in his new car. He said his dad bought it for him after he had gotten accepted to Grambling. Usually I wanted him to walk me home so we had more time to spend together, but I was so tired from work. And, plus, I was in a hurry to share the news that Caesar had invited me to his parents' house for dinner, and maybe in a bigger hurry to get there just to rub it in her face.

I warned him not to get involved with any of those college chickens.

"Don't worry. As soon as I get into the fraternity, I'm sending you my sweater.

"Fra who?"

"I'm pledging for Gamma. My daddy was one, so he expects me to be one."

"Do you want to be?" I asked.

He seemed like he was examining the question like he'd never thought about it. Maybe no one had ever asked him before.

"Yeah, I guess."

I stroked his head.

"I just have to pledge."

"You'll get in. I know it."

He turned to me and smiled.

When he pulled up to my aunt's house, I didn't want to leave the comfort of his car.

"Can I have one more kiss?"

"You sure can." I leaned over and kissed him, my eyes closed. I was really into it, learning how to use my tongue and trying to maneuver my lips so he didn't deliver so much saliva into my mouth.

He abruptly broke the kiss.

"What?"

He was looking behind me. "It's the same house I dropped you off at last time, right? 'Cause if it is, something is happening, baby."

Through the windows of my aunt's house, I saw her throw something that busted out a window. "Oh shit." I opened the car door and ran up the steps and into the house.

My auntie was struggling with my uncle, who was buck-ass naked. "Get the fuck off me, you bastard! And get the fuck out of my house!"

I almost laughed at his wrinkled ass. When I heard Caesar's feet behind me, I placed a hand up, telling him silently not to enter.

Aunt Ruby swung at Uncle Byron, knocking him into the coffee table. He hit his head and lay sprawled out, his dick dangling back and forth and a milky liquid leaking from it.

I turned away disgusted. Then a sinking feeling hit me. No, she couldn't have. "Auntie, what happened?'

She spun around quickly. "What happened, Cashmere? I'll show you what happened." She pulled me by my hand to me and my sister's room.

I looked over my shoulder at Caesar, who looked confused and concerned from the porch. "I'll be back," I told him. I shrugged 'cause I was just as confused as he was.

Aunt Ruby barged in our room and pulled me with her. "This is what happened! This slut was fucking my husband in my own house. And, bitch, like I said, get out! Get out! You got five more seconds to pack your shit!"

I looked at Desiree with a shocked expression that asked her silently, "How the fuck could you?"

Desiree gave me a glance that said she was sorry then changed her sorry expression to a malicious one, twisting her mouth to one side and rolling her eyes at our aunt. "Shit, he came after me and he was willing to pay. Shit, I don't want your man. Don't trip."

"After I give y'all whores a home, this is how you repay me?"

Desiree tossed a bag my way. "Cash, I packed your shit too."

I shook my head. "What? I'm not leaving, Desiree. I'm staying."

My aunt turned to me. "I want both of you out."

"We'll be out, bitch."

Aunt Ruby took a step toward her.

A naked Desiree stood and balled her fist, fire in her eyes. "Touch me, bitch, and get fucked up like my mom used to whip on you!"

Aunt Ruby stepped back.

"Aunt," I whispered.

"I want you both out!" She turned on her heel and marched out of the room.

"Don't judge me. I needed the money, since you giving me that bullshit you made at the café. He offered, so I took it."

"So you tricking now?"

"Shut up, Cashmere, and let's go." Desiree zipped her duffel bag with her shit and rushed out. "Bye, bitch!" she yelled.

I walked out the house slowly behind her.

My aunt didn't reply. She just rocked back and forth in her chair. And despite how mean she was to us and how bad she made living with her, I felt bad for her. She just did, after all, catch her husband cheating red-handed. Her pride and joy, the man she boasted about at her card games with her friends and constantly brought up in her phone conversations, and always found a way to praise him on being a great husband, father, and lover, when all her other friends either complained about what a piece-of-shit man they had, how their men wouldn't stop hitting them, cheating on them, or commit to them. Or some just complained because they just didn't have one. Now she was sitting in a chair crying her eyes out. But don't get me wrong, she was going to take him back. He'd already cheated on her before. But, still, to see her hurt, I was hurting. I couldn't imagine that happening to me and Caesar.

"I hope everything gets better, Auntie. And I'm sorry for your pain." I tried to pat her hand, but when she saw my hand moving toward hers, she snatched hers away and rested both her hands on her lap.

I smiled tightly and said, "Thanks for letting us stay here."

"Cashmere, come on. Damn! Your man said he would drive us to a hotel."

I walked out of the house, and down the porch steps to Caesar, who had just helped my sister in the back seat and was rushing to open the passenger door for me to get in.

Broken woman, I thought. I gave him the best smile I could manage, but the truth was, I was worried out of my mind. I didn't feel comfortable or happy about leaving my aunt's house. There was no telling where we would be now, and since my sister wasn't the most reliable person any damn way, I knew we were going to be in some shit.

I snapped on my seat belt and took a deep breath when I felt my eyes tear up. Before Caesar could make it back into his seat, I wiped them away quickly and glared in the rearview mirror at my trifling-ass sister. This bitch's scandalousness had no gotdamn fucking limit!

I squeezed Caesar's arm as he made a U-turn and drove past our aunt's home. The whole time, watching my sister in the mirror.

"Stop fucking looking at me like that!" Desiree yelled.

"Like what?" I yelled back.

"Like I'ma—"

"A what?" I continued to eye her in the mirror like one would look at shit on the back of their shoe, hoping it would make her ass feel bad.

"You know what? Fuck it!"

"Yeah, let's . . ." I held off on what I wanted to say.

Desiree crossed her arms around her chest and stared out the side window. I hoped her ass was freezing in that skimpy-ass summer dress she wore.

"You ain't perfect, Cash," Desiree said, her head rocking back and forth with every word. "That's all I got to say."

I finally turned around and faced her. "You sure?"

"Sure about what?"

"That that's all you have to say?"

"Oh, you trying to get smart and shit." I tossed a hand at her.

"Forget it, Desiree, just forget it."

"I know what you thinking. You ain't gotta say it. It's all over your little face. You thinking I'm a ho because I slept with our uncle."

Caesar coughed, and his eyes widened, but he kept them on the road. I closed mine briefly, embarrassed out of my mind. "That's what you thinking, ain't it? Or some shit like that? But sometimes you gots ta do what you gotta do."

"Yeah," I mumbled, "but not with family. You have to draw the line somewhere, don't you?"

"Shut the fuck up! You don't know shit, with your young, dumb ass."

I know you ain't shit, I thought to myself. Finally she silenced her mouth. Desiree had a way of pissing me the hell off 'cause she didn't know how to stop.

Caesar rubbed my thigh, and I smiled at him again. "Make a right here, boyfriend-in-law," she spat out nastily, crossing her arms under her chest and twisting her head to one side.

When he did, she told him, "Now pull into that motel." I cringed inside when I got a look at the place.

"Desiree, here? This place looks horrible!" I cried, my eyes wide.

"Well, shit, Cashmere, I ain't eighteen until next month, and I know the manager here. It's the best that I can do for now, so shut up."

"How?"

She didn't answer until she opened her door, stepped out, and poked her head in my face. "How what?"

"How you know him?"

"We just cool, Cash, that's all. Stop asking me questions that are not your business."

I gritted my teeth as she sashayed away to the office. I leaned over and kissed Caesar. "I'll see you tomorrow after school, okay."

He chased after me as I got out of his car and tugged both me and my sister's bags. "Cashmere, are you sure you're okay here?"

I dropped Desiree's bag and reached up to stroke his cheek. "You so sweet, worrying about me. I'm so lucky to have a boyfriend like you, Caesar. I hope you know that."

He kissed my hand and said, "I know it. But, baby, I'm worried about you."

"Don't be. If me and my sister are anything, we are some survivors, and we'll be okay. I'll be at work tomorrow, so you don't have to worry." I tiptoed and gave him a peck.

Desiree strolled up to us and yelled, "Hey, dude, get your ass off my fourteen-year-old sister."

Caesar dropped his hands immediately, but I waved her away and put them back around my waist.

"No, I need to get home before Mother starts to worry about me."

My sister mocked him. "'Before Mother starts to worry about me'? Nigga, where you from?"

He ignored her, waved at me, and got into his car and drove away.

After his car vanished, I asked, "What room is it?"

"Girl, they gave us the honeymoon suite!"

Desiree bumped her booty into mine. Whenever she did that, I would laugh and say, "Girl, watch that bone 'cause we all know you ain't got no rump and that bone hurts." And she would laugh and say, "But I got titties."

"Come on, Cash, you ain't gonna say it?"

"Say what?"

"You know. Say it, Cash. Please, say it!"

I repeated the line in a flat voice. "Girl, watch that bone 'cause we all know you ain't got no rump and that bone hurts."

She laughed. "But I got titties! Girl, you still crazy."

And despite the situation and my anger, I laughed alongside her as we went to our honeymoon suite.

Chapter 13

I was on pins and needles the day I was to officially meet Caesar's whole family. Would they like me? Hate me? I wanted them to love me, because I knew his family meant a lot to him. I prayed everything went well. Since me and Desiree were currently living in a hotel, there was pretty much no way that I could afford to buy myself something to wear, get my hair done, or a manicure like I wanted.

Caesar said to wear something conservative, so I pulled out a linen dress I wore last Easter, one that dropped to my knees.

Since Desiree was trying to be on my good side, she painted my nails, toenails, and did my hair in a pretty style for me. She said, "You look real good, Cashmere, honestly."

I bit my bottom lip and studied myself in the cracked mirror in the bathroom. "Just make sure you remember all that stuff Mama taught you."

I turned around and gave her a funny look. "Mama ain't taught me shit."

"Well, Daddy sure did, 'cause you know one thing he had a problem with, and that was not having proper table etiquette, and presenting ourselves like young ladies."

I nodded. That, I was cool with. But what if they had other questions for me? Questions I wasn't just ready to answer.

Desiree read my thoughts. "Your daddy is an accountant, and your mother is a nurse."

"Okay." I took a deep breath. I wondered if Caesar would be okay with me lying to his parents.

The knock on the hotel room made me jump. I gave myself one last glance in the mirror. From the corner of my eye, I saw Desiree switch to the door and open it. What was up with the switching? Like Caesar wasn't what he was—my damn man!

She stood in front of the door, and pulled it open, her hands on her hips.

"Hello, sexy."

"Hi. Is Cashmere here?"

Before she could say anything else, I rushed to the door and shoved her ass out of the way and went straight into Caesar's arms. "Hey." I slipped my hands in his, and we walked to his car.

Desiree smacked her teeth. "Here we go with this love jones bullshit," she muttered.

When I looked back, I caught Desiree spying on us from the hotel window. I ignored her and sat in the passenger seat, careful not to wrinkle my dress.

"You look real nice, so don't worry, Cashmere," Caesar said.

Shit, I hoped I did. But his words didn't stop me from stressing. Maybe I should have told Caesar no about meeting his family. I was, after all, a stripper and an orphan Annie. He was getting ready to go to a good college. There was no way anybody could see me as being on his level or good enough for him. Shit, sometimes I doubted it. What did this fool see in me any damn way? Maybe if things were different for me, when Mama was actually a wife and mother, and my dad was of sound body and mind, when we were just a middle-class family.

Caesar's family lived in Ladera Heights, a part of California I'd never heard of. Now I thought before our dad got sick that we were doing pretty good in our middle-class neighborhood, but these big-ass houses made our house look like one damn room.

"Caesar, your house looks like a mansion."

"It is one," he said casually, like it wasn't nothing.

"It is?"

"It's nothing, Cashmere. Just extra space to clean."

But I found that hard to believe as we drove around the wraparound driveway and I saw a damn near perfect manicured lawn and the marble entrance with the French double doors.

As we walked up the steps, I saw a fireplace from the outside. And when he used his key and we stepped inside, there were windows in the damn ceiling, which he called skylights. A winding staircase overlooked the living room, so at any given time people could look down on us. I made sure I kept a smile on my face and didn't curse. The hardwood floors were white and shiny, like someone had just polished them, so I took small steps, afraid I would bust my ass.

"Are we the only ones here? I don't hear anybody else, Caesar."

He chuckled. "The walls are sound-proof."

"Oh." I felt so stupid and scared, and both feelings got the better of me.

I turned and was about to run out the damn house, but Caesar grabbed me and whipped me around in his arms. "What's wrong, Cashmere?"

I shook my head and avoided his eyes. "You know damn well I don't belong here. You know you met me at a strip club. What you doing is nice, but I'm not going to ever fit here, and it's cool."

He studied me carefully. "If you don't belong here, I don't belong here. I can't judge you for being in a strip club 'cause I was in one that night too. So I'm no better than you are. Coming or not coming from money does not define a person. And I think you are special. Even that night I met you, I felt you didn't belong there. And you didn't. You were just doing what you had to do. That makes you a better person than most people I know. So if you wanna leave, say the word. I'll leave with you."

I thought about it as he waited patiently for my reply. And he was right. Yes, I could be mischievous, I had a dirty mouth, but I wasn't a bad person, was I? If he didn't see me as one and saw me as someone special, why couldn't I? I used to. I pushed all the negative thoughts away. I would work them out later.

"I'll stay." As I looked around, all I saw was luxury and money—expensive paintings, crystal, fur-lined couches . . .

The double doors across the living room slipped open, and I could hear a woman's voice, her heels clicking against the floor. I guess she didn't care about scuffing them up, or falling.

"Caesar, honey, is that you?"

Caesar's mother wore an expensive, sharp-looking suit. She was very pretty, and Caesar had a lot of his features from her. But it was the bling coming from so many places on her neck, ears, wrist, and fingers that really caught my attention. She was full of diamonds. She had on some sharp shoes too, the ones Mama use to drool over on the Internet (Jimmy Choo) that she never had enough money to buy, and her hair was slicked back in a thick bun. Judging from that house, all that shit on her had to be real.

She walked down the long path from the dining room to the living room. "I thought I saw your car drive up, son."

"Hey, Mom." Caesar untangled his hand from mine and embraced her.

As he did, her eyes pierced me as her chin rested on his shoulder, so I offered a smile. She did too, but she might as well not have, 'cause it was a cold-ass one at that. I knew I was gonna have some shit with her.

When she pulled away from her son and turned to me, I stuttered out like a damn retard. "Hi, ma'am."

"Hello." Her hands barely touched mine when I held out my hand to shake hers.

Bitch!

"Is this the girl you were telling me and your dad about? That has been helping you at your little store." She was now wiggling, rubbing the hand she shook mine with, and looking at it disdainfully, like she had just dipped it in shit.

Caesar smiled. "Yeah."

She raised a brow. "Yeah?"

"I'm sorry. Yes, Mother, this is Cashmere, my girlfriend."

I stared down at the slick floor as I felt her eyes dissect me.

Wasn't shit warm about her reception.

"Well, everyone is waiting on you, so let's go in inside so we can eat."

"Right, Mom."

We followed after her into the dining room then walked down some stairs into another big room.

When I stumbled on a step, Caesar rubbed my back, soothing me. "Relax, Cashmere."

The dining room was bigger than the whole café.

I was introduced to everyone there, from his dad and grandparents, to an aunt and uncle, who were cool. But his evil-ass mom mean-mugged me the whole time I was there. Then his older brother, Angelo, wouldn't stop looking at me, and when I held my hand out to his ugly-ass girlfriend and said hello, she brushed right past me like I wasn't shit. Caesar's brother would not leave me alone, though.

The food was cool. Everything was set up like a buffet, and you pretty much got what you wanted, some stuff I had before, some I didn't. There was regular stuff like pot roast, stuffed chicken, salmon, filet mignon, shrimp, lamb, lobster, lobster bisque, crab, clams, pasta, rice, potatoes, some shit called keish, artichokes I wasn't gonna bother with, and asparagus and whatnot. I ate light as hell 'cause his mama watched me more than she chewed.

I rose from the table to get some more food and avoided her eyes, which were making me dizzy.

"Try the crab. It's sweet and tender. Like you."

First, I thought it was Caesar getting a little freaky, but when I turned and saw it was Angelo, I frowned, grabbed some shrimp, and rushed back to the table.

Questions during dinner ranged from where I was from, how old I was, what my parents did, to what I planned on doing with my life. The shitty part of it was that the mama was the one asking all the questions and didn't give anyone else the chance to ask me shit. She damn near choked when I told her I wanted to do hair for a living, but Caesar held my hand under the table and squeezed it, letting me know he was okay with my dream.

The dad cut in and said, "Well, we own a couple—"

The mother cut him off and drilled me some more. She wasn't gonna rest until she made me feel like uncomfortable, I guess. But I answered each question and kept eye contact with her ass. I know one thing, if Daddy was there he would have been proud of the way I handled myself. And Caesar was proud of me too.

After dinner, people scattered around the house. The grandparents went into the family room to watch TV on this big-ass wide-screen TV. I know because I helped his grandmother in there.

Everyone went out on the balcony, leaving Caesar and Angelo, who were attacking the left-over shrimp, lobster, and crab like little boys in a candy store.

My bladder started talking to me, so I asked, "Caesar, can you take me to the bathroom?"

Before Caesar could answer, his father called out, "Angelo, take her to the bathroom."

Then before I could say, "Never mind. I'm cool. I'll hold the shit," he rushed off.

A smile curved around Angelo's lips. He looked identical to his brother, but he was just so trifling. Hitting on me despite the fact that he had a fiancée, and that I was his brother's girl made him ugly as hell to me.

"No problem, little bro. Follow me."

I smiled, trying to be polite, but quickly changed my expression to a stern one, the way Daddy used to look at me when I did something wrong, so Angelo didn't think I was inviting his advances.

He slipped a hand around my waist.

I pulled away and shifted my body to the left 'cause he was on my right.

"You don't remember me, do you?"

"Naw, so please stop talking to me and show me the bathroom, please." I was trying my best to not curse.

"Bitch."

His eyes slid over my body, making my fucking skin crawl. I stopped walking and started to shake 'cause I was holding a fist back that I wanted to fire on him.

"Your ass wasn't so proper when you was popping your pussy on my dick or slapping your titties in my face for dollars at that house party, now were you?"

Heat rushed to my face. I was having a hard time remembering his face. I mean, I had stripped for dozens of men and couldn't help it that the only one that ever stood out to me was Caesar.

"What house party, nigga?"

He laughed. "That's more like it. Your sister was there too."

Oh, shit! It came back to me now. A while back we did this private party for these dumb-ass college dudes, and Angelo was the drunk one who'd offered me an extra three hundred dollars to fuck him. I had told him to kiss my ass. I guess he couldn't handle the rejection and was holding a grudge against me.

"Is it coming back to you . . . slut?" Even as he insulted me, he reached over and tried to grab one of my breasts. "Now play nice, and I won't mention it to Caesar."

Oh, he had me fucked up. I slapped his hand away. "Muthafucka, let's get this straight. Caesar know what I do, but do he know his brother a piece of shit, trying to push up on his girl?" I rushed off before the muthafucka could answer, but deep down, I was too embarrassed to mention it to him.

After I peed I couldn't find Caesar, but his mother was still alone on the balcony, sipping on some wine.

I approached her slowly and planted myself to her right, leaning slightly forward and looking out at the view. "You have a really nice house."

She assessed me coolly. "You're very pretty, and you have a very beautiful body."

"Thank—"

"But that's really all you have going for yourself. And why have you attached yourself to my son?"

"No, I—"

"You what . . . came from a gutter and got your hands out for a prize? My prize, my son. Not going to happen. He's going away to college soon, and once he gets his little dick wet in some pussy, trust me when I say he will leave you alone and go on to college like a good little boy. I've worked too hard to raise my boys with class, morals, and values for you to come up in here trying to interrupt the program. So I'm gonna say this to you once and only once—stay the fuck away from my son, you piece of shit!"

Chapter 14

I was silent on the ride home, suppressing the urge to cry, or just tell Caesar to stop the car and find a bus and use my last to get a cab to take me home to the hotel.

"Why you so quiet, babe?"

I didn't respond. My heart was aching. I knew sooner or later his parents, well, his bitch-ass mom, was going to make him get rid of me, dump me like I was some trash. I don't think my feelings had ever been as hurt as when she said that shit to me out on the balcony. The words wouldn't leave my head. All I could do was walk away and find Caesar, tell him my head was hurting, and that I needed to get back home.

"I'm just sleepy," I said in a quiet voice. "Well, go ahead and take a catnap. I'll wake you when we get there." I closed my eyes, but I couldn't sleep. In fact, I didn't sleep at all that night.

And, yeah, Caesar's mom damn sure wasn't playing when she told me to stay the hell away from her son. I went to the café the next day, and it was closed. Not knowing where else to go, I walked home, only to find Ceasar pacing in front of his car, which was parked outside my room.

When he caught sight of me, he walked up to me quickly and hugged me. "Hey."

"Hey."

He pulled away and looked me over. "You hungry?" Before I could even respond, he snatched my arm, ushered me to his car, and sped down the street, not even giving me time to snap on my seat belt. Then he pulled into the park and parked, all done in five minutes.

I was almost scared to ask him what was wrong, but I had a feeling that I knew what it was about.

"Mama is really tripping, Cashmere."

My heart started pounding. I knew it.

"She has it in her silly, materialistic head that you're not girlfriend material. She also gave me an ultimatum."

Now I wasn't born in Laden Heights, or even too old. Still, I knew what that word meant. Mama gave those to Daddy all the time. Either take her out, or get no pussy. Buy her a purse, or get no pussy. Put some money in her hand, or get no pussy. Yeah, the word placed a sinking feeling in my stomach.

"What was the ultimatum?"

"Get rid of you or lose my café."

I figured which one he chose, and it damn sure wasn't me. I couldn't hate on him for his choice.

He'd be a fool to pick my poor ass. I had no family and probably no future. Thinking this way, I guess you could say, logically made my eyes tear up even before he got his next words out.

"So I guess you gonna have to find another job."

Man, did it make me smile to hear that.

"My mom is crazy if she thinks I'm giving you up. She's just a snob who lets money rule her head. Either way, nothing is going to stop me from seeing you, Cashmere." He tucked his hands in his front pockets, looked at the ground then back at me. "'Cause I love you. And, Cashmere, I don't give a fuck that you stripped, that your mom is gone, that your sister is what she is. And I feel that you care about me just as much as I care about you. And I do want to take care of you, baby. And in time I will. It's just I can't offer you much now, but my heart."

I reached over and rubbed my knuckles across his cheek, and he kissed the inside of my palm.

So all his dumb-ass mama did was bring us closer.

We spent a lot of time together during that time. But time was also ticking, and he would be leaving soon to go to Grambling. He was on speaking terms with his father but still wasn't speaking to his mother, who used to blow his cell phone up, but he never answered. He took me all over the place, Disneyland, Magic Mountain, bowling, to the movies. He would even offer me money, which I didn't really want to take, but necessity made me, so I could get Desiree off my back.

Desiree stopped selling drugs too. How she was racking in dough, I didn't know, but we had just moved to a much nicer hotel, that's for sure.

After another day of fun at a golf course, Caesar helped me out of the car and followed me to our room.

I turned, gave him a big hug.

"What do you wanna do tomorrow?"

"Oh Lord, look at the fucking lovebirds," Desiree said, a blunt dangling from her lips and she was smiling. She never smiled when she saw me with Caesar 'cause she was too busy hating on me.

"Well, I got some news for y'all. Now I got a boyfriend too. In fact he's taking me out shopping tomorrow."

The look I gave her told her I didn't give a shit.

Caesar gave me a quick kiss, promised to pick me up tomorrow, and rushed off. For some reason, he always rushed off when Desiree was around.

"Bye." I waved to him and turned back to Desiree. "Get your ass out my way, Desiree."

Chapter 15

As time wound down and Caesar had only a couple days before he left, I was starting to really stress. Despite how cool I had been that past month, knowing damn well he was leaving now, it was getting to me. I was about to lose him and I was mad at myself for being sad. He was doing the best he could by me. But, shit, I loved him. Because of my age, it may have been puppy love but, this puppy love was killing me, just like the thought of not seeing him again.

"Where the fuck is he?" I yelled out loud as I stood outside me and my sister's hotel room.

A husky voice said, "Right behind you."

I turned around quickly and shoved him playfully. "Boy! You scared me." He pulled me in his arms. "Everything okay, babe?" I tried my best not to cry yet again like a punk. I pulled away and turned my back on him. "When you leaving?"

"Remember I told you my plane leaves on Friday."

Shit, today was Wednesday. "Guess I forgot," I mumbled.

Truth was, I was hoping he'd say something like, the semester was pushed back, which sure as hell wasn't possible. Or that his flight was cancelled, and every other flight going to fucking Georgia. Or, fuck it, he just smack-dab wasn't going to go. But I'm glad he didn't say any of this 'cause I knew my ass was being hella selfish to continue to not want him to go, when this was about his future and he wanted to go. If the shoe was on the other foot, would my ass just up and forget about cosmetology school for him? Hell yes! Sadly, I can say I was a sucker for love.

"You know this is going to be hard as hell for me, Cashmere."

"What?"

"Leaving you."

"Look, you been dreaming about going off to college and pledging since forever, right? So don't trip. I'll be all right. Plus, you gotta make your dad and mom—"

"Fuck her!"

Damn, he rarely cursed. "Proud. And don't say that 'cause, no matter what goes down between us, she will always be your mother."

He shook his head. "After the way she treated you?"

Yeah, the bitch was pretty cold, but I chalked it up to her loving her son and wanting the best for him. And maybe it wasn't for the best that we be together.

"I wish I could take you with me."

"I wish I could go."

"Listen."

I faced him.

"I know this is a lot to ask you, being that we're going to be thousands of miles away from each other, and you being out here and being as pretty and smart as you are. Promise me you won't—"

"I won't shit. I should be worried about you with all them older country-fed heiffas who going to be—"

"Ten of them couldn't measure up to Cashmere."

That's when I made a choice. I grabbed Caesar by his hands and pulled him into the hotel.

I was shaking when he stripped me of my clothes, but when his lips were on me, my nerves disappeared and was replaced with a need to make love to him.

I stood before him in my panties and bra. I closed my eyes and waited to feel his lips on mine. They were soft and demanding at the same time. He sucked on my bottom lip and slid his tongue inside. I rubbed mine against his. His mouth dipped down to my neck, where he placed more kisses. He then pulled the right strap down so one of my breasts was exposed, and he caressed it with his hand and placed more kisses there, before taking my nipple in his mouth.

My breath quickened. "Ahhhhh," I moaned. *Sorry, Daddy.*

Caesar led me to the bed and laid me down. Towering above me, he slid my bra and panties off slowly, asking, "Cashmere, are you sure you wanna do this?"

"Yes, I'm sure. No, I'm not! Yes, I'm sure."

"Okay." He chuckled.

"Save yourself for your husband, baby. You got a flower down there and ain't no man worthy of that, but your husband." Those were Daddy's words. I shook my head, tried to focus on Caesar.

"You know you are the prettiest girl I have ever seen."

Daddy's words entered my head again. *"You pretty, baby, but you gonna look a whole lot prettier in white than off-white."* I lowered my lashes, trying to forget that thought as well. "Thank you."

Caesar stood there and admired me. His hands traced the outline of my body, making me quiver, before he took off his clothes and joined me.

"You got a flower down there."

I shivered when his tongue dipped further to my belly, where he placed more kisses. He was treating my body so gentle, it was almost like I was a baby. He split my legs open and placed his head there.

"Stay pure and innocent. Unless he swore before God, you don't owe him nothing below the knees, baby." Fuck! That was Daddy's voice again.

Caesar split my legs open and placed his head there. Desiree was right! Having a man go down on you is some pleasurable shit. But it did get sloppy, 'cause shit must have been new to Caesar too, 'cause he had slobber all over me.

The voice in my head came back. *"Baby, before you do it, ask yourself, is he worthy? Will he love you for a lifetime? If it takes even a second to answer, baby, you making a mistake."*

Then the shit felt bad. As his mouth loved me down there, his hands reached up and massaged my breasts and my nipples became so hard. It felt good again. Everything he was doing felt so good, all I could do was moan, my legs curled around his neck.

"Keep your doors closed, Cashmere." Fuck!

My hands were buried in his head as he kissed the lips, blew on my clit, and glided his tongue around my pussy in a circular motion. He dipped his tongue further in the folds, causing my legs to tighten around his neck. He covered my body with his and curled his strong arms under my legs, so I was positioned carefully.

"This may hurt a little, but I promise, the pain will disappear quickly."

I nodded.

"Save yourself for your husband."

When his penis was positioned at my opening, I took a deep breath. Then when I closed my eyes and waited for the pain, I saw Daddy looking at me. It wasn't Caesar. What the fuck? "Stop!"

"You okay?" he asked, looking down at me.

I pushed him off of me and covered my face with my hands and said in a muffled voice. "I can't, Caesar. I can't do this. I wanna"—yeah, 'cause the way this boy was making me feel? Wooo—"but I promised Daddy . . ."

Annoyance was on his face. It wasn't like the Caesar I was used to seeing. Nothing I ever did made him angry.

But he said, "Okay," and began to get dressed. He slammed out the hotel room with, "I'll see you tomorrow." And that was it.

I knew I'd made a mistake. I should have gave my man some. But what about what I promised Daddy?

I figured out what I could get as a going-away gift for Caesar—a sketched portrait of myself. Now, I would have preferred to get one painted, but I wasn't rolling like that. A sketch was all that I could afford. I remember they were doing them at the pier he took me to in Long Beach one day, but I was too busy stuffing my face on a chocolate-covered ice cream cone to want to go and get it done. Plus, the line to get it done was long as hell, so we said next time. And it wasn't expensive either, only about twenty bucks.

I skipped school that day and took the long bus ride there to have it done. I asked Desiree if she wanted to come, but her dumb ass wouldn't get up. She was sleeping the day away, I guess, because she got in late from her date with her so-called boyfriend, whom I still hadn't seen. And judging from Desiree's taste, case in point, our uncle-in-law, I didn't want to see him.

Once the bus dropped me off and I walked to the pier, I prayed the dude that sketched the portraits was there. He was sitting there twittering his thumbs because he didn't have any customers. Cool. I damn near ran up to him. The funny thing was, the dude could draw, but he was blind in one eye. Crazy. He had pictures of Tweety Bird, Goofy, and sketches of celebrities like Elizabeth Taylor, Janet Jackson, James Dean, and Tupac hanging up in his little corner of the pier.

"Sketch me please," I told him.

He snatched my twenty from me. "Sit there."

I did and I pulled my hair back from my face, but the damn wind was blowing it right back.

"Don't move."

I tried to give him my best smile ever, like I was auditioning for a Kool-Aid commercial. But the thing was, every time I thought about what I was doing and why I was doing it and who I was doing it for, my eyes got shiny with tears, but none of them dropped, though. My leg twitched as I tried my best not to drop my facial expression.

In about fifteen minutes, he gave me my sketch. The tears showed on the picture, stuck in the corner of my eyes like little diamonds.

"Damn, you couldn't have drawn around them tears?" I snapped, gesturing toward the picture.

He shrugged. "You didn't say."

"Draw another one."

"You have more money?"

I sucked my teeth. "No, I don't."

"They make you look more beautiful. Real."

"Kiss my ass," I huffed out as I walked off.

I had to admit the whole bus ride home that the picture did look good. It was like someone took a picture of me. I hoped Caesar would not only like it, but put it in his room and say, "That's my girl, Cashmere." And if any other chicken thought about stepping to my man, they would see my picture and step.

I rushed to our hotel door to show the picture to Desiree. I knew Caesar would be there soon.

I was out of breath when I made it to the half-way open door. But as soon as my eyes focused on what was taking place in the room through the crack in the door, I was horrified and frozen. Desiree was buck-ass naked and moving on top of Caesar, who was just as naked as she was. And she was moaning like I was moaning the night before, rocking back and forth on him. He flipped her over and was riding her like I should have let him ride on me. Then, maybe this shit wouldn't have happened.

"You giving this big-ass dick to my sister, huh? Can she handle it like I am?"

I felt powerless, like my ass was gonna straight pass out. Tears burned beneath my eyelids. My breath came out in pants, and my legs felt like jelly beneath me. The picture dropped from my hand before I screamed, "You bitch! You punk-ass muthafucka!"

They saw me standing there. Caesar's eyes widened, and Desiree, that bitch, smirked. Caesar tried to jump from the bed and go after me, but I was too fast.

I ran outside and spotted his car. I picked up a rock and threw that shit right in his window and shattered the glass. Then I spat on it over and over. I wished I had a key to scratch it. Instead, I took my foot and continued to kick the car until I dented up the sides. Then I ran off, just as he managed to get his pants on, the image of them fucking still in my head, making me cry.

Chapter 16

Day turned into night, and I couldn't stay at the home Daddy was at forever. I hadn't moved from the spot that I was in, crouched in Daddy's bed, my head on his chest. The only comfort that he could give me was the feeling of his chest rising up and down on my cheek and the sound of his heartbeat against my ear.

I left as they were locking up. The only place I could think of to go was my aunt's house.

I took a deep breath and knocked on the door. She opened it a crack and glared at me. "What do you want?"

I looked down, and my eyes teared up again. I couldn't say it. I struggled to, but my mouth was dry, and my voice cracked. She did the dirty work for me.

"You thought that boy cared about you, huh? Well, I hope you didn't give him none." I swallowed but couldn't get rid of the gargantuan-size lump in my throat.

"She probably got to him too, huh, like a damn virus. That's what your sister sure is."

"Can I come in?"

"No, I don't want you in my house."

My heart sunk.

She stepped outside, her arms under her sagging breasts, and studied my long face. "She ain't shit, just like yo mama."

I knew it was off the subject, but I asked anyway, "Why do you hate your sister so much?"

"The same reason why you hate yours. Now."

A black car pulled up on the street near us with tinted windows. I ignored it.

"You know them?"

I glanced at it as it parked. I shook my head. "Can I—"

"You can't stay here."

"I can't stay with my sister anymore, Auntie, not after what she did. I should have kicked her ass, but I been fighting her my whole life. It wouldn't have solved nothing. It wasn't until now that I understand what you been saying, and what Mama said. Desiree ain't shit, if she can do what she did to me, and she knew I cared about him."

"Coming over here with his nose in the air like we beneath him. What he got to say about it?"

"I ain't talked to him."

The car started up, pulled out of its space, and drove away.

"Why you didn't confront him? It takes two."

"Couldn't." Tears dropped as the scene flashed before me again. "Couldn't see his eyes after that. I need, I want to remember his eyes like they were before. The last time I saw him he was smiling at me. If he had done it or not done it, he's leaving and I wanna remember him like that, not like I saw him." I shook my head. "See, you ain't gonna understand, so forget it."

Aunt Ruby could understand, if she tried to, if she looked at herself and the situation with her husband and Desiree.

"The thing is, the best punishment I can give her is to not deal with her ever again."

She nodded as if she agreed. Then she repeated, "You can't stay here."

"But I have nowhere else to go."

"No."

"Why, Auntie?"

She glanced back at her house and said the craziest shit to me. "I don't like the way he looks at you."

I started sobbing. "Please. I would never."

"Her destiny has been fulfilled, and your destiny is hers. You can't run away from it."

I bawled and took a step toward her, my arms outstretched. "I don't understand. Auntie, please."

She took a step back and opened her door. "Cashmere, get the fuck off my property and don't ever come back, ever."

A gust of air hit me as she slammed the door in my face. I started walking, having nowhere to go. I would've slept on the street before going back to the hotel to stay with that trifling bitch, Desiree. Fuck that!

The wind was blowing heavily. For some reason Mama's words came back to me. "In other words, life gonna be hard as hell on you, baby girl."

A car honked loud as hell, scaring me. "Fuck you!" I flipped the bird and kept on walking.

Another passed, and a man was hanging out the passenger side and leering at me. "What's up on some pussy?"

"What's up on getting your ass kicked?" I yelled, showing him my middle finger again.

A man was walking toward me on the other side on the street. Now if I wasn't by myself or even if it was daytime, I wouldn't be bothered in the least by him. But for some reason he just so happened to cross the street and continued to walk behind me.

Seeing no one else around me, like a mom pushing her baby in a stroller, some kids my age walking by with cell phone playing some Jay-Z song, or some old lady wheeling groceries away in a cart, I was scared. Especially since he looked like a damn pimp, going, "Psst, psst," to me.

I turned the other way just as the black Cadillac I had seen earlier at my aunt's house sped past me. I opted to go down the alley instead. The biggest mistake I ever made in my life. A mistake so bad that, after I made it, I promised myself that if I ever had kids, the first thing I would teach them before reading, writing, or looking both ways before crossing the street was to never, ever go down a dark alley at night, and hope they didn't forget about it like I did. 'Cause Daddy sho 'nuff told me, since I had silky pigtails in my hair and hadn't had teeth yet, not to ever do it.

I took off running for my life. After looking over my shoulders at least five times, I noticed the man was no longer behind me. The new threat was that black Cadillac that, just as I made another turn and was a couple feet away from the other opening of the alley that would put me on the main street going in a different direction, sped in the alley and stopped me from exiting.

Some dudes I had never seen before jumped out, leaving me no choice but to run back into the heart of the alley to get away before they did God knows what to me. But my running didn't do shit, and since I had already been running, I was tired and worn-down, so they easily caught me, two of them, and dragged me back to the car, covering my mouth to silence my screaming. They tossed me in the trunk, shoved me all the way in, and slammed the top, making me feel like I was having a heart attack, and sped off.

The drive was quick, which was good, 'cause I felt like I was hyperventilating. They dragged me from the car. I was so fearful about what was going to happen that I kept my eyes closed. I felt myself being carried then shoved hard.

I opened my eyes and glanced around the room. I was in a living room. I was alone. I jumped up and looked for an exit. Once I saw it, I stood to run.

Desiree came out of a room, ass buck-naked. "Cashmere, it's gonna be okay."

"Fuck you! Where the fuck you bring me to, you tramp?"

Her eyes were glazed, and her face looked weird." Oh, honey, I know you're hurt, but don't be. I did what was best for us. I've entered a new world now, and well, it's only right that you enter that world also. I had to get you away from Caesar, one way or another, 'cause he was bad for business."

Despite my promise to myself, I rushed her, my fist cocked, when a man walked into the room. I paused and mean-mugged him. "Nigga, who the fuck are you?"

"Cashmere, stop looking like that, honey."

Why is she talking like that? What the fuck is going on?

"Remember I was telling you that I got a boyfriend. Well, here he is. I just call him *Daddy*."

I paused and studied him; everything about him, his dark-as-hell skin, full lips, and wide-bridged nose with flared-out nostrils. He was tall and lean, and carried himself like a panther. After my inspection, I knew exactly what he was.

"Bitch, are you crazy? That's a pimp."

She laughed. "This where we stayin'."

"Oh, bitch, you crazy! I'm getting the hell up out of here." I ran for the door.

Desiree chased after me.

"Move!" She was pulling on me.

He came behind her.

"Calm down, little sister. Everything gonna be okay."

"Move!"

My eyes were wide, and I was crying at the same time. He had my arms pinned behind me, and she was stuffing something white into my nose that burned at first then had me dizzy. Then they stuffed a pill inside my mouth and forced a bitter liquid down my throat.

His husky voice was in my ear, saying, "It's okay, Cashmere. Daddy gonna take care of both of you."

I was halfway out, and you don't want to know what happened after that. One thing was for sure, it was far from over.

I felt Desiree's hands all over me, peeling my clothes away, my shirt, pants, underwear, bra, shoes, and socks. I really felt like I couldn't move my muscles, which gave out on me. I can't describe the feeling, but I know it was drug-induced. "I don't wanna." I slapped at her hands.

Desiree held my head and whispered in my ear, "It's okay, Cash. He did the same thing to me the first time. He has to break you in. It won't take that long. I'll be right with you, Cash."

Her voice was going in and out, and I could barely see.

Everything was moving in circles, and their voices kept echoing. I couldn't keep my head up.

"Yeah, she fine. Thank you for bringing your sister to be put on, Desiree."

"No problem, daddy."

My tongue was heavy in my mouth, and I felt like I was floating. He was touching me, and I didn't have the strength to push his hands away.

Desiree's hands were in my hair, and his tongue was on my titties. He put his hand between my legs. I groaned and moaned when he put his tongue down there. Couldn't help it.

He started kissing me and whispering, "You daddy's property now. Daddy gonna take good, good care of you, Cashmere."

Smooth voice, smooth like water. Soft, soft for a man.

Hands were on me again. And his dick was in me. I felt a tiny pinch then it felt good. Real good.

He grunted. "Daddy's pussy now."

I couldn't push him away, since my legs were held up in a firm grip.

Desiree whispered in my ear again, "It's almost over, Cash, and then you'll be like me."

When he pulled out, I moaned again. *This is bad, bad, Cashmere. Stop fucking enjoying this shit!*

My legs were lifted higher, and he slid a tongue in me again, making my moans louder.

Then he slid his dick right back into me. I was wet, wet like I was for Caesar. *Does that make me bad? A ho? Damn! Daddy, I'm sorry.*

He slid out and went into me again, twisting his body.

My legs were shaking, and I felt like I had to pee.

Auntie's words came back. *"Your sister's destiny has been fulfilled, and your destiny is hers."*

Felt my eyes lids flutter gave a deep moan from the pits of my tummy. He was licking my titties again.

"Almost over, Cash." That was Desiree. The bitch.

"Cum for daddy."

I think I did. Wetness was all I felt before my eyes rolled back in my head.

And that was my introduction into the ho game.

I blinked rapidly. The damn mascara was irritating the hell out of me. I wasn't the same Cashmere. Well, that's what my clothes said. I was dolled up in this gold sequined tank top with thin straps across my titties, and some linen shorts. On my arms were shimmery gold bracelets, and a gold choker on my neck, forcing my thick hair to stay planted to one side in a ponytail. I had on all this damn makeup like I was a damn gypsy.

But on the inside I was the same, just a little angrier and a little more shamed. And right about now, I felt like I was a piece of fried chicken. The last piece in the bucket. That's how these four dudes were staring at me. This was to be my first trick-turning experience.

Only, it would be a series of tricks because, while it was me and Desiree in the room, three out of the four wanted to fuck me, not her. And the way the fourth dude was eye-balling me, it seemed he wanted to fuck me too.

That nigga Black had laid out the pimp commandments to me.

1. Never run away, 'cause if you do, no one will ever find you. Literally.

2. Never try to juggle more than one pimp. You'll pay for it with your life.

3. Don't try to keep even a penny of the money before turning it over to your pimp.

4. Don't look other pimps in the eye.

5. The only one that can hit your pussy raw is your pimp.

6. Don't ever do anything else besides ho'ing. That's your job, what you on earth for.

7. Number three again.

8. Don't fall in love with tricks. Fall in love with the fucking.

9. Pimps always come first before anybody, period.

10. Number 7 and 3 again.

Of course, Desiree explained all this shit to me while I glared at the bitch like she wasn't shit for getting me involved in this shit. But, according to her, if it wasn't for Black, we would've been in a lot of shit 'cause he was the one paying for Daddy to stay in that home.

"What you been doing with the money you were making and the dough I been giving you?" I wanted to ask but didn't. It wouldn't matter. We were stuck. Destiny was a son of a bitch. After they transformed me from the girl I was to this shit, I hated looking at the mirror.

When I thought about the day they'd drugged me and Black fucked me, I kept tugging at my palm with my nails, to wipe the thoughts away. Afterwards I woke up to find him cuddling me like I was his wife and shit. When I tried to pull away, he snatched me back and said, "You home now. You got a real nigga now. And I'm gonna take care of you."

"I don't wanna be here," I mumbled, tears pouring from my eyes when the reality of where I was and what just happened hit me again.

"You'll adjust," he said.

"Cash!"

I ignored my sister and looked back at the dudes. One was tall and ugly, one was short and ugly, and one was fat and ugly. There was no way

I wanted them all up in my fourteen-year-old pussy. Well, I was turning fifteen next month, but that didn't matter.

I shivered. I pulled on the edges of my shirt so that the material would loosen up and wouldn't fit to my chest the way it did.

Desiree tapped me. She laced her hands in mine."We gotta get this started."

I finally turned a cold eye on her and snatched my hand away from her. I closed my eyes as shame filled me.

She shrugged and pulled her shirt over her head.

Just then, I jumped up from the bed and ran in the bathroom. I locked myself in there and sat down on the edge of the tub.

A few seconds later, I heard Desiree sigh and knock on the door. I ignored her.

"Cashmere, come on, open the door."

"Fuck you!"

"Baby, we got paying customers."

"Fuck them!"

I heard laughter.

"Black is waiting outside. These his clients and friends. You can't disrespect him like that, and plus, they already paid Black."

"Fuck him too!"

She huffed a deep mouthful of breath. "Come on."

I unlocked the door and sat back on the edge of the tub.

Desiree stepped in the room with a glass and two plastic baggies in her hand, both her titties hanging out. She sat down next to me. "Listen, I know that you're still mad, but face it, this is our life now and you gotta accept it. We need someone to take care of us. Every woman needs a man, and ain't no man harder than Black. We his hoes and we both broken in now. Ain't no turning back now, Cash. One day you going to love me for the choice I made for us."

I turned to her. "Just so you know, I hate you, Desiree. Hate you more than Auntie. Hate you more than Mama. I wish you wasn't my sister. I hope you die one day."

Seemingly unaffected by what I said, her reply was, "Here take some of this. It will make you feel good like the other day."

I glanced down at her hand, balled in a fist and some white powder on the edge of it. She pulled it to her face, pinched one nostril, and sniffed deeply. Her face screwed up for a second, and she shuddered. Then, eyes closed, she smiled like she was floating.

I shook my head at her. "I don't want that shit." That was what she gave me that night Black did what he did.

She shook her head and placed a pill in my hand. "Then try this, Cash. It's not coke. It's like a painkiller, and it's not addictive. It will get you through this. However you wanna feel, it's gonna make you feel like that—happy, high, horny, funny, all of it. Because, despite how much shit you talk, you gotta do it. And you know it too."

I needed a painkiller, all right, to kill this pain I had inside. I dropped it down my throat and took a long swallow of the bitter brown liquid she'd poured in a glass for me.

She patted my back and said, "That's it, little sister. Let the pill do its work."

And after a few moments I was feeling good.

She helped me undress, and I slipped back into the room with her. The dudes were leering at me.

Desiree went straight to her trick, dropped on her knees in front of him, pulled his pants and boxers around his ankles, and took his dick in her mouth. I watched, feeling good, but horrified nonetheless. She bobbed her head on it quickly.

I jumped when a hand stroked my behind. I gave him an evil-ass look.

He winked at me, the tall ugly one, and asked, "You ready, baby?"

I closed my eyes and nodded. I guess I was expected to do the same. Whether he was ugly or fine, I still wouldn't want to do this shit.

My sister pulled the dick out of her mouth and said breathlessly, "Cash, make sure he puts on a condom."

He did.

The other two men stood around the bed and watched the action, my naked ass sprawled up on it and him jamming his dick into me. I kept my eyes closed, squinting to keep the tears from falling out of them. To ease my mind and to keep from screaming, I thought about everything I could think of that would halt me from jumping up and pushing him off of me as he stabbed me. And it hurt like hell, 'cause his shit was hard, big, and fat, and my pussy was dry, little, and tight. I moaned in pain.

He thought I was enjoying the shit, so he got rougher. "You so pretty," he murmured.

I opened my eyes and looked at him. He had to be in his forties. Had to have a kid, a niece, a godchild, or something my age. But that didn't stop him from wanting to fuck me. Then that's when his dog chain hit me in my face. Had a reflection of a girl looking back at me, smiling. I turned my face to the side to avoid it hitting me again, or seeing it.

"Man, come on with all that shit."

I ignored the voice. The belt buckle on his pants kept slapping me in my ass as he entered and exited my pussy. I kept singing songs in my head, recited The Holy Prayer.

When he busted, I rolled away, and for the first time in my life I sucked a man's dick. Through it, in my head, I recited the "I Have a Dream" speech. I grimaced every time he snatched my hair up to jam his dick deeper in my mouth. His balls were in my face, and he smelled like some old sweaty boxers. I tried not to gag.

The worst part was having to swallow his cum. His grip on the back of my neck grew tighter and his legs shook. After that I knew when a man was going to cum.

The next guy, unlike the other guys, had sympathy in his eyes. He also had a little dick that didn't hurt as much as the other bastard. He stroked my pussy gently and smiled down at me. He was the short, ugly one. I just prayed the shit would be over soon, 'cause the other three dudes were watching me and saying what a fine ho I was, and how good my pussy was. And Desiree was nowhere to be seen.

And finally he came.

For all that shit, I received three hundred dollars, but I felt like I did the shit for free, 'cause

I paid a high price. My sanity and self-respect started chipping after that.

Afterwards, feeling dumb for doing it, I went directly to the shower. I felt like I was on TV. And it was one of them movies where a woman was raped and she always showered afterwards, as if it would wipe away the act. I guess I was delusional like them chicks in them movies, 'cause I couldn't stop scrubbing myself, and still it didn't get rid of the shame that I felt.

I slipped on my clothes, left the hotel, and climbed in the backseat of Black's car. Desiree offered me a smile.

I stared out the window. The hot tears ran down my face so slow, by the time they got to my chin, they were cold. And I cried all night.

Chapter 17

After my first trick, I found two things to get me through the rest—Grey Goose and ecstasy—which enabled me to sleep peacefully. Desiree's drug of choice was coke. I, however, wasn't fuckin' with that shit! The ecstasy and Goose was cool. The only time that I didn't get high was on Sundays when we went to see Daddy. Our real Daddy! Being there always made me feel like shit, 'cause I was far from being Daddy's little girl now, from being the perfect girl he always thought I was.

Black called us his "prime bitches," and often took us to special clients. We got the rappers who flew into Cali and wanted a little pussy, or the actors, basketball, and football stars, so he kept us pretty clean. But Black said when these clients showed a decline, we would be back on the track. But, see, I never hit the track. I had seen it when we would roll by and collect dough. Desiree was on the track, and I know it pissed her off. Still, we got preferential treatment, compared to the other bitches.

In that short time, I had fucked men of all kinds and ages—thugs, hustlers, Wall Street dudes, lawyers, even celebrities. The shit was crazy. A lot of times we'd show up at parties dressed to impress then I'd see a nigga point at us, or murmur, "I want that bitch."

Then Black would nod, and it was on. Black said I was a high-priced ho. I didn't like the title. I felt like I was being insulted when he said it was a compliment.

"Cashmere, baby," he told me, "you sure are hard to please." But he also said I was too special just to be standing on a stroll.

So the niggas I fucked with wined and dined me before fucking the hell out of me, poking tiny holes in my young-ass soul that didn't get a chance to be nurtured. Sometimes I had the same trick request me again. I'd just slip a pill and do what I had to do. All these niggas raking in dough for him should have made Black happy, but all it seemed to do was piss him off more.

But then again Black was a weird dude anyway. He didn't eat no meat, and every morning he woke up and exercised. He prayed to Allah, and yet he pimped hoes. And he did all this pimping without ever raising his voice. Bitches acted like they worshipped him and moved whenever he snapped his fingers, including Desiree, who acted like she was obsessed with him. And his ass, hell, he acted like he was obsessed with me.

Now, at first, Black never laid a finger on me. In fact he never yelled at me. But even still I knew he was dangerous, so I never crossed him. I'd heard stories of what he'd done to other hoes who got out of pocket. Beatings, burnings, and shit I didn't wanna hear, far less repeat. Yep, I could tell Black was no joke.

Mama always said, "The heard muthafuckas are the ones that don't have to say shit. They rep speaks for itself. So if somebody wolfing shit, that's really all the hell they doing, and shouldn't be no problem taking their ass out."

Whatever. I didn't want to be one of them girls. Desiree neither. I also knew that Black had spent nearly half his life locked away at Pelican Bay. One of the hoes told me that though. She said he had no problem killing, and if a ho ran away, he had no problem killing again.

"How long was he in jail?" I asked her.

"How old you?"

"Fourteen."

"Longer than you been living, and he did some cold shit in that bitch too. So don't go getting too independent. Just try to be a good little ho. Suck and fuck as many niggas as you can. Do that shit good, don't fuck up the count, and don't try to run away, or you gonna find yourself in a dumpster."

Even though she wouldn't tell me what Black went to jail for, I knew it was something horrible. But she added, "He don't plan on going back anytime soon in this lifetime, and I'm sure he'd take a bullet before allowing the po-pos to take him in."

I was taking a shower and was about to step out when I felt a presence in the room. I almost jumped when I saw Black in the bathroom studying me through the sheer plastic shower curtain. Though he was gentle with me most of the time, I still feared his ass.

"Cashmere, you following proper protocol on them dates?"

His voice was so soft, I had to turn the shower off to hear him fully. "Yeah."

He studied me for a long moment, ignoring his ringing phone. He pulled the shower curtain back, pushed his fingers in my hair, and kissed me on my lips.

I pulled away but not too quickly. I walked into the bedroom to dry myself off. He grabbed my arm and pulled me into his arms and walked me backwards toward the bed. My heart started pounding. I hated him and I didn't hate him—that's the only way to describe how I felt about Black.

See, he wasn't mean to me, he was nice, treating me like I was his woman sometimes. I knew he was attracted to me and desired me, 'cause he fucked me just as much as the tricks did. But I hated him for making me be a ho. His fingers made me melt too, and I hated myself for that.

"You know I let a lot of stuff you do slide, Cashmere?"

I nodded, pulling my lips in.

He tilted my face up to his. "I do it 'cause I know you're special, Cash. Your sister ain't got the pizzazz that you have. You givin' my bottom bitch a run for her money. You sure are."

I looked in his smoky eyes, as his hold tightened on my arm.

"Just don't do anything to fuck up my good graces, Cashmere."

"I won't, Black." I looked at my feet.

His hands slid up and down my back. "Daddy," he corrected.

I gritted my teeth and repeated what he said.

"Who am I?

"My folk, my pimp."

"And what does that mean?"

"That I belong to you. I serve you."

He made me say this all the fucking time, like he thought he was gonna brainwash me.

"You love those fools?"

"No. There's only one man that I love, and his name is Desmond Pierce."

Black frowned. He must have thought I was going to say him, but I wasn't the lovesick puppy my sister was, I was just playing the game I had to play.

"Lay down."

I did as he told me, and as usual, panic rose in my chest. The way he made me feel made me hate myself later because he was controlling everything I did.

He crouched on his stomach and knees and skipped my naked legs over his shoulders. His tongue slipped into my pussy, past my lips, into my crevices. All of them. Sensations built up inside of me. I couldn't deny or fight them for shit on this earth. It was always like this. I knew Black had a gift. He could eat pussy and fuck. And these gifts allowed him to have seventeen hoes under him.

He made love to my pussy, kissing it like it was my mouth, sliding his tongue in it like he was exploring it for lost treasure. He bit my clit gently then tongued it. I moaned loudly, even though I didn't want to, tightening my legs around my neck as tremors pulsed throughout me. And right when I felt that sensation like I was going to cum, he stroked me, and I felt my cum splash out of me.

Black left and came back with a rag and cleaned me up. "Can Daddy make you feel like that, Cashmere?"

I lowered my lashes. I knew he was jealous of my love for Daddy, and might have thought it was taking away from the love I had for him.

Ninety percent of the time Black treated me like I was his baby. If ever he slipped away from treating me that way, it made Desiree happy as hell, who was in love with Black as deeply as a person could fall for a man, even though he treated her like shit and had her on the track day in and day out.

We didn't really fraternize with the other hoes because Black didn't really approve of that shit. He felt that any free moment we had should be reserved for making dough. But sometimes we sneaked and had little parties and watched movies together. Not too many were with the program, not wanting to risk Black finding out.

I befriended one of the hoes, Peaches, who had been down with Black for over four years. Ol' girl was twenty-two but looked like she was in her thirties. They said that's what the game did, age the hell out of you.

Black kept her around because, according to him, she could suck a mean dick. And I knew for a fact that he dibbled and dabbled with all the hoes in the building. Once I caught him, Desiree, and Peaches in bed together. I almost vomited at that nasty shit. Peaches was a tow-up looking ho. Just being real. She'd been getting a weave in her hair by some chick named Crystal, who lived in Carson, but was on maternity leave, and some other chick ended up burning her hair out. So she was taking a break from it.

So I offered to braid her hair for her and had been working on it that whole morning.

"Girl, you must have some magic fingers," she exclaimed, touching her hair.

I just laughed. It felt good to be able to do braids again. I had just finished the first half of her hair when Black slammed into the house. See, we had snuck, 'cause her ass said he was going to be making rounds on the track.

"Hey, Black," she said nervously. "Your girl Cashmere here was just doing my hair. Now I know you said we couldn't hang, but I needed to get my hair right, so I can go out and make them ends for ya. I wasn't doing too good on that, since the weave come out. You said presentation is everything, right?"

He stood in the doorway, where we couldn't see his face, there being no light there.

I bit my bottom lip, feeling uneasy.

"Go home, Cashmere." He walked past me.

Before I made it to the door. I glanced back and saw him walk up to Peaches. He took one look at her, and hauled off and slapped her in the mouth, and she started crying.

"Go home, Cashmere," he repeated.

I slipped out the doors, but heard him tell her, "Bitch, go out like that and make my dough looking stupid just like that, and if you short, I'm fucking you up!"

My heart started to pound as I dashed out and went to me and Desiree's apartment.

When he came back to the house. I was sitting on the couch.

"Go in the room."

I did, and he followed after me. I was waiting for him to slap me like Peaches, but instead, he told me, "Take off your clothes."

I did quickly and stood in front of him. His eyes raked my body. The only real change these past couple months was my titties were bigger and my hips slightly wider.

"Listen, Cashmere, and listen well. You are a ho. That's what you do. You are not a hairstylist. You fuck, suck dick and assholes, and even feet, if need be. You get ambitious again, and I will fuck you up."

There was fire in his eyes, but not once did he raise his voice above a whisper. But he still scared me so much. I nodded my head over and over again. But instead of fucking me up, he fucked the shit out of me.

My punishment for getting "ambitious" was being put on the track that night with fat-lipped Peaches. Desiree got my trick, and she couldn't have been happier about the shit. That night out there, shivering like a damn fool, part of me wanted to take a chance and run away. It wasn't the first time I thought about doing it. But every ten minutes Black would cruise on by, letting me know not to try it. I didn't bother to even look at him as he slid down the street past me.

Another pimp casually approached me talking that dumb shit. "Say, ho, you need to get with a winna, that's a winna like myself. They broke the mold when they made a pimp like me, ho. I'll make all your ho wishes come true."

Black told me whenever a pimp approached me with that lingo to keep on pushing, so I kept my head down and brushed right past him. But every time I turned around, his silly ass was on my heels.

He must've said, "Say, ho," at least forty times, until I couldn't take it anymore and ran in the opposite direction.

He got the hint and went after another ho. He did it in the nick of time too, 'cause Black sped by me again and hit the corner. He was probably going to check on another ho.

I took a deep breath and froze when I felt something poke me in the small of my back.

Whoever had something in my back said, "Walk."

I nodded, scared out of my mind. Judging from the prick, I thought it was a knife. I walked slowly and said, "I don't have any—"

"Shut the fuck up! It's not your money I want." The knife slid up some more, making me stumble. "Keep on walking." He guided me into the empty parking lot.

Just my luck. I was crying and holding my breath at the same time, not knowing what this man planned to do to me.

I finally looked at him when he shoved me further into the lot and paused between two cars. He was tall as hell with a cap on his head. It was so dark, I could barely make out his features. And I only got a second's worth of a glance.

"Get them pants down."

"No, please." Then I sobbed and felt my shoulders moving up and down with my crying.

He reached over and slapped me in my face. Blood trickled down my lip, as he held the knife to my neck. "I'm gonna repeat myself just one more time—Get them pants down."

My fingers were shaking, but I managed to do as he told me to, crying the whole time and begging him with my eyes not to hurt me. Once my pants and panties were around my ankles, he shoved roughly me on the concrete, making me skin one of my knees.

I cried but couldn't fight him because he had the knife pressed against my throat and an arm pressed around my neck.

"Bitch, don't move."

"Okay," I said in a weak voice, still crying.

He kneeled behind me. "Where you want me to fuck you?

"Huh?"

He slapped me again, and heat filled my face.

"You want it here?" He slid the knife to my pussy. "Or here?" He slid it to my asshole.

"The first place, please."

"Naw, your pussy probably run-through." And without reprieve, he pressed his dick in my asshole.

My screams were muffled as he had one hand over my mouth, the other around my neck, the knife clutched in his fingers, and he kept on jamming.

When it wouldn't go in, he yelled, "Fuck!" and repositioned himself, leaning back and jamming himself all the way into me, making a growling sound.

He slipped out of me, and right back in, hard and fast, breathing harshly and gripping my neck harder. I screamed as heat and burning spread throughout my body. I could feel my skin tearing.

He heaved in loudly and jammed me and started moaning as he rocked behind me. Then he pulled out and went in, out, and in, shoving me forward each time, pressing my kneecaps into the concrete and making them chafe.

I couldn't describe how the pain felt, except to say that I felt like I was being stabbed. I sobbed and kept my eyes closed and prayed it would be over soon, as he gripped a tighter hold on me, slid it in my pussy, then back into my ass, moaning loudly and busting into my ass.

I was sure I was bleeding now, and it was my blood mixed with his cum that was leaking down my legs.

Then he left me out there.

If I was never the same and lost touch with reality and who I was, it was in that moment.

Desiree was acting real weird. She couldn't stop bragging about getting one of my clients, and the fact that for once I had to be on the cold-ass track. She claimed she was able to stay warm with the dude, who spoiled the hell out of her on their date, and that he had requested her again and again, which pleased Black.

I told her, "Kiss my ass. I don't care how many times he requests you." Any reminder of that night brought back to mind what happened to me with that dude who raped me on that cold-ass concrete.

My butt bled for three days straight, and I couldn't stop crying. I couldn't shake the feelings of wanting to die, so I took a pill to help me forget, and when that didn't help, I went back to digging in my skin.

Then I worked on getting back into Black's good graces, so I never had to be out there again. But for a whole week Black had me out there.

Desiree wasn't on Black's jock anymore and kept bugging him to see if the trick named Raphael had requested her again. If Black said yes, she'd nod coolly, but once he left the room, she couldn't stop cheesing. I just assumed he paid her well.

Chapter 18

A couple weeks later I found out what the deal was. I was knocked out when Desiree woke me up with a kick in my ass. I ignored her and turned my back to her. "Cash, get up. This is serious. God, this shit is serious."

I sucked my teeth and rubbed the sleep out of my eyes. "What?" I narrowed my eyes at her as I sat up in the bed and saw her fidgeting and tapping on something behind her back.

She cleared her throat and bit her lip. "Ummm, I need you to help me do this."

I slid out of the bed. "Do what?"

She shoved a box in my hands so quick, I didn't have time to grasp it before it fell. When I bent over to retrieve it and read the label, my eyes widened. It was a pregnancy test.

"Is it Black's?"

She gave me a long stare and picked at her nails. "If it was, do you think I would be tripping? But we always use condoms." She looked down and offered a weak smile.

"Desiree, don't tell me."

"I love him, Cashmere. Finally I found someone to love me for me."

Desiree was a sucker for chances. Fucking with the trick, like she was doing, was suicide, but obviously she didn't care. She went on and on about how good he treated her, but I was half-listening.

Desiree was eighteen now, but the bitch read at a third-grade level, so I was reading the instructions on how to do the pregnancy test. And it turned out that she was very, very pregnant.

She screamed and kicked the laundry basket. "I'm not prepared for this!"

"You stupid."

She paced around in a circle. "Shit, Black don't show me no love. All he ever has his mind on is you. Now he showing me some attention 'cause he mad at you. But I didn't care anymore 'cause I was getting caught up in ol' boy. And he has some good dick. But it's not just that." She had a dreamy smile on her face as she continued to pace.

I waved a hand at that bullshit she was talking. "What are you going to do?"

She stopped pacing and gave me a dumb look. "Whatchu think? The man loves me. He was begging me to leave Black for him, and now that I'm pregnant, I have a reason to. But, to be quite honest, the last thing I need is a snot-nosed muthafucka to take care of, but hell, like I always tell you sometimes, you got to do what you got to do. So I'll go on and ride this baby thing out to get my man, 'cause I love my boo-boo, and I think he'll make a good daddy."

I shook my head at her, as she made the decision for us to leave Black.

How Desiree got the money up to get us the bus tickets, I don't know, since Black pretty much controlled the dough we made. But she was sure able to get up enough for us to take the Greyhound to Oakland, and enough for us to get us both burger specials at some café. I was happy though. I didn't want to be with Black, or to hook, anymore than she did.

When we got there with our backpacks and a few clothes, Desiree and I walked about three blocks until we made it to a Motel 6.

"This where we always meet," she said excitedly. "He'll probably call a cab to come scoop us up."

I shrugged, not sharing her excitement. I just had a funny feeling the whole way there. I stared down at the crisscross cuts all over the back of my hands and wrists while she made her phone call at a booth. Whenever Black saw them, he told me I needed to stop doing that to myself, but he didn't know what was going on in my head, and he damn sure couldn't take the pain away. He was partly the cause of it.

My thought was interrupted by Desiree's yelling, "But I thought you said—"

He must have cut her off, because she paused her loud-ass voice and started tapping her foot on the ground, frowning like our mother used to.

"But, baby, we out here and we—"

I chuckled when he cut her off again.

Suddenly she yelled into the phone at the top of her lungs, "You lying muthafucka!" Then she took the earpiece and beat it against the base of the phone over and over again, yelling, "Fuck! Fuck! Fuck!" Then she crumbled to the ground and started crying.

My sister wasn't very smart or resourceful, but when something became an issue of bodily harm and possible death, she knew what moves to make. Case in point, we ended up selling drugs yet again in Oakland for some dude named Rocco, out of this abandoned house. In all honesty, we were only lookouts for the dude, Desiree on one side, me on the other. We sat outside and alerted them whenever we saw the po-po coming, so it wasn't as risky as it was before. Since there was nothing but dudes there, we didn't have to worry about nobody fucking with us. Plus, Desiree was fucking Rocco. Since she was now eighteen, we stayed in a pretty cool hotel, and she was even talking about me going back to school.

That shit didn't last long, though. We showed up one day to find the place abandoned. None of the usual dudes were there, and the next thing we knew, cluckers were crowding the room for shit we didn't have.

"Where Rocco? Where Rocco?"

"He ain't here. We don't know where the fuck he is," Desiree snapped.

That's when Black walked in the room.

Before he could even look me in the eye, I was running and yelling for Desiree to do the same, but he easily reached out and snatched me up by the back of my neck and held me so I couldn't move. Hell, I could barely breathe, because of the pressure. Then he grabbed Desiree by her ponytail, yanking her back.

Desiree did all the talking. "Black, I'm—"

He ignored her and turned to the three cluck-heads. "I'm sorry y'all didn't get what y'all need-

ed. Maybe I can accommodate y'all with something just as good."

The three cluckers turned to Black curiously.

"Black!" Desiree screamed.

"Shut the fuck up, ho." Black's hold on me
tightened.

"Y'all can have a go with her, and the shit is
for free."

I struggled against him as he held me firmly,
giving me no choice but to scream at the top of
my lungs. He shoved Desiree so hard, she fell on
the ground, and the crackheads were given the
opportunity to get a free fuck from her.

I tried to pull away from Black, but this time
he twisted my arm, making me cry out. I closed
my eyes but couldn't help but hear her crying,
slapping sounds, and the cluckers' moans.

Black said, "You wanna run away from me?"

Somebody roared, "Yeah!"

My sister was bawling like a baby. "I'm sorry!"

I just wanted the shit to be over.

I peeked at Desiree laid out on the ground, the
dude over her. When he finished, he didn't even
bother wiping his dick. He shoved it in his pants
and ran out the warehouse.

She had one dude to go. As he fucked her, there
was no expression in her eyes. After that dude

busted quickly and vanished as well, Desiree struggled to put on her clothes.

I thought I was next, but I wasn't.

We were both shoved in his car. I was still nervous as hell 'cause I knew my punishment was far from over.

Chapter 19

Once we got back to L.A., Black dropped Desiree off on the track. "You got tonight to make up for the dough I lost, ho, or I'm fucking you up." In the rearview mirror, I watched her sadly limp away to the corner.

Once we made it home, Black hissed for me to go straight to my room, like he was my Daddy. I did it though. He was behind me and closed the door softly. When he pulled the belt from his pants, my eyes widened.

"No, Daddy. I'm sorry."

He pulled me in his arms and said gently, "I have to, baby. You can't be running away from me."

Instead of hitting me, he sat me on the bed, and pulled off his pants and shirt so he was in a wife-beater and boxers, and walked into the bathroom. A few moments later I heard water running.

Black came back and began stripping me of my clothes. Then he shoved me on the bed. He walked back in the bathroom.

I dug my hands in my flesh again. The shit was really starting to be a habit. It went from every once in a while to all the time. After each trick I always ended up with a new mark, and ended up with five more after the dude raped me.

"Cashmere."

I walked naked in the bathroom, expecting to be burnt with an iron or a cigarette. I met him there sitting on the edge on the tub, his head in his hands. There was water and suds filled to the rim of the tub.

He raised his head and looked at me. "I was losing my mind thinking I lost you."

I lowered my lashes.

"Get in the tub."

I slipped in with the quickness. Even though the water was warm. I was shivering.

Black kneeled down and grabbed a wash towel, and began washing my body with it. "Do I make it real hard for you, Cashmere?"

I didn't reply.

"I took you and your sister in. Gave you a home. I pay for yo Daddy. I'm more than fair to you." He clutched the washrag and soap so hard, the bar of soap slipped from his fingers.

"You treat me and my sister like shit," I wanted to say, but instead asked, "Why I'm not out there with Desiree? I ran away too."

"Desiree don't have what you have, Cashmere. I can't just treat you like you generic. Like I said before, you got the potential to be my bottom bitch." He poured some shampoo in my hair and lathered it up. "You know you're special to me."

Maybe if it wasn't coming from a pimp, it would have been nice to hear.

"Niggas been blowing my Sidekick up for you. I can probably let the other hoes go and live off of you alone.

"You really think I'm giving that up?" He tilted my head back and rinsed the soap out of my hair, which hung down my back.

"But I hate what I'm doing, Black. I—"

He placed a finger on my lips. "This is where you belong. This is where you gonna stay." He locked his eyes with mine. He was serious. "That was some cold shit, coming home and you not being there. I felt like I lost a part of myself, Cashmere."

He rinsed off the washrag and washed the soap off my body. "I'm not liking the way I feel, Cashmere, when it comes to you. Man, this is some way-out shit."

He stood and held a towel open for me to step into once I rose from the tub. Then he led me back into the bedroom. I was silent as he dried me off. Then he laid me on the bed so he could rub baby oil all over me. And I was feeling those feelings again, which I didn't want to, the shame, guilt, and fire.

Black fucked me so good, I ended up going right to sleep in his arms.

I felt the heat of a whip on my flesh. First I thought I was dreaming. Then I felt it again. I opened my eyes to find Black standing over me. "Black, what—"

He struck me again, but the shit didn't feel like a belt, which it was; it felt like a damn whip.

I screamed when it struck me on my ass. I rolled over and hit the floor and ran to a corner of the room. I held my hands out to ward him off. "No, Black."

He easily yanked me back on the bed, on my stomach, and straddled me with his body. He struck me over and over, till I felt pieces of my flesh pop open. My body was burning like someone had thrown some boiling water on me.

I kept yelling, "Okay! Okay! I'm sorry, Black!"

In my ear he whispered, "You run away from me again, Cashmere, and I'll kill you for sure."

Seconds later I felt something soothing on my back, down my spine, and my butt. Slowly, it took the sting away. Then he kissed me all over my back and tear-stained face, before saying, "Go to sleep."

Desiree quickly got over that dude she claimed she was in love with. She dropped that baby like it was hot—in the abortion clinic—and went back to her obsession with Black. The dumb bitch got his initials, BM, tattooed on her neck, like the rest of the hoes. It stood for Black Mitchell. I refused to, though, but I knew eventually he would want me to.

She also had something else she was in love with, and I couldn't figure out which one she loved more, Black or crack. Every time I turned around, she had a burnt-looking plastic tube smack in her mouth. So I'll wager it was the latter that she loved more.

Black was actually the one who'd turned her on to it, saying to her one day, "Why you stuffing your nose with that shit? Soon your nostrils are gonna fall off, and you gonna look like a damn fool, girl." He waved a pipe and some yellow shit in a bag that looked like a small piece of soap in front of her.

I peeked from the corner of the bedroom as he stuffed some Brillo pad (I knew what it was 'cause we used it to scrub pots when she cleaned dishes) at the bottom of the pipe, put the piece of look-like-soap shit in it, lit the shit, and shoved the other side in Desiree's mouth.

"Now breathe it in, Desiree," Black told her, "nice and slow . . . that's it."

Desiree did what he said. Then I watched as she fell back against the couch like she just bust the biggest nut of her life.

And, boy, was she starting to look jacked-up. She didn't get private clients anymore, which pissed her off. But, hell, we talking about rappers, athletes. You think they want to fuck a crackhead? Be for real, honey.

In fact one day she was at the kitchen table, and once again the burnt-looking tube was shoved in her mouth. Black grabbed her by her hair and said, "You better not let Cashmere try this shit, or it's over for you." Then he stuffed another bag in her hand before shoving her away.

He didn't have to warn me. I wasn't putting that shit in my body any damn way. I didn't know who I hated more, him or her.

And after the last stunt she pulled, having us both run away from Black and landing us both in shit, you'd think she would wise up and get with Black's program, since, like she always said, we married to the game and there was no such thing as divorce.

Word was, Desiree had tried to pocket some of the tricking dough, and Black found out about it. All I knew was that I woke up 'cause somebody was screaming at the top of their damn lungs. I ran outside, because that's where the sound was coming from, and found people crowded in a circle around the middle of the street. I pushed through them all when I recognized Desiree was the person screaming. Once I was able to bust through, I understood why she was screaming. She was buck-ass naked, and Black was striking her with his belt, foot, and free hand. And though there was fury on his face, he never uttered a word.

Desiree was wailing and, at the same time, trying to cover up her pussy and titties. She tried to crawl away on her knees.

I stood in the crowd shivering. I shook my head and resisted tears.

"Come here, ho." Black snatched her up by what was left of her hair, so that she was standing, and walked her down the line of neighbors and hoes. "Bitch, don't you ever steal from me."

"I'm sorry, Daddy."

As my eyes teared up, I frowned at myself because I didn't understand why I was crying. This shit should've made me feel good, to see him stick it to her for all the shit she'd done to me, but it didn't. It was killing me.

Black punched her in her face, and she fell with the impact, as did a tooth. The belt flew again, getting her in her face and body. Soon her body welted and swelled up. As she coughed and sobbed, he kicked her over and over again, till her screams turned to moans. Black then took three steps back, nodded, and all the hoes joined in and commenced to whipping on Desiree, throwing punches, slaps, kicks, and spitting on her.

Without thinking, I rushed forward and dived into those bitches, blindly throwing punches at whatever I could come into contact with, and spitting right back on their asses. I felt my fist connecting with heads, faces, titties, backs, but then somebody lifted me clear in the air. I continued to swing but was only hitting air because my feet couldn't touch the ground.

"Let me go!"

Black had me and he wouldn't release me, but still I struggled all the way, so he had to practically carry me in the house. A glance over Black's shoulder showed me that them bitches were still whipping on my sister. And I couldn't do anything about it.

Once we were in the house, Black didn't release me until we were in the room I shared with him. He sat me gently on the bed and sat down next to me. I scooted over as far as I could away from him. He took a deep breath, rose from the bed, and walked out the room. As soon as he did, I dug in my flesh so hard that an area of my skin popped open and blood gushed out. I ran into the bathroom and rinsed it off, and placed a Band-Aid on it. As I turned around to go back into the room, I collided with Black, who held his arms out for me like he really thought I was going to hug him.

I sidestepped him and looked down at the carpet. The belt he had just whipped my sister with was dangling halfway on the ground, mocking me almost. When he reached for my arm, I took a step back, crossed my arms over my chest, and looked at him with fire in my eyes.

He took a step toward me, but then his cell phone went off. He paused, flicked it open, turned on his heels, and left the room. I walked back in the bedroom.

I sat back on the bed, waiting to see if my sister was okay.

Five minutes later he came back into the room. "Put some clothes on."

Chapter 20

We went to the usual hotel I met my "dates" at. Black always waited outside for me, and once the deed was done, I would go on about my business. The dough was always handed to Black though, but sometimes they gave me tips, which he always took too. He didn't let us hold much of shit. A couple dollars here or there for drink and ecstasy, that's all.

I knocked on the door and waited for the dude to tell me to enter. Once he did, I walked in the room and sat my purse down on the table. The dude's back was to me, and he was staring out the window.

"What's up? My name is Cashmere. I'm with Black." He spun around quickly, and my eyes and his stretched to the sky. It was Caesar's brother. I shook my head and laughed. "You got the game twisted, homie, if you think I'm fucking you."

Angelo marched up to me and snarled his lip, looking ugly as hell. "Bitch, I already paid. It's a little too late for you to be playing the siditty role, ain't it? You are, after all, a dirty-ass, low-down, sleazy ho at that."

Can you imagine that coming from a nigga who was the lowest of the low, fucking scum of the earth? Without much thought, or any fear that this shit would come back to bite me in my ass, I spat on his punk-ass and ran out of the room.

I walked down the hall to the elevators. When it beeped open, I stepped in and pressed the button for the lobby. I'd planned to tell Black no. I had never said it to him before, so maybe, just maybe, he wouldn't trip and would understand the situation if I explained it to him. My stomach floated as the elevator sailed down to the lobby.

As soon as the elevator doors opened, I jumped. Black was facing me, a calm look on his face. He stepped on silently and pushed the button for the 16th floor. I bit my lips waiting for him to speak, but he didn't.

"Black, don't make me do this shit. I fucking know him."

"You will go back in that room, Cashmere." He slipped closer to me, so his breath was on my cheek. First, he tried kisses, shushing me, as I continued to bitch and whine to the point where I was about to cry. When that didn't work, he hemmed me up against the wall by my neck. "You getting far too ambitious, Cashmere. Maybe I made a mistake of handling you with kid gloves. Did I, Cashmere? Huh?" He applied pressure to my neck.

Tears popped out of my eyes. "No, Black."

"You lucky I love you, girl, else you'd be hurt. Listen to me and listen well." His angry eyes pierced through me, and he aimed a finger in my face. "You don't make the rules in this game, I do. You're going back in that room to do old boy."

I nodded, my heart beating fast as hell.

"Wipe your face."

I obeyed.

Once the elevator door opened, I had no choice but to follow Black into the room I'd just abandoned. Black knocked, and as we entered, I hid behind him.

"There's been a mistake. Cashmere is down for anything." He stepped to my right, exposing me to Angelo. "Ain't you, baby?"

I nodded, closing my eyes and sobbing.

"The bitch spit on me. Can I spit on her back?" Angelo's nostrils flared out with anger.

"Like I said, she's down for whatever."

And spit on me he did, on my face, as the bastard rode me like he was a disc jockey, and all over my back and ass as he fucked me doggy-style. Then he spat all over his hands and smeared it all over his dick before I had to put my lips over it. And when it was time for him to cum, he sprayed me all in my face with the shit.

I didn't talk to Black after that, but he didn't give a shit. He was just as pissed at me for my "ambition," and that landed me out there on the block after he gave me a beating like never before.

Chapter 21

Life for me wasn't no beach chair. Hell, life was infectivity. I felt like walking cancer. And my sister? She was walking death. Crack was now her middle, first, and last name, and she was chasing her own ass to get it. I personally wasn't fucking with any more drugs. Since the last time I popped ecs after that shit with Caesar's brother, I popped two pills and ended up in the hospital. And seeing my sister practically dead on her feet, I put an X to taking ecs and made a promise to myself not to ever use drugs again. My dumb ass thought I was taking the high road with ecstasy. But I found out that shit had damn near every drug imaginable in it.

Now even though it had been a year and a half since Daddy had his accident, he still had not gotten any better. I flew there solo today. Sadly it was now to the point where, just to breathe, he needed to be connected to all those damn machines. He couldn't function without them, kind of like how Desiree needed to get a hit of her pipe to handle her business. And Black had no problem supplying her with the shit, just as long as she took her ass out on that track and got him his money.

Now I knew I looked a mess, and I don't mean a mess in the physical sense. I still looked decent, still had all my hair. I had all my teeth, unlike Desiree, who was missing one of her front teeth, and was the same size pretty much, except like Mama always said, my titties would grow once they got sucked on. But I don't think Mama anticipated that they'd be licked, sucked on, gnawed, chewed on, and bitten. But there was other damage, like the crisscross scars on my palms and wrist, but I usually wore gloves even when I fucked tricks. I'd be ass buck-naked, but I'd cover up the scars. The tricks just thought I was being freaky.

What I mean by mess was how I felt on the inside. I felt like people could see how fucked-up I was, that they could look me in my eyes and instantly know about all the alcohol I had consumed, all the ecstasy I had popped, and all the niggas I had fucked.

Once I left my visit, Lanette, the nurse who me and my sister always spoke to in passing, stopped me. "Why do you always look so down, Cashmere?"

I shook my head. See, I had no problem with her. In fact, I liked seeing her smiley face. I wish I had a reason to smile back, but I always gave her a nod. Still, I couldn't disclose all the shit I had been through and was still going through.

She grabbed me by one of my hands in a firm grip that made me want to follow her and said, "Come with me." She held my hand all the way to the chapel, which was empty when we got there. And she didn't let it go, even after she sat down.

To tell the truth, I didn't mind her hands being on me. They were rough, yes, but oh so warm; they gave me comfort. I remembered I didn't have on my gloves, so I tried to snatch them back, but she wouldn't let me.

"I remember when my kids were your age. I was never able to be home with them much, working all these hours, but they understood." She tightened her hold on my hands.

I nodded a bottomless nod. I shifted my body, hoping that, as I did, my hands would slip from hers. They didn't. She didn't see my scars, I guess, or maybe she did, but didn't acknowledge them.

"Tell me something, Cashmere—have you ever had a conversation with God?"

I shook my head and twisted my lips to one side.

"Do you believe in Him?"

"I used to."

"Why don't you anymore?"

"I been in too much pain to believe in a God."

"Belief gotta stick around, even through the fire. It's just a test, anyhow. This is not going to be the way it's always going to be, honey. It's a hump in the road, not an opportunity to turn in the towel, 'cause it's your life we talking about. And, baby, you are far too young to be carrying all that weight on these little shoulders."

How she know what I was carrying? Was it that apparent? Obviously.

As she searched my eyes, I shifted mine to the ground.

Quietly she asked, "Well, Cashmere, can I please pray for you?"

I nodded slowly. "Go ahead." I bowed my head and closed my eyes.

She did the same, grasping my hand tighter again.

"Father God, I ask that You move Cashmere through this, Lord. Lord, Cashmere is a beautiful girl, Lord, with a broken spirit, Lord. Father God, Cashmere is out of faith. Lord, I ask that You show her just how important her life is to this earth. Lord, help her to understand that she is needed, Lord, that she is loved. Lord, help her to believe in You, Lord, to see that, through You, all is healed, aches can go away, broken bones can be fixed, Lord, a split heart can be put back together, Lord, depression wiped out, Lord. Cashmere has pain in her heart, Lord. She's been hurt, Lord. Help her find joy again, Lord, in the name of the Father, the Son, and the Holy Spirit. Amen."

Crazy as it sounds, I did feel better. I left the home feeling so much better that I couldn't wait to go back.

Eagerly I showered the next Sunday, put on something pretty to wear, and dashed into the living room. I was sure that if Lanette prayed for Desiree, it would make her feel good about living again too. I asked breathlessly, "Desiree, you ready?"

She was laying across the couch, looking half-dead. "I'll pass."

"What?"

She rolled her red-looking eyes at me and repeated herself, "I said I'm not going."

I didn't want to argue with her, so I took a deep breath and smiled at her.

She smirked.

"Desiree, we gotta go, so we don't break tradition. We been doing this for almost two years, you know—"

"I know what? Huh?" She held a hand out to me as if I had something to hand her.

I rubbed my eyes wearily. She was draining me.

"He can't see me. He can't do shit, Cashmere. Really, if you think about it, we wasting perfectly good money."

"Desiree, how can you—"

"Don't call me that shit!" She threw a cup at me, and it fell at my feet.

I scooped it up and sat it on the table calmly. I couldn't understand why she was tripping, or what had made her so insensitive when it came to Daddy.

Black stepped in the room. His voice silenced and confused me. "Y'all both need to sit tonight out, Cashmere."

"What?"

He placed a hand on my shoulder, and I shrugged it off.

"Cashmere, money is low. I need you both on the track tonight."

"Fine wit' me," Desiree said.

"I'm not—no, we not!"

Black studied my face, his jaw twitching. "You saying no to me, Cashmere?"

"Yes! I do whatever you ask me to do, Black, but this is something I cannot do. I won't. So beat my ass, fuck me, throw me out, whatever, but you can't stop us from seeing our Daddy!" My eyes were on his, and I saw my reflection staring back at me. I was shaking and walking around in circles, and as I spoke loudly, my voice was cracking too.

The room was silent for a minute. Desiree was frozen on the couch, waiting for what was about to happen next. Maybe Black would knock my head off my body or throw me off a cliff.

"You can't stop us from seeing Daddy," I repeated.

Black studied me, a hand resting under his chin.

"Desiree, get your ass up and get dressed," I told her.

"When Black tells me to."

"Desiree, go on and wash your ass. You got ten minutes." Desiree gave Black a shocked look. I didn't miss it. Two minutes later, she went in her bedroom.

Chapter 22

Desiree was acting weird again. Pacing in Daddy's room, she kept glancing at the clock and leaving the room and coming right back. The more time went by, the more she tripped.

I should start calling her ass 51/50.

"Fuck!" She turned her eyes to me and snapped, "Let's go."

I ignored her.

"Come on."

I continued rubbing lotion on Daddy's legs.

"Fuck it then. I'm leaving."

Just as she stood, Lanette walked in the room and offered a smile. Desiree muttered, "Shit." My eyes narrowed when she gave Desiree a white envelope. She was holding something in her hand also. "The rest of the staff and I also made a scrapbook for you ladies to take."

My eyes passed over the blue photo album that had Daddy's name on it. "What's this for?"

Lanette's smile slid off her face and was replaced with confusion, the same look that my
face wore. She turned to Desiree. "You didn't tell
your sister?"

Desiree didn't speak.

"Tell me what?"

"Desiree, are you gonna tell—"

"I ain't gotta tell her shit."

"Man, what is going on?" A sinking feeling
came back to me again. I closed my eyes and
tried to control the shaking of my hands.

"Ladies, I don't mean to get in your business.
But, Desiree, you should've of—"

"Look, I'm grown and I'm the next of kin, not
her." She pointed at me. "She ain't even seventeen yet, so I'm running this shit and I"—she
poked herself in the chest—"I make the decisions
for Desmond Pierce."

Instantly I knew what she did. That's why she
didn't want to come to the hospital today. I asked
her quietly, "You authorized them to pull the
plug on Daddy, didn't you?"

Her look confirmed my fear.

I ran to try to reverse this shit, but her yelling
stopped me.

"It's too late to change it. It's going down, and
you can't do nothing about it, 'cause I'm grown.
I'm the oldest. And don't think you can run to

Black and he gonna fix this shit to your fucking favor. He ain't!"

I spun around and got in her face. "Bitch, you ain't cutting shit. I don't get you. He is all we have left. And you wanna cut the cord on him? He did nothing but love you, Desiree—all of us! This is how you wanna repay Daddy? Man, you truly ain't shit."

She shoved me. "And what the fuck makes you any better than me? Last time I checked, you was a ho." She pulled down a finger like she was counting. "You do dope. So how in the hell can you say I ain't shit? And, to tell the truth, I wanted Daddy to die. That night. 'Cause I hated him. 'Cause he loved you more. It made no sense for me to do shit right, 'cause he loved you more than me."

"No."

"Shut up! He did. Everybody did. I hated him for the way he looked at me like I was nothing. Everybody loved you more than me, no matter what I did. Even Black. And all my plans to break you down failed 'cause you always found some fucking way to win."

"Plans?"

Desiree smirked again. "I set all this shit up—fucking Caesar, our uncle, getting with Black. I wanted to see your downfall, Cash. I was sick of the world praising you like you was better than me 'cause you had a big ass, a prettier face. 'Cause you were smarter, funnier, could cook better, talk better, fuck better. I wanted you not to be shit. And I was willing not to be shit, just to achieve that. So I guess you can say I achieved my dream, 'cause you ain't shit but a dirty, ecstasy-hooked ho."

That's when I snapped. Rage was all up in me as I went after her, trying to punch and kick her at the same time. I wanted to rip that miserable bitch apart. My fist went to her face. *Bloop. Bloop. Bloop.* I bust her bottom lip.

She swung back, but the bitch was high. I ducked and drilled, weaved and drilled, fucking her face up some more.

Lanette yelled for us to stop, but I was far from being done. I socked her in her titty, making her come forward. Then I went for her face again. I leaned her face down and socked her in her neck.

She bent over coughing, and that's when Lanette grabbed me. "Cashmere, calm down."

"Get off of me please," I yelled, trying to yank away.

The diversion gave Desiree the opportunity to grab the bedpan from Daddy's neighbor, which she threw on me.

I sputtered as piss was all in my face, and the smell of shit and piss rose up to my nose. I wiped my face and saw the bitch run from the room. I pushed Lanette off me and went after Desiree's ass. "Bitch, I fucking hate you!"

I chased after her down the hall, passing nurses and doctors. As she speeded up, I increased my speed as well. When I was close on her heels, I swung and knocked her upside her head. The blow slowed her down, and she shook her head. I then cocked my left foot back as far as it could go and kicked her in her ass, pitching her forward.

All I thought that would happen was, she would fall and I would continue fucking her up. But she flew forward, her legs folded beneath her, and slammed her head on the hardwood floor. She shook for a minute, blood leaking from her head.

Then she was stiller than Daddy was.

Okay. Here I was trying to make a change, only to find myself caught up in the same shit. My sister was very much dead. And I was very much the killer. So all that shit the nurse said to me went straight out the window.

They were wheeling Desiree away in a bag, and I couldn't see her face or body, just the imprint of her body. Who could I be mad at? My mom? Auntie? God? Myself? Black? He sure was nowhere to be seen, now that I was caught up in this shit.

I was facing a murder charge. I was in too much shock to cry, too shook to be scared, as handcuffs chafed my skin and I stared blankly out the window of the squad car.

The car sped off. Where were they taking me? A maximum-security prison? The electric chair?

Chapter 23

They took a mug shot and fingerprints. Then the officer got on the phone and called somebody, and the next thing I knew, I was being transported somewhere else.

Some black lady was in the room. She asked me a series of questions: Do you need to see a doctor? Do you have any cuts or bruises? Do you have a history of medical problems? Are you allergic to any foods? Do you use drugs?

To her last question, I thought, *Now is as good a time as any to use some.* Instead I said, "I used to, but not anymore."

"When did you last eat?"

"I'm cool."

"When?"

"This morning."

Then I was asked if I heard voices, or ever thought about killing or hurting myself. I said no to all. Then they had me sign all these papers.

"This is an OC warning." She explained to me that staff there used pepper spray and, if an OC warning is given, I am to drop. Then she gave me my charge and my court date.

I was then taken to a room, where the doctor examined me. They took all my shit, did a strip-search, and gave me a pair of pants, two tops, a sweatshirt, and some "bubblegum" tennis shoes.

"Now grab a bedroll, young lady."

She was referring to a black burlap-looking blanket that was rolled up. I grabbed one from the stack.

"Now follow me." She walked to the door, paused, and looked at me over her shoulder. "Now when you step out, young lady, you need to be quiet, with your hands behind your back." She demonstrated, her hands behind her back, the top of her hands resting on her back, and her forefinger and thumb pressed against each other.

I obeyed her.

"You also need to look straight ahead. If you see a rival gang, don't—"

"I don't gang—"

"Quiet!"

She guided me down this long hallway. The place looked more like a funeral hall to me, with all these old-looking buildings and all this grass.

We stopped at one building that read *East B* on it. My eyes narrowed 'cause I didn't know what it stood for.

"Hold up!"

I stopped in my tracks, assuming the command meant stop.

As she unlocked the door, I was fighting because I needed some ecs now more than ever. Despite my promise to never touch it again, I was craving it. To erase the image of my sister lying on that ground still, her eyes open. Fuck that shit about staying clean.

And damn praying to God. After Sunday after Sunday of going to church with Daddy and praying to God, trying to live my life right and honoring my parents, I was in some shit like this for killing my sister. I winced.

I followed behind her down a hall that had doors on each side. Each door had a skinny piece of glass on it.

The lady took me into an office set in the center, with another hall on the other side of it. She said, "This is Ms. Pierce. Here is her chart."

The black lady with the all gray hair, and long-ass nails studied me quietly. She said, "You need to put your hair up," and handed me a thick rubber band. *She must be the supervisor*. I thought.

I pulled it all back till it was in a ponytail.

There were two other women in the room, a Latina with long, straight, black hair, and an older, heavy-set, brown-skin black woman with soft brown eyes.

"Rino, put her in room seven."

The Latina chick stood and said, "Come on."

I didn't say shit, just followed after her.

She unlocked a door and said, "Step inside."

Once I did, she locked the door. I watched the bolt slip into the opening in the wood of the door. I didn't bother putting the blankets and sheets on the bed because I couldn't sleep. I just sat on the bed and stared out, looking at nothing in particular.

I was able to get a little sleep, until I heard a male's voice bellowing down the highway, "Step the fuck out and face your muthafuckin' doors!" He unlocked our doors in a rush.

Once we did, he continued, "Listen up, bitches! It's been far too much shit going down in this unit, and I'm not gonna stand for it no more. Keep in mind, I have no problem locking y'all up in your rooms."

I took a look at the short, black man, who looked like George Jefferson, his shoes knocking against the hardwood floors.

"Y'all crazy bitches hear that? So y'all best to take y'all meds and run a decent muthafuckin' program or I'm fuckin' y'all up for sure!" He peered in all our windows as he spoke, pausing when he got to mine, maybe because I didn't bow my head as he talked his shit.

I looked right back at him.

"Let the supervisor call me again 'cause y'all silly asses wanna act stupid. Step out your rooms on the two-count . . . one, two!"

We all stepped out.

"About face!"

I stayed the way I was because I didn't know what he meant, but the other females moved.

"Bitch, step the fuck back in the room!"

I heard the brown-skin lady, Ms. Clark, say, "She just got here."

"I don't give a muthafuck! All y'all hoes, step back in your room." Then he walked on the other side to the opposite hall and repeated the same thing. I found out later that he ran the facility and gave those speeches once a week to scare the new kids that came in. Sound like he had short man syndrome to me.

The next voice I heard was Ms. Clark's. She walked down the hall and said, "It's time to get up, get groomed, and dressed."

Once my door was opened, a box with a toothbrush, toothpaste, and a comb was slid in my room.

"Make sure, when you're ready to step out, you have your clothes on the right way and your hair is combed."

I went to the small sink and brushed my teeth. I didn't even bother combing my hair. It didn't even matter 'cause I ended up eating in my room and, boy, was it some nasty-ass shit—some cold-ass eggs with no white in them, two pieces of bread, a banana, and a carton of milk.

When it was time for lunch, I was able to step out because I got it right. As I stood in line, there was a bunch of mumbling from the other chicks as we waited for the next command.

"Where she from?"

"She got pretty hair."

"La-La said that bitch from A tray."

"No, she from Hoover."

"Big-booty hoes!"

I heard snickers, but I wasn't tripping off them bitches. And they damn sure didn't wanna see me. I didn't have shit to live for and didn't mind breaking one of those bitches in quarters, but for now I was gonna leave it alone.

"Hold up!"

I stood quiet, but a bitch behind me bumped into me.

When I ignored her, she whispered, "I can't stand nappy-headed sissies."

Now the last time I checked, I didn't have nappy hair, and I wasn't no sissy, so I knew she wasn't talking to me or about me.

The girl in front of me whispered, "You gonna let her diss your set like that?"

"Set?"

"Quiet, ladies," Ms. Clark said, shoving a plate in my hand.

I followed after the girl in front of me to the rec-room, where tables were set up for us to eat, and sat down.

"Fuck sissies!"

Here this bitch goes again.

When she stood, I stood. I wasn't gonna get hit sitting down at all. But staff was on us. Before we could do shit, they were dragging us both away. She kept on calling me bitch and ho, but I never responded.

The next morning was pretty much the same. Bitches fucking with me, dissin' my 'hood.' I didn't bother telling them that I had no hood, other than the ones on my sweatshirts. Them bitches were weird as hell. Most of them looked like fucking boys. We wore the same clothes, but their pants sagged, and they either had fades or cornrows. And the hoes, they looked feminine, but they were trying to fuck each other.

I was placed on the other side of the hall for my protection because, according to the short-ass supervisor, there were no gangbangers on the other side. They placed me in this double-bunked room with some heavy-set, freckle-faced, light-skin chick called Basil. As long as she didn't fuck wit' me, it was cool. And she was cool.

I was making up my bed, fastening the sheet around the edges, when she asked, "This your first time here?"

I nodded.

"What did you do?"

When I paused, she smiled. "It's okay. You don't have to talk about it if you don't want to. Just making conversation, girl. To tell the truth, I don't like talking about what I did either."

I managed a half-smile.

She tossed something my way, a plastic bag with a white substance. I narrowed my eyes and frowned.

She giggled. "It's not what you think it is, girl. It's salt! The food here is fucking terrible." She rubbed her bulging tummy. "Man, I sure miss Mama's food. She makes the best smothered pork chops. And her fried chicken, girl, it taste better than KFC."

I nodded.

"Can your mom cook?"

I stiffened and said softly, "Yeah, she could cook."

"I been here ten times, girl. My mom is pissed at me. I gotta get my shit together, so she won't have to keep missing work to come to my court dates. When you go to court?"

"The 14th."

"Whatever you do, girl, don't piss the judge off, 'cause he can put our black asses away for a long time. My homegirl just got fifteen years in YA."

My eyes widened. I wondered what YA was. I later found out that YA stood for Youth Authority and it was no joke.

"But you don't look like you did anything too bad, right?"

I eyed her. It was just a slick way for her to get in my business, to trick me into telling her what I did.

Basil talked me to fucking death, until we went down for showers. When we came back, it was lights out, and I drifted off to sleep.

"Aye! Aye!"

First my vision was blurry from sleep. I shook my head and rubbed my eyes. I gasped to see her sprawled across her bed, and finger-fucking herself, her legs bent out like chicken wings. I placed my hands over my mouth. Basil had her head thrown back and kept stroking herself so hard, I thought her pussy was gonna rip apart.

"Look! Look, Pierce!" she said, breathing hard, three fingers jammed inside her vagina. She sat up in the bed, moved closer to the edge close to me, and held her fleshy, fat-ass legs open. "Come on, come on!"

"Come on what?"

"Come on, you know, eat me, Pierce. Then I'll do you too." Her feet and legs were in the air shaking as she tried to hold them up. She dropped them and grabbed them back.

"I'm not doing that gay shit. Take your nasty ass to sleep!" I threw the covers over my head and turned my back on her, so I didn't have to see that nasty-ass bitch.

She got real silent, so I thought she was doing like I said, and was gonna go to sleep.

A few moments later, I felt my eyelids start to get heavy and was about to drift right off when I felt a draft of air. I turned around to find the bitch in my bed, my blanket on the floor, and her fingers inching up my thighs to my pussy, her ass naked as a newborn baby.

"Bitch, I told you to stop that nasty shit!" I leaped on top of her big ass and punched her in the face, big-ass titties, and stomach until she started screaming loudly like a wild animal.

When she wouldn't fight back, I pounded her in her face. "Hit me back, nasty ass!" I jabbed her in her stomach, and she curled into a bowl of fat. I kept on punching her.

Her screaming got louder. Then footsteps were heard running down the hall to us. Staff was on me trying to get me off her naked ass.

"Move, shit! Y'all shouldn't have put me in the room with her nasty ass!"

They pulled me out of the room and dragged me down the hallway. Then they shoved me in another room, this time by myself.

After that incident, I was pretty much isolated because she was gang-affiliated. She was supposed to be a real hard bitch that was gunning for me. Ain't that a bitch. They were all a bunch of silly broads to me, so it didn't bother me much that I had to eat breakfast, lunch, and dinner alone. Cool, since I didn't really taste it anyway.

After lunch I was sent to this small office to see some psychologist bitch. *I'd like to see her white, privileged ass diagnose me.* With her perfectly straight blonde hair and headband that had a C written on it in glitter, she had some glasses on and some lip gloss. What the fuck was she gonna do for me, but give me a headache?

"Pierce, I'm your psych, Corliss."

"Who?"

"Corliss."

I nodded. I guess that's what the C on her headband stood for.

"Pierce, tell me why you here."

"You read my chart, didn't you? I'm here because I was arrested."

"Yeah, you're here on a mur—"

"It was an accident."

She looked like she doubted me. My nostrils flared, and I pursed my lips.

"Were you abused as a kid?"

"No."

"Molested, raped, assaulted?"

"I don't want to talk about it."

She jotted something down on a yellow pad. "Why don't you want to talk about it, Pierce?"

Why this bitch had to bring that shit up? I dug my hands in my flesh.

"Well, you have a lot of scars on your hands and forearms. Most girls who cut on themselves have had a history of sexual abuse. Did you?"

I never talked about it, and I shouldn't do it now, but maybe, just maybe I thought if I mouthed what happened, she could help me get over it because, to be honest, it was bothering me. And the more I was in that room, the less I slept and the more I was thinking about the day that man raped me.

But it wasn't just that. I couldn't help but think about all them dudes I had fucked for Black.

"Yes." I gritted my teeth. But just as soon as it came out, shame filled me. I wanted to run out of that room and hide forever, vanish off the earth, so I didn't have to hurt no more. Mouthing it didn't do shit for the pain I was feeling inside, or the lump in my throat that I couldn't cough up and spit out.

"Tell me what happened."

I took a deep breath. "I was on the track and—"

"Prostituting?"

"No, running cross-country," I said sarcastically.

She licked her lips nervously. "Should you have been out there?"

"What the fuck you mean?" I was snapping because I was back there in that alley, hands on me. I shook my head and blinked rapidly.

"Pierce, you here?"

He pushed me on the concrete. I couldn't get it out of my head. "You want it here or there?"

"Pierce?"

I screamed. He shoved me to the ground. The shit was happening in my head yet again.

"Pierce."

I opened my eyes and saw the white bitch. "I don't wanna talk about this shit!" I rose.

"Pierce." She grabbed my hand.

"Bitch, don't touch me. I'll fuckin' kill you!" I ran out of the office, ignoring her as she called my name, and kept running down the hall.

The next thing I knew, I was being tackled to the floor. "Man, get the fuck off me!"

They had parts of my arms and legs, and were carrying me to my room. They placed me on my bed and locked the door.

The thoughts were coming back. I jumped off the bed and beat on the doors. "Let me out!"

"When you calm down. You can't run down the hallway."

"Fuck you!"

I kept kicking, but nobody answered. I was stuck in that room staring at them white bricks.

My mind started fucking with me again, like it did in the office. After a while I didn't know if I was dreaming or awake. I saw Mama, and she said the same thing she'd said before she left us. "In other words, baby girl, life is gonna be hard as hell on you." Then I seen my sister in bed with Caesar, saw myself fucking him.

Then the same dude was raping me. Then Caesar's brother, Angelo, was raping me.

Daddy was flipping over on the freeway over and over. It wouldn't stop!

Mama was fucking Caesar. Then Black.

The dude in the alley was chasing me again.

I rose and beat on the door again. I cried and screamed at the top of my lungs, "Somebody help me. I'm going fucking crazy. I can't be in this room!"

The girls were laughing at me, and staff didn't come down the hall to let me out.

Somebody yelled, "Punk bitch!"

"Fuck all of y'all! Y'all don't fucking know me! Y'all gonna ignore me? Fuck y'all bitch-ass staff too!"

I kicked and banged, and kicked and banged, till my feet were throbbing and my hands felt numb. Still, them images kept on coming, and dude that raped me, his voice was in my head. I could feel his hands on me and smell his odor.

I screamed again, crawled to a corner, and slid my finger across my flesh until my skin tore again. I must be going crazy.

Chapter 24

I knew for a fact that I didn't make any friends in that bitch. Even the staff hated me. I bit my bottom lip, swallowing my apology, when Ms. Clark unlocked my door.

She gave me my plate of food and said, "Eat, groom, and get dressed. You going on movement."

"What?"

"Court." She closed and locked my door without another word. "Humph!" Like I gave a fuck. So when old girl came back down the hallway to fetch me, I showed all them just how much of a fuck I cared. As we walked up the hallway to the exit, I yelled, "Fuck all y'all bitches—insanes, insects East Coast, cheese toast, hoovers, pyru—fuck all y'all hoods! All y'all gang-banging dykes can kiss my ass too!" This was all stuff I heard them say.

Boy, did I get them riled up that early in the morning. They beat and kicked on their doors, calling me every name but a child of God. They wanted to get to me so bad and they couldn't. I almost felt sorry for them bitches. Almost. Shit, that was my introduction to just not giving a fuck about anything. Hell, not even my damn self.

Shit was no different when I went on to court. I had nothing to live for. Why should I act like I cared what they did with me? So I met with my public defender, and he didn't have much time to discuss shit 'cause he was a damn paper-shoveler.

I gave him nothing but a grimace.

The bailiff gave the judge a file and said, "We are about to proceed for *The People* versus *Cashmere Pierce*."

The judge slammed his gavel, and with it, my heart thumped against my chest so hard and loud, I heard it. But what that bailiff said—the people versus Cashmere Pierce—that shit was true. Wasn't nobody in the world for me anymore. The only one that ever was, was lying dead right now.

The district attorney said, "Your Honor, we are here for the preliminary hearing of minor, Cashmere Pierce, arrested for alleged murder."

The judge with his droopy-ass eyes was half-listening. I guess he had done his job for the day, hitting that loud-ass gavel. And Daddy's hard-earned tax dollars had kept this nigga warm at night. Supplied his fat ass with golf balls.

My public defender spoke up, "Your Honor, Ms. Pierce has never been in trouble before."

The district attorney held up a hand, silencing my lawyer. "Counsel, according to her file, this minor has not been attending school, and there were drugs found in her system. There's a difference between never being in trouble and never being caught."

I rolled my eyes 'cause, once again, muthafuckas were running their mouth and didn't know shit about shit.

The judge glared down at me. Should I be intimidated?

I glared right back at his old, grouchy-ass. Couldn't no worse happen to me. Daddy was gone, Mama and my sister. Like I said, there was nothing on earth that I cared about, not even my own damn self.

The judge coughed up some cold, swallowed it, and cleared his throat. "Well, young lady, what have you been up to?"

"Hooking, fucking, sucking dick, taking it up the ass." I was lying about the ass part technically, since I never let a man come through the back door except one, the dude that raped me. "I probably did you, Judge, and it was so good, I

put your ass to sleep. I done the officer outside,"
I said matter-of-factly.

There were whispers in the room and a couple
of laughs.

My public defender looked at me with a shocked
expression on his face.

"Watch your mouth in my courtroom, young
lady."

I smiled and tilted my head to one side, showing him I didn't give a damn.

"Young lady, you are facing a pretty hefty
charge—murder. That's a huge charge for someone so young. It says here you just turned fifteen.
And your sister is deceased. Do you have anything to say on your behalf before I make a decision based on the evidence?"

"Yes, sir, I do," I said loudly. "I wanna say,
Fuck the United States, George W. Bush, my
public *pretender*, the court, jurors, Mama, God,
Allah, the Church of Christ, the Church of Scien-
tology, Bishop Don Juan, 'cause pimpin' is easy,
but trickin' ain't. And, you, Judge, fuck your old,
flabby ass."

He turned beet-red, and his gavel swung in
the air like he was gonna hit me with it. "Get her
out of here now!"

***

The only thing I liked about going to court was my mandatory phone call. The only person I knew to call was my aunt. But her punk-ass husband seemed to answer every time it rang. I told him to tell her I had called and could only hope that he would.

They ended up putting me on the other side permanently. All them bitches wanted a piece of me. At first it was about five; now it was about twenty-five.

I had to shower and eat separately. When it was time to go to school, I had to sit it out in my room. The more I stayed in my room, the crazier I got. I wanted the fuck out of that room and the fuck out of that facility.

Chapter 25

Over the next week I plotted an escape. I figured out the first step how to escape. In the paneling of the door, there was an opening where a bolt slid in once the door was locked. Because of the position the door opened and closed in, it appeared locked even when it wasn't. I noticed this when staff forgot to lock my door one day. The best time was when laundry came, because the exit door would be open and stayed open during this time.

The next day I took some tissue and, on my way back to the room, stuffed the opening so it looked like it was already locked. Then I waited for them to deliver the laundry. Shit, for hours I waited and stayed on my door until they came. Like clockwork I heard the knock 'cause males always had to knock before coming in. Once the staff went down, I listened for the click, and I pushed my door open and ducked down. I creeped up the hallway while the staff was signing the paper and sped past her and the dude.

"Pierce!"

I kept on running around the building, through the grass, trying to find a way out that bitch-ass establishment. I crept around the church. I saw three members of staff looking for my ass, Ms. Rino, Ms. Clark, and some muthafucka I'd never seen before.

I ran the other way past a building called North C. Nothing there. There had to be some exit I could get through, some gate I could climb.

"There her ass go!"

Shit, they were close on my heels. I took off running.

"Stop, Pierce!" It was Ms. Rino.

"Hell no!" I was kicking my legs at the air, trying to get away. Only, there was nowhere to go.

I went the opposite way again, and they got closer, to the point where they were only a few feet away from me. I faced them and kept on backing up.

"Drop, Pierce." It was Clark.

I was so sick of her ass. "Naw, fuck this! I don't want to be here, gotdammit!" I backed up some more.

"OC warning!" Ms. Rino said.

My heart pumped. I didn't want to get pepper-sprayed. Somebody must have been creeping up on me 'cause, when I turned around, a dude tackled me to the ground, knocking the air out of me.

The dude laughed and said, "You ain't no joke, huh, Pierce?"

"Kiss my ass, you fat, black bastard!" I swung my fist and feet wildly.

I grunted when someone placed a knee on my stomach. It was Ms. Clark. Then Ms. Rino and that fat nigga pinned my legs and arms. I guess they showed me.

I screamed at the top of my lungs, "Get the hell off me!"

They pulled me to my feet, and once again dragged me back to my room.

Sunday came, and it was time for visits. Five days had passed, and I was able to behave myself. Well, except for the little incident at court. I'd cursed out the judge again, who had no choice but to kick me out when I said, "I'll piss on your old ass."

I even scooted out of my pants, like I had many times before, to show him I flat out didn't give a fuck. The reason being, eventually when I stopped talking shit and stopped pissing off the DA, public defender, and the judge, all they gonna say was that I had to spend the rest of my life behind bars. Even if it was true, who wanted to hear that? It's like an overweight woman who knows she's overweight but would hit the roof if you called her fat. It sucks to hear your fate, so I never went in there serious.

But this Sunday I had something to look forward to. After the way I'd behaved, the staff didn't want to give me my phone call, but they did, and finally I was able to reach my aunt.

She asked briskly, "Who is it?"

Damn, her voice sounded like an angel to me. "It's me, Cashmere! I been calling you for the longest, Auntie."

"Um-humph. How you?"

"Cool." I wasn't, but still I said I was. I knew she knew I was locked up.

"It can be lonely in there. I'll bet you want a visit, huh?"

"Yeah, Auntie. I'm tired of being in here. It would sure help to see a familiar face. Every week the other girls here have visits and I don't. It would be so good to see you."

Maybe some of my hope could be restored, and I would have a reason to be good. I don't think I was finding a reason to be bad. I always did the right thing before, and look where it got me. I wanted to revert back still. I just needed a reason. I needed support from family, and right now, my aunt was the only family I had left.

"What day is the visiting, Cashmere?"

"Every Sunday. Starts at one."

"Is there anything you need?"

Hell yeah! Some ecs, flip-flops, so my feet weren't touching the dirty floor in the shower, some shampoo, conditioner, lotion, deodorant. "Some flip-flops."

"That's all you need?"

"Yeah, and you to come see me just for about fifteen minutes," I said quickly.

"I'll be there. And I'll stay for forty minutes."

I almost cried tears of relief.

On Sunday I paced up and down my small room. I kept hearing staff come down the hall, the clinking of doors being unlocked, and the call, "You have a visit."

I couldn't wait till they came to my door and let me out to see my aunt. I would explain how I got in this mess and hope she would understand. I smoothed my baby hairs back off my face. I needed a trim badly. I made sure my white tee was tucked in, and I stood on my door, waiting for my aunt to arrive.

Doors opened and closed, just not mine. I stayed on my door, peeking out. Then I sat down, only to pop up on my door again when I heard the shuffle of feet. But they were on another door, not mine. Hell, they were right down the hall.

I grew impatient and banged on my door.

Ms. Clark came and asked, "What do you want?"

"What time is it?" I asked

"Four."

"Will you tell me when my visit arrives?"

When she nodded and went back down the hallway, I remained standing near my door, but no one came to get me out. My window in my door fogged up, and my legs were cramped up. I sat cross-legged in front of my door. Minors were being locked down, feet shuffled down the hallway, and I heard laughter, excited voices. Visiting was over, and my auntie didn't show.

"Fucking liar!" I pounded on the door. "You fucking lying fat bitch!"

I took my longest nail and began poking my skin. Tears popped out of my eyes, but I kept on jabbing myself till there was nothing but gaping holes staring back at me. Then I bent my fingers and slammed then into my arm with such force that blood was pouring out of me, gushing out of all of them. One cut in particular was so deep, the blood wouldn't stop flowing. And it shot out more quickly than the others too. Soon I was feeling weak, then dizzy, then weak and dizzy. I had to lay down, so I curled up on the floor. I felt myself slowly going out. Then all I saw was darkness.

There were bandages on me and I was in a hospital bed. I tried to stretch, but one of my legs couldn't. I pulled the blankets away to find it shackled to the bed. I was still in jail, I suppose. My arms were sore. I winced.

I glanced over at a woman sitting in a chair across from me. She was probably here for my ass, to make sure I didn't run away from the hospital. And once my eyes passed over her badge, I confirmed it.

Then a doctor walked in the room. "Hello, Cashmere."

His voice was echoing in my ears.

I nodded slightly, my eyes going in and out. When I felt too weak to keep them open, I closed them.

He said, "You lost a great amount of blood, young lady. You are going to have to find some way to get your emotions out besides cutting on yourself."

I nodded.

"I'm going to keep you for another twenty-four hours for observation. Then I'm going to release you back to the facility you're detained at. I'm also going to prescribe some Seroquel for you. It will help with your depression. The staff there are going to keep you under twenty-four-hour observation and keep you as a status three."

I nodded again, too weak to talk. Then I drifted off to sleep again.

Two days later, I found myself being transported back to the juvenile hall. Getting out should have been a good break, but I was so doped up, I didn't know any better.

I was taken to a room on the other side of the hall where the status three's were. Let me explain: Status 1 is what you call standard. You could be in a room by yourself without a staff member staring in your face to make sure you didn't try to harm or possibly kill yourself. Now if you are a status three, then your crazy-ass had to be isolated from the other minors, and staff sat in front of you twenty-four seven 'cause you were a danger to yourself and, sometimes, the institution. And that's what I now was. You also had to wear an ugly-looking Velcro-like jumper.

I didn't bother explaining that I had only cut myself too deep and had no intention of killing myself. But who gives a damn? So they stuffed me with meds so I would sleep, and took all my shit. I guess they figure that no one admits to trying to kill themself.

As soon as they took the handcuffs off of me, I laid on the bed and went right back to sleep. That became my salvation from all of this. Give me them meds and let me sleep.

"You can observe on Pierce. She ain't gonna give you no trouble. She'll probably sleep for the majority of the shift. All you really gotta worry about is getting relieved on time."

I turned over in the bed, and my eyes opened just a slit, adjusting to the light. I stared at a black woman, who didn't look much older than I was. She was dark brown with some pretty brown eyes.

"Hello, Ms. Pierce. My name is Ms. Hope, and I'll be observing on you."

I nodded, turned back over, and went right back to sleep.

I continued with the same routine—sleeping, waking to take my meds, eating, and going right back to sleep. Nothing could get better than that. Didn't have to deal with no bullshit, didn't have to feel nothing, but my breath pumping in and out of me. I still didn't bother to tell them that it wasn't a suicide attempt. I had been cutting and scratching on myself for the longest and had never went that deep before. It just happened like that. Wasn't nothing scarier than passing out, 'cause I didn't know if I was going to really wake up from that shit. Still, I didn't want nothing to fuck up what I had going now, not a gotdamn thing, and that's just the way I liked it.

For the longest, I was placed on status three, and that staff they had observing me would not shut the hell up. Every time I turned around, she was asking me if I wanted to hear a poem.

I always shrugged, hoping she'd cop an attitude and just say forget it, but she always pulled out some shit she called, prose, sonnet, haiku, and whatnot. She usually started once I woke up to eat, and I would get out of bed, grab my tray of food—I had grown accustom to the nasty shit— stuff it down my throat. Then I would crawl right back in the bed, and she would still be rambling. I wanted to say, "Will you shut the fuck up!"

I'd be going out, and she would still be going with that bullshit.

Chapter 26

After what seemed like damn near forever but was only a few months, the psychologist bitch and the short-ass supervisor Ms. B came down the hallway to my room. They interrupted Ms. Hope from her daily quote of the day. I couldn't even remember the first half of it because, as soon as she asked me if I wanted to hear it, I tuned her ass right out.

Ms. B said, "Pierce, you coming back to the world? It's a fucked-up one, but you still gotta live in it like the rest of us, baby."

I laughed but, really, was considering what she said.

"What the hell! Did you ladies see that?" Ms. B looked from Ms. Hope to the psych. She smiled wide. "Pierce laughed. All we been getting from her is, 'Fuck you! I'm not doing shit! Fuck you, bitch! I'll kill y'all!'"

I laughed again and shook my head. "Was I that bad?"

"Yes!"

Ms. Hope was shuffling her stack of poems.

"But we took into consideration the fact that you was coming down from drugs, and plus, you got issues, baby girl, issues your little ass needs to get out."

I didn't smile at that.

The psych bitch spoke in a soft voice. "Pierce, I talked to Ms. Hope and the Ms. B, and they feel you have been conditioned and fit to run your own program now. And a decent one. You've been on this side for almost six months. How do you feel about being moved to a status one?"

My first reaction was to tell her to kiss my ass, but I had to think. What would that do? Lead me right back to lockup.

Ms. Hope said, "Cashmere, she's talking to you."

Who asked your poem-reading, won't-shut-the-fuck-up-so-I-can-sleep ass, fake-ass Maya Angelou?

"Hello, Cashmere. You going deaf?"

I took a deep breath. That smart-ass Ms. B sure could talk some shit for someone the size of an elf. "I can't say that I'm ready. Really, I'm in a place where I've never been before. All I can say is, if nobody fucks with me, I won't fuck with them."

Ms. B narrowed her eyes at me then turned to Ms. Hope. "What do you think? You been sitting on her for a minute?"

If I didn't know, how in the hell was Maya Angelou's impersonator going to know?

Ms. Hope studied my face, as if in serious concentration.

Boo, bitch. I frowned and stared at the wall. Why was I having so much trouble locking eyes with Ms. Hope?

"Yes, I think Cashmere is ready to be a status one."

I was knocked out on meds when my seventeenth birthday passed on by. Now I was in a regular program like everybody else. All the bitches now wanted to be cool with me, which was nowhere near what I expected, so I ate in that rec-room (where we ate our meals, went to school, and did programs) surrounded by all of them. My eyes kept scanning the room, and none of them seemed to be tripping off of me.

Ms. Hope surprised me by coming into the rec-room and relieving Ms. Clark of being the unit leader, the person responsible for all the minors in the unit. They tell you when to enter a room, exit a room, when to eat, talk, and shit. It was synonymous with a babysitter, if you were to ask me. They also talked to us about different topics, and every day they gave us a "word of the day." We were supposed to shut up while we ate, so they could do their lecture. Then they told us about their expectations of us. Which meant no gang-banging, fighting, fucking, disrespect to minors or staff, and to go to school and get your schoolwork done.

Since I had been on the other side, I had yet to really run a program, let alone a good one. And even though two years had passed, I was yet to be sentenced, 'cause I had pissed off the judge so much.

"Okay, ladies, I'll be the unit leader this week."

Oh shit. Now I'd have to be up and hear that shit she talk?

Somebody mumbled, "Awww shit! Not this new-booty bitch."

Now if Ms. Hope had heard the comment, she pretended she didn't.

We ate our lousy breakfast while she talked.

"Ladies, your word of the day is *change*. Pretty much, the word speaks for itself. It means to do something different, modifications, rearranging. Ladies, something that I'm gonna propose to you every day is to think about the word and know that, despite what you have done in the past, you can make a change, whether it be the way you see things, changing your attitudes, behavior, lifestyle. At any given moment, you can change it. Any second that goes by is the opportunity. You just gotta take it. But keep in mind that seconds become minutes, hours, days, weeks, months, and the moment to make a change passes you by.

"Now I brought a poem in for you, ladies. It's by Maya Angelou. Keep in mind, ladies, that some of you don't want to hear this, some of you do, and some of you don't know what you wanna hear. So I ask that, if you don't want to hear it, you sit quietly and keep your opinion to yourself, or you could sway the one confused about what they wanna hear to feel the way you feel."

Why the fuck am I not surprised? Maya Angelou had a stalker for sure.

She surprised me because her voice was powerful. She read it like she was on a stage and not in front of some juvenile inmates. It was so loud that I had a hard time tuning her ass out like all the times before. And I also noticed that through all her talking I had barely touched my food.

Why was I so damn eager to step back into the rec-room when the food tasted like shit? Reason was, I wanted to hear some more of what Ms. Hope had to say, now that I wasn't drugged out on meds.

"Ladies, I think we have a lot of issues between us as females. But those issues stem from one thing in particular. How we see ourselves. Chances are that if you are not happy with who you are, you're not gonna be happy, period. And you are more likely to pick on somebody else. The reason being, ladies, is that if you can find flaws in other people, it forces you to take the attention off yourself, and you don't have to acknowledge your issues. But what you have to understand is that type of thing is self-destructive. So if you are constantly putting others down, chances are, ladies, you need to stop and check yourself. Ladies, know that self-esteem is connected to so much. How we feel about ourselves, why we make some of the choices we make, deal with the people we deal with. Why we sell our bodies, engage in drugs, be around people that are no damn good for us. But, ladies, what it takes to get out of this is changing the way you think . . . your logic, your reasoning."

I bit into my banana and chewed quickly.

"Confidence and self-esteem are vital to your livelihood. And I think there are a lot of women in here that need to work on those two areas, but again, it's about your logic and your reasoning. I brought another poem in I'm sure a few of you have heard. It is pretty popular. It's called 'Phenomenal Woman'. I listened intently as she read the poem to us.

When she finished, she said, "Now, ladies, I'm not going to go over the whole poem line for line. We don't have time. But think about this first stanza. 'Pretty women wonder where my secret lies. I'm not cute or built to suit a fashion model's size.' She is saying she is not perfect. But yet and still women wonder what it is about her. It's her confidence. How she sees herself as a powerful woman and the women see it also. And the men trying to find her 'mystery.' It's her embracing herself. It's in her conscience, ladies. She has a certain 'umph' about her strut." Her head high in the air, Ms. Hope switched around the room, making us laugh.

"And the men see that umph and they want some of that. And then, ladies, the line in the next stanza that says 'Now you understand just why my head's not bowed. I don't shout or jump about or have to talk real loud.' She's proud of herself. She can be who she is and still be appealing. Ladies, before we go back down, I wanna show you something. It's a triangle I came up with." She drew a triangle on the board with a marker. "I call it the levels of steps to self-confidence. The first step is understanding. Ladies, understand that no one is perfect." She drew a line in the triangle. "As perfect as we think Beyonce, Jennifer Lopez, or Jessica Simpson are, ladies, they don't see themselves as perfect. Nobody is. That's the logic no one is perfect. Now here is where your reasoning comes in, ladies. Ask yourself, If no one is perfect, why in the hell would I be? Ladies, once you get there, you have mastered the first step. Now the next step is acceptance." She drew another line. "Here, once you passed the understanding stage, you start to accept yourself for what and how you are. Then you start waking up and being happy with the person you see in the mirror." She drew another line. "That is where you boost your self-esteem and you now, ladies, have self-confidence. And remember this—once you realize this, you realize what your worth is, and no one can ever say or do anything to change how you see your-self. And what you ladies are gonna realize is that your worth is a lot higher than you think. It's at a level that not fifty of them fools on them tracks can measure up to. Ladies, you can't put a price on it because, ladies, your worth is priceless." She turned and looked directly at me.

I closed my eyes and tried my best not to let any tears drop.

Chapter 27

The next morning I ate my food quickly so I didn't have to look up and down. I didn't want to miss nothing.

Ms. Hope began, "Ladies, last night when I was at home, I was trying to think of something I could bring in. I didn't want to burn you out on poems. I thought about all the things you ladies have shared with me. All lot of you have been raped, molested, abused physically or mentally, robbed, and sadly maybe all of these things happened to you. So, ladies, when we say move forward, don't think we're being insensitive to what you've been through. I'm not. We are all victims at one point. We all start out as victims, but it's better to be a survivor. A survivor is someone who was once a victim like you and through time and healing was able to move forward. Ladies, if you are doing drugs or in here because of what has happened to you, chances are that you are still a victim, because what you are doing is defining yourself by your pain. I don't know about y'all, but I wanna be a survivor, so I can pull somebody else up with me. So again as I thought about you ladies last night, all the sad stories I heard, it reminded me of one thing: baggage. So I brought in this song by Erykah Badu called Bag Lady."

She lost me there, but once I kept listening, it made sense.

"Ladies, 'Bag Lady' is a metaphor for baggage, issues, all this weight on this lady's shoulders. 'Bag lady, bag lady, you gon' miss your bus.' Ladies, the writer of this song is saying the baggage or issues is holding the lady up. 'You can't hurry up 'cause you got too much stuff,' meaning that this baggage she is carrying is slowing up her progress. The line, 'I guess nobody ever told you all you must hold on to is you'—if you don't have anyone else, know that you'll always have you. Ladies, we talk about steps all the time, and the first step is facing your demons. Ladies, a lot of you engage in drug use to forget the issues you have, but when your high comes down, you still have those issues, or you self-destruct, sell your body, your soul. Ladies, I know why you hate being in that room on lockup." She raised her voice as she scanned our faces. "Ladies, you get in that room and you have nothing but time, time to think about choices you made or the thing that happened to you. Then you start cutting, to avoid that mental pain, I know. But, ladies, all you doing when you engage in stuff like that is, again, prolonging your progress."

My eyes watered. The room was quiet.

"Jay-Z has this really powerful line in one of his songs. He said, 'Don't run from the pain, run toward it; things can be explained what caused it.' Ladies, it takes you facing it, getting it out. You need to cry, cry! If you need to scream, scream! If you need to beat the wall, beat the wall! But you have to grieve. You have to hurt, ladies, so that you can move to the next step. And the next step is being strong enough to let go so that you can move forward, 'cause if you don't, what you find is that you in the same spot. Ladies, tap into that strength you never thought you had, but first you gotta handle the unfinished business of what's going on in here." Ms. Hope tapped her chest.

Before I knew it, I broke down crying. Me! I cried like I hadn't cried in a while. Cried over Mama, Daddy, losing my sister, being raped, selling my body. I screamed as I fell out of my chair and hit the ground with my fist.

Ms. Hope helped me to my feet, and we walked out of the rec-room. I continued to sob.

"Ms. Hope."

"Yes, Cashmere?"

I rubbed my snotty nose and followed her to my room. "I wanna see the psychologist."

"I'll put in a request for you."

I sniffed again. "Ms. Hope."

"Yes, Cashmere?"

"Thank you."

I continued my crying and screaming 'til I couldn't cry or scream any more. Once I was done, I lay on my bed shivering, yet feeling like my strength was really being restored.

I heard Ms. B yell, "What's wrong with Pierce?"

Ms. Hope said, "Nothing. She's grieving . . . finally."

I never thought it was possible to love a woman more than I loved Mama, but I loved Ms. Hope just as much. She always had these stories to tell us. I always went to bed thinking of the stuff she said and woke up wanting to hear more. And it seemed like everyone else did. They didn't start on shit on her watch because they admired and respected her so much. Sometimes even staff would come in the rec-room and listen to what she had to say.

She had us all laughing today, telling us this crazy story. "Ladies, we got to stop hating on one another."

I smiled as I looked at Ms. Hope trying to get hip.

"It causes so much animosity. And awkwardness. Ladies, one day I went on this date with this handsome guy to this play."

She was sitting next to Ms. Rino.

"And, ladies, we were able to find our seats and once we did, I was to sit next to a black girl who looked like she was the same age as me. As soon as she saw me, she shifted her body the other way and turned her head, and not once during the play or during the break did she turn back around because she was sitting next to me. Anyhow, there was a part in the play where the singer said turn to your neighbors and give her a big hug, so I turned to her and she wouldn't look at me. So, ladies, I"—she scooted next to Ms. Rino and hugged her—"threw my hands around her, and you know what she did?"

"What?" a few minors asked.

"She laughed and hugged me right back. Ladies, sometimes it has to start with us. Imagine, if you picked a different person every day and said something nice to them, what good that would do. When you see another minor who is homesick, stressed about their court date, or just came back from court, just a nod or telling them it's gonna be okay will do. We gotta start looking out for each other, and we gotta show each other more love."

When Ms. Hope was sending us down to our room, I reached out and hugged her tight, like I didn't want to let her go.

She just laughed and hugged me right back. "Cashmere, you so silly."

I had made a lot of progress. I didn't get into fights or disrespect staff anymore. I also learned from Ms. Hope how to get out what was in my head, and once I was able to do this, I no longer felt the need to scratch or cut myself.

I took every opportunity to help Ms. Hope and jumped at the chance of being her helper. Most girls liked being the helper because you got extra food and stuff from staff, and mostly because it kept them out of their room. I liked it because it allowed me to spend more time down the hall with Ms. Hope. Helpers were picked by how many points they earned. We had a Latina chick named Roxie, who was fired as helper because she'd gang banged the night before.

"Pierce."

"Huh?" I rubbed the sleep out of my eyes and shielded the light from my face. I was surprised as hell to see Ms. B and Ms. Hope at my door.

"Ms. Hope wants to make you a helper. Don't start no shit, or I'll kick your cute little ass."

I laughed. "Yes, Ms. B."

Like I said before, Ms. B talked a whole lot of shit for somebody so short, but mostly she was bullshitting. She had a good heart.

The job wasn't too bad either. It was just a whole lot of cleaning.

It was hallway clean-up time. Which was what we did every day after the girls had breakfast—mop, sweep, and wipe down every room. Ms. Hope would open one door, and I would sweep out the room. The fun part about hallway clean-up was listening to music while we cleaned up.

While I pushed the trash out the room, I asked her, "Ms. Hope, how you get so wise at such a young age?"

She laughed. "You think I'm wise?"

I grabbed the mop and rubbed it on the floor of the room till the dirt came up. "Yeah."

She closed the door back.

"You know how many times I heard 'Bag Lady.' I never thought about it the way you made us think about it. And a lot of stuff you say is so deep." I smiled. "You know, before, I couldn't wait for you to shut up."

"What?" She poked me in my back playfully.

I laughed too. "I used to. Now I don't want you to ever stop talking. I could listen to you all day. The shi—"

She pierced me with a look, interrupting me.

"Sorry—stuff you say is like therapy for me."

She smiled. "That feels good hearing that from you, Cashmere. It really does."

We stared at each other for a minute. Then she said, "Now, come on, Miss Leader. You can't be lazy."

"Okay." I went to the other room and started cleaning on that one.

Another thing I was good at in the unit was doing hair. Staff would bring us fake hair and gel, and I would braid hair on my downtime. It made time go by fast as hell in there. That and crazy-ass Ms. B recommending I study for the exit exam so I could graduate from high school.

My hair styling in the unit became so profitable, I ended up braiding staff's hair. They always treated me to some ice ceam or a burger or some candy as payment, which was cool with me. But I still had my craving for chocolate pound cake and strawberry shortcake on my time of the month.

Ms. Hope was writing a report outside the recroom while I braided Frankie's hair, a quiet, black girl. I was doing some French braids that had a tight little swirl design. Ms. Hope said, "Cashmere, you getting better and better at them braids."

I smiled as I parted a section of Frankie's hair. "I can do you too, Ms. Hope. I braid a little tight though."

She smiled and stared at Frankie. "She killing you, Frankie?"

Frankie chuckled. "No, miss."

Ms. Hope placed her chin underneath her hands and studied. "You still want to do hair for a living, Cashmere?"

I shrugged and started on a new braid. "I use to. Naw, I still do, but I don't think I'll ever get out of here."

"Why wouldn't you?"

"Ms. Hope." I finished the braid. "Do you know what I'm here for?"

"I know. I also know by the person you have come to be that it wasn't intentional. And you still have a chance to make something out of your life like anybody else. Why can't you?"

I didn't have an answer for her. I never thought about it in that way.

"Cashmere, don't ever think you can't do what you dream of doing. I can't continue to have all the hope for you. You got to have some for yourself."

I nodded.

"Keep doing good and don't stop believing in what you can accomplish." She rose and patted me on my back.

I grabbed her hand and kissed it. She called me silly again, and walked into the rec-room.

When all the other girls were in school, it was my time to study for the exit exams. So when the other students were in class, I would sit outside the rec-room with Ms. Hope and study, while she did her paperwork.

Ms. B's crazy ass was in the office dancing to Tupac. Ain't that some shit? What did her old ass know about Tupac?

Instead of studying, I was tapping on the table with my pencil to the beat of the Tupac song playing, "Hail Mary."

"Cashmere, you out here to study, not to goof off," Ms. Hope said sternly.

"Yes, ma'am." I went back to the book and worked on a tough problem.

Out of nowhere, there was a commotion in the rec-room. Me and Ms. Hope heard yelling and looked up at the same time and saw a book fly. Ms. Hope jumped from her seat.

I watched through the glass windows as a teacher pointed and yelled at another minor, Roxie. "I want her out!"

Roxie yelled, "Fuck you, muthafucka!"

"Let's go, Roxie," Ms. Hope said.

Roxie walked out of the rec-room slowly, and Ms. Hope followed after her. I stared at Roxie as she paused a few feet from me. Ms. Hope placed a hand on her back and guided her down the hall.

She jerked back and pushed Ms. Hope. "Bitch, don't fucking touch me!"

Then I was up. I jumped from the chair, pushed Ms. Hope back, and fired on the girl. I got her in the cheek. "Bitch, don't you ever touch Ms. Hope!"

"Pierce!"

I drilled her face like it was a beanbag before Ms. B and Ms. Clark pulled me off of her ass and dragged me to my room.

While Ms. Hope tended to Roxie, I yelled, "Let me go. She shouldn't have touched Ms. Hope!"

Neither responded.

They locked me in my room, and I stayed on my door staring out the glass.

A few moments later, Ms. Hope was on my door. I smiled at her, but she didn't return my smile. I hadn't kept my part of the bargain not to get into any shit.

"I'm sorry, Ms. Hope. I just couldn't let her sit up there and try to hurt you."

"Honey, I appreciate you looking out for me, but you can't fight your way out of everything."

I nodded.

"And, Cashmere, as much as I don't want to, I have to put you on lockup."

I nodded again, looking down.

"But I want you to read this to keep your mind clear. You been doing so good. You in a good place, Cashmere. Don't stop that. When your lockup is over, I expect you to be done with the book, and I want you to tell me who your favorite lady in the book was. And if those thoughts come back, Cashmere, I'm gonna need you to pray, and if that don't work, call my name. I'm staying over tonight so, Cashmere, I promise I will come." She unlocked the door and slid me a book. It had a long title. *For Colored Girls Who Have Considered Suicide When the Rainbow Is Enough.*

By the time my lockup was over, I'd missed breakfast but was able to come for lunch, to listen to some more of Ms. Hope. I had only managed to read half of the book she gave me.

"Ladies, we have to learn to embrace each other and offer support," she said. "I bet y'all don't think that's possible, huh?"

A lot of us, including me, nodded.

"Ladies, we also have to aspire to do more with our life, have hope that we can get out of the circumstances we in now. Ladies, I'm gonna go around the room, and I want all of you to tell me one thing you want to accomplish."

One girl said she wanted to go to college, one said to get off drugs, one said to take better care of her kids, one said to get a good job.

The closer it got to me, the faster my heart started to pound in my chest.

My partner said, "I want to be a teacher."

I took a deep breath, paused, then looked over at Ms. Hope.

She nodded.

So I went, "I—I want to go to cosmetology school and own my own hair salon one day."

And nobody said anything bad, no one laughed at me. In fact, a few other girls nodded their heads and said they wanted to do the same thing.

Ms. Hope opened her mouth and took a breath as if she was gonna say something else. "Naw, never mind."

Minors at the same time said, "No, miss. What?"

"Okay." Her eyes scanned the room. "If you agree to do this, you have to take it seriously."

We all nodded and waited.

"I want you look across at the person in front of you and—be serious now—tell them, 'You can do it.'"

After we completed the exercise, Ms. Hope, her eyes shiny, took a deep breath. "Ladies, I don't know if you realized what you just did.

Not only did you instill confidence in that minor across from you that they can accomplish something, but you also did something you said you could never do. You unified."

When we went back down to our rooms, the dumb chick that pushed Ms. Hope was on her door, mean-mugging the hell out of me. She was still on lockup and was the only person that was left out of our activity.

The day that Roxie was taken off of lockup, two more Latina chicks were transferred to our unit. You would have thought Roxie would have forgotten that shit, me whipping her ass, but she didn't. I was outside during field time, shooting hoops, and every time I shot and went to retrieve the ball, her and the other two chicks were huddled in a corner talking, looking at me.

I ignored them. My P.O. said that she had been faxing my daily behavior charts to the judge and that nothing but good were on them. I didn't want anything else bad on there either.

After a little while, I went inside to use the bathroom. I grabbed a seat cover and some tissue and sat down on the toilet to do my business. I noticed my piss was a lot clearer, now that I had been drinking all that water and milk.

I wiped myself, got up, pulled up my pants, and turned to flush the toilet. That's when I felt a sharp blow to the back of my head.

Before I could swing back, someone snatched my ponytail from another direction. "Do some shit now, bitch." It was Roxie and the other two girls. They all were swinging on me.

I hit back, but six hands to two were no match. They were coming from different directions, but I kept on fighting.

One bitch grabbed me from behind so the other two could go to work on me. I gagged and fell on the floor, where they were kicking me all over—my face, back, thighs—and I couldn't fight back anymore.

"What the fuck is going on?" It was Ms. B. "Lay down flat! Down flat!"

The kicking and punching stopped, and somebody rushed over to me. "Pierce, you okay?"

I moaned as pain pulsated through my body. I spat out some blood.

"On your feet!"

I peeked at the girls rising and stepping out of the bathroom. Then I heard the Ms. B say, "I was taking a shit. Then the next thing I hear is shuffling of feet. Lock them down and call the nurse for Pierce."

Ms. Clark was helping me as I limped down to my room. A black chick named Reese stared out at me through the slim glass in her window. She asked me, "Pierce, you okay?"

I didn't answer.

Another asked, "Who jumped you?"

I kept walking and glanced down the hall at Ms. Hope. She couldn't leave the status three she was on, but she waved at me. I struggled to wave back.

I sat down on my bed and waited for a nurse. Them bitches fucked me up. I had a big knot on my forehead, my lip was busted, and I was sore in my stomach, legs, and back.

And even though the nurse treated me, I was still in a lot of pain. So I didn't come back up. I slept the pain off. The last words I heard Ms. B say were, "You did good, Pierce."

Chapter 28

Some shit was going down in the unit. I could feel it. It couldn't have happened at a worse time. We had no supervisor that day, and all the regular staff, except for Ms. Hope, had called off, leaving us with new staff that had never worked East B before. We were in for something because, whenever we had different staff working in our unit, fights got started. To make matters worse, Ms. Hope wasn't unit leader either. She was wearing too many damn hats, 'cause there wasn't enough staff. She was backup and acting as the supervisor.

The unit leader didn't know what the hell she was doing. The three chicks that jumped me pulled some slick shit by all three of them tying sheets around their neck so they looked like they attempted suicide, meaning they would be placed on status three with a staff in front of their door. And the chick named Reese did the same, so she was down the hall with them.

I was on my door when Reese did the shit. Then, as she passed down the hall, she looked at me and gave me a nod. Some other chicks locked down gave her a nod back.

Aww shit!

When the unit leader let us up to go in the rec-room, I whispered to her, "Disturbance." All she said was for me to be quiet. I shook my head. Disturbance was another word for riot.

A girl started humming, "*Meet me in the club, it's going down.*"

Still, the dumb-ass staff didn't get it.

I asked to use the restroom, so I could catch sight of Ms. Hope to warn her. She was gone. I peered down the hallway. None of the staff was regular staff on the status three's.

Down the hall I heard Reese yell, "I want another tray!"

I went back into the rec-room, and there was a speaker talking about safe sex. I didn't want to look like a snitch. I couldn't concentrate on the speaker. Every time I looked up a black chick would nod at me.

Two chicks were humming now.

The unit leader stood near me. I was near the door. I mumbled, "Disturbance." She ignored me again.

The yelling down the hall grew louder. "I want another muthafuckin' tray!"

The humming again.

Someone was banging down the hall on the window, I think, and yelling, "I want another tray, bitch!"

Humming again.

Three girls asked to use the restroom, and she let them at the same time.

Dumb-ass. Where is Ms. Hope? God, where is Ms. Hope?

The yelling and banging grew louder. "I! Want! A! Tray!"

Ms. Hope slipped back in the unit and took a deep breath. Just then we heard glass shatter. Ms. Hope took off down the hallway, yelling to the unit leader, "Send your girls down!"

The humming started again.

The unit leader had us all get up at the same time. No! No! That's not how you should do it!

As we exited the rec-room, we saw the three girls who went to the bathroom shoot through the office down the hall.

"Stop, ladies! Go to your room," she yelled.

I watched from the office window as they ran down the hall with the opened doors of the status three's. A window was shattered for sure.

The staff were frozen as Reese joined the three girls who were in the bathroom, and they attacked all the status three girls, the ones who'd attacked me. There were now seven girls in the middle of the hall fighting.

As more girls went down, bumping past me, the staff stood frozen. Ms. Hope did her best to break it up, but she didn't have her pepper spray. Like the other staff, the punk-ass unit leader stood frozen too, while the kids on my side ran wild. The staff ran into the office, leaving Ms. Hope to handle it on her own.

I ran past them down hallway. I felt my heart pumping against my chest so hard, I thought it was gonna pop out. From what I could see, it was now Blacks against the Mexicans.

Ms. Hope was pulling them apart and yelling, "Back up, ladies!"

It became a full-out race riot, and I was punching through girls, I didn't care what color, to get to Ms. Hope. "Ms. Hope, go in the office!" I yelled.

She ignored me or just flat-out didn't hear me.

A girl tried to punch me in my mouth, but I cracked her fast, with my elbow, knocking her down.

Two chicks came after me. I dodged them and saw Ms. Hope push a girl so hard, she slid backwards into the glass from the shattered window. Then my eyes widened at what the girl did next.

"Ms. Hope, watch out!"

The bitch grabbed a thick chunk of the glass and stabbed Ms. Hope in her back with it.

I screamed as Ms. Hope froze. Then blood gushed from her mouth and she fell to the floor. I tried to get to her, but two girls tackled me down.

That's when the back door opened and I heard, "OC warning!"

Then a mist filled the air.

The other girls dropped, started coughing, and covering their face. But I didn't cover up. I was too busy screaming and pointing at Ms. Hope, who was lying in a pool of her own blood.

Ms. Hope died. She was killed in that riot. And now I didn't see a need to get out of the bed, much less run a program. All I did when I woke up was cry, which was why I was placed on status three down the hall again. For a while I refused to eat, bathe, or even leave my room. And my existence was just cool with me.

Until Ms. B came down the fucking hallway and stood in my doorway, a hand on her hip. "Pierce, get yourself up and groom."

"No."

"You know you got court coming up, right?"

"Fuck that! I don't care."

"What do you care about?"

"Nothing."

"Nothing?" She stepped further in the room. "Listen, you been through hell and back, and you mean to tell me that, after all of this shit, you giving up now? What? You gonna stay on status three for the rest of your life? That's some bullshit, Pierce. Ms. Hope instilled enough in you to want more for yourself."

I blinked. At the mention of Ms. Hope, tears slid down my face and rested on my chin.

"You ain't crazy, Pierce, you just angry. That's what depression is—anger turned inward. And after all the things Ms. Hope taught you, you got all that shit out now. What you trying to hold on to now? We all miss her, but we gotta keep going. You wanna shift right back? Don't go so deep that you can't come back this time." She slapped her hands together and repeated. "Ms. Hope instilled enough in you to want more for yourself."

More tears came.

"Let me see your arms." She ran her hands along my hands and arms, and scanned them, I guess, looking for new cuts or scratches. Then she smiled. "Something Ms. Hope said stuck."

I smiled through the tears.

"Think about what I said." She walked away.

I lay back on the bed. Ms. Hope's words were in my head like she was standing in front of me. *"Don't become defined by your pain. Ask yourself, ladies, Are you a victim or a survivor?"*

As I turned over in the bed, something caught my eye. A book was sticking out of the edge of my bed. I stretched a hand to retrieve it. I grasped the tip, and then it fell out of my hands. I pulled myself closer to the inner edge of the bed, toward the wall, and grabbed it again. It was the book Ms. Hope had given me, the one I'd only half-finished, *For Colored Girls Who Have Considered Suicide When the Rainbow Is Enough*. As I flipped through the pages, something fell out onto my lap. It was a folded up letter.

I took the folds out and was surprised to see Ms. Hope's writing, which was addressed to me.

Cashmere, there are times I don't want to come to work. Y'all girls work the hell out of us sometimes. And when I reach for the phone to call off, you come to mind. Cashmere, you may look up to me, but I look up to you at the same time. I tell myself, if Cashmere can get up, manage a smile, or even a laugh, I can keep going as well. Cashmere, I know you been through a lot, but you gotta keep going. You have made so much progress, and I know things can only get better for you. You been through the fire, and you came out. Girl, you have so many blessings around the corner, you just have to be open to receive them. And now you are. Believe in Him, and know you are truly something special. See ya in the morning, Hope.

I read the letter over and over until it was crinkled up in my hands. Then I leaped out of the bed and yelled, "Ms. B!" scaring the hell out of the staff that was sitting on me.

Ms. B came running down the hallway, her eyes wide. "What? What is it?"

I smiled. *Don't run from the pain, run toward it.*

"Fool. I thought you were whipping on my new staff."

I shook my head. "Naw, it's nothing like that. If Ms. Hope was here, she would kill me."

"You know she ain't never left, Cashmere." Ms. B winked.

I got it, what she meant.

"Ms. Hope's spirit is gonna always reside in East B."

I laughed and felt more tears come, but they weren't bad ones at all. I felt good as hell. "I hope so, 'cause these heiffas need it, just like I needed it."

If I didn't know any better, I would have sworn Ms. B's eyes had teared up at that moment. Turned out I was right, and tears did drop from her eyes.

"I'll make a deal with you, Ms. B. I'll shower if you give me a pen."

She placed her hands on her hips. "Normally, I don't make deals with kids, but your ass stinks, so come on."

She wrapped an arm around my shoulders and walked me to the showers. "Just out of curiosity, Pierce, what do you need a pen for?"

"I want to write the judge. You said I had court, right?"

She nodded.

Chapter 29

It was like a ceremony, me going off to court. They didn't forget when I had tried to AWOL, and since I was at their facility the longest before being sentenced, I was transported with two staff.

The first thing I did when my public defender greeted me was politely ask him, "How are you?"

He looked surprised and stuttered. "Fine, and you?"

"Better, sir, much better."

I was the same way with the judge, who glared down at me again, like he did last time. "And how are you, sir?" I asked. He narrowed his eyes. "Ms. Pierce, I have been pushing your court date back. Do you know why?"

"No, sir."

"I had no desire to see you in my courtroom."

People in the room laughed, but I remained poised. Ms. Hope would've been proud. Even Daddy. "I must say, Pierce, I am pleasantly surprised. All I have been getting is positive behavior files and letters from the facility where you're detained. But I'm tired of reading. I want you to tell me where you are now."

I took a deep breath. "Well, sir, I'm in a much better place. See, for the longest I been fighting 'cause I been angry about my dad, my mom, being put in the situations I been in. When I was fourteen, my dad was in an accident and was never the same. Mama abandoned me and my sister. That's where it started, my anger. I let my anger consume me, and when I came here, I gave up on myself. On life, period. I already knew my life was over, so I felt no need to pretend that I cared about anything. I was abused, raped, degraded, and I couldn't do anything about it but scratch myself to avoid feeling it when those flashbacks came in my head. This may sound crazy, but I never wanted to die. But then again I never wanted to live, 'cause I felt I had nothing to live for. Then, sir, someone came into my life and, man, they were a sheer blessing. They taught me one of the most important things anyone could teach me—how to be a survivor."

"How so?"

"She taught me that everyone is a victim once, but you don't have to remain one. You have to come to terms with what you been through so that it won't be a crutch for the rest of your life. So it doesn't trap you. Then once you acknowledge what happened to you, you let go, so you can progress. And, sir, I had to do a whole lot of letting go."

There were chuckles.

"Letting go was such a weight lifted off my chest. I didn't have to be angry anymore. And, most of all, I started caring about myself. It's been a while since I started doing that. I started feeling like I was worth something. And I am. I'm priceless. And I want the chance to get out of here and accomplish something eventually. I have so many reasons to, and most importantly, I owe it to somebody. 'Cause if it wasn't for them, I wouldn't be here."

I didn't want to start crying, but I got like that whenever I thought of Ms. Hope.

"Sir, I did not intentionally kill my sister. It was an accident, and if I could change that day, I would. The only thing I had then was taken away. And I was always taught to handle stuff by fighting, but in the end, all I end up doing is hurting myself.

"So, sir, I have changed, but I accept whatever you choose to do with me. I just ask for a second chance to do things right now."

"What do you want to be?"

"I always wanted to be a hairstylist and open my own shop, sir."

The judge didn't look convinced by what I just said, and no one was saying anything. I licked my dry lips, as the judge seemed to be studying my face. He shifted some papers, read them again, and wrote something down.

The judge gave me my sentence, and my whole body wobbled. I didn't hear him right. "What?" I blurted out.

"I said, 'Ms. Pierce is having a birthday in two weeks. Release her on probation on her birthday.'"

"I don't have life, sir? No electric chair?"

"Pierce, if you don't leave my courtroom, I'll change my mind."

My smile was so wide, my face ached. I hugged my public defender and was about to go for the judge, but changed my mind. I smiled graciously, feeling like I'd just won a million bucks. I kind of did, getting my freedom back.

Damn, Ms. Hope. Thank you for everything. You saved me.

Since I didn't have any relatives I could stay with, they placed me in this emancipation program. The first thing I did was find out where

Daddy was buried. The hospital was so kind. They told me they'd paid for Daddy's tombstone. They gave me the address in case I wanted to go see him. I did. I put flowers on his grave.

The program I was in provided me with a place of my own. I was even given spending money to purchase furniture and clothes. It was a little studio, but it was mine. The program paid my rent and utilities, and for me to go to a school of my choice. I picked a beauty college within walking distance of where I stayed.

Now, finding a job was another thing. I couldn't find one because I had no real work experience, except for Sweet Tooth Café. And that was only for a short period of time. And I had no reference, except Caesar. But he was part of my past, and I had no intention of dealing with him again.

My P.O.'s name was Ms. Chisolm, a buff-looking black woman that always had her nails and hair done. She said to me, "You know you violating part of your probation by not working, don't you, Cashmere?"

"I can't find anything. I don't have experience with much, except for hair."

She laced her fingers together. "That's right, you are in hair school." She put her purse on her desk, opened it pulled out a card from her wallet. Then she took a pen and circled something and slid the card to me. "I'm only doing this because I see you really trying. And sometimes other sisters gotta help other sisters out. Then what you in turn do is, do this for another sister."

I nodded. "Thank you."

"Tell Bev, Bosey sent you to her. She know I'm a good voucher."

"Thanks again." I walked out of her office.

The next day, I skipped school to visit the salon, hoping Bev would hire me. It was on the same street as the café I used to work at with Caesar. Pain tugged at my heart, but it passed after I thought of how fortunate my ass was. I was given a fresh new start. Man, I was going to make the best of it.

I took a deep breath, smoothed the skirt on my business suit, checked my stocking to make sure they had no runs in them, and stepped inside the salon. The salon was pretty big. It was decorated in leopard and candles were all around the place. They were also burning incense. I hated that scent, 'cause Black used to burn it all the time. I could hear Too Short when I walked further in the salon past the lobby section.

I tried to keep a smile on my face as I passed stylists pressing, perming, flat-ironing, and curling hair. You could smell hair being burnt. Customers waited on the leopard print couches yelling at each other, some on their cell phones, others flipping through magazines.

I got a couple of strange stares as I walked a bit farther. I ignored them.

One stylist whispered to her customer, "You know who that is?"

I ignored that, although I didn't want to.

"Well, rumor is—"

I tuned it out and asked another stylist, "Excuse me, is Bev here?"

A couple of females were now checking me out. Fear rose within me. What if they recognize me from the track? Well, that wasn't real likely, 'cause I wasn't on there too much. But maybe they'd heard about me and my sister.

I pushed those thoughts away and waited for a reply.

The tall, slim woman said, "On the end with the loud voice." She used her curlers to point to a woman in the far back booth putting relaxer on a woman's hair.

I went up to her. I caught the tail end of her conversation.

"Yeah, girl, if the dick is good, the dick is good. Pass that shit around, if you gonna brag about getting dicked the fuck down!"

Her client burst out laughing. "Girl, you know you crazy!"

"Bev?"

She spun around and said, "Yeah, babe?" Her smile was genuine.

Cool. I cleared my throat but still managed to stutter. "I-I'm Cashmere. Bosey said to see you about a job."

"Bosey? Oh, that's my husband's P.O. Well, girl, welcome to the family." Bev reached over and hugged me. She was a stranger, but it felt nice. Genuine.

"All right now, dig it, girl—you work on commission. It won't be much, and that all depends on what you can do." Bev blew out a cloud of smoke. "What can you do?"

"I can braid, press, perm, and weave, and I'm working on my license right now."

Her eyebrows rose when I said braid.

"Well, without a license, you can't do very much, so for now you can be my 'poo-poo' girl."

"What?"

She put her weight on one leg. "Shampooing, and you said you could braid, right?"

I nodded.

"That will work too, 'cause I do a lot of sewn-in weaves. You can braid the shit down for me."

"Okay."

"Five for every shampoo you do, and eight for every head you braid." She yanked me by my hand before I could answer. "Come on."

Now all the chicks were staring at me as I stood with Bev in the center of the salon.

"Y'all listen up! This is Cashmere, the new poo-poo girl. Don't give her no shit."

Somebody said, "Murderer!"

Color drained from my face, and I felt cold. I almost walked out, if it wasn't for Bev grabbing my arm and holding me there.

"All the reason not to fuck with her, right?"

I managed a smile at that; a few others did as well.

"Y'all bitches don't even know her, and I'll bet she ain't got half the skeletons y'all hoes got. So don't fuck with her! Everybody deserves a second chance."

Some of the women nodded.

The bitch who called me a murderer shrunk in her chair, and my eyes penetrating hers made her shrink deeper.

Someone said, "Don't judge a book by its cover."

I smiled. I now had a job. I was really getting it together.

Bev was crazy as hell. And her craziness always had me cracking up. Every time I turned around, her ass was sending me to get her skinny ass some fried fish, hush puppies, and potato salad.

And the thing was, staff gave me a bit of hell at first, but once they saw how quick I could braid, they showed me love. One thing hairstylists that did weaves hated to do was braid hair. It hurt their wrists.

And another thing about working in a salon with females is that you always learn the latest gossip, whether you want to or not. Who was back in town, who left town, who got arrested, who got robbed, and the most popular topic, who was fucking who.

I listened quietly as I placed a cap over this lady's head and sat her under the dryer in the back of the salon.

Gee Gee, this buck-tooth stylist with gray contacts that could press good as hell, was talking and usually the one to initiate the gossip, her and Rona, and this short stylist named Quida, with the squeaky voice and childlike face. The other ladies who worked in the salon were usually tight-lipped but always listened in.

"I don't know why she with that fool, always coming up here bragging about how good her man is to her. He ain't shit."

Rona, the pretty, brown-skin stylist with freckles, added crimps to a lady's hair. "Okay, girl."

"You know you ain't never lied," Quida said.

Gee Gee laughed. I wished she would close her mouth on her buck teeth. They weren't a pretty sight.

"Shit, yesterday, girl, I was getting me some chicken from Louisiana Chicken, and that fool was picking up a raggedy hooka."

Rona laughed and stomped her feet, almost burning a client, and Quida giggled as well. Some of the other ladies in the salon laughed with Gee Gee and Rona.

"I'll tell you, that's why I stay the fuck alone." Gee Gee had her pressing comb in the air like she was testifying. Then she snickered and pulled the cape off of her client. "But I will participate in some good dick every now and again. Okay, baby, you done."

"Cashmere!" Bev was calling me from her office.

When the door opened, I heard somebody mumble, "Speaking of the devil," but I didn't get the chance to see who they were talking about until I came back from seeing what Bev wanted.

After getting the letter back from her to give to my P.O., I dashed back outside. When I did, I gasped at my auntie sitting at the rinsing bowl, her head back and her eyes closed.

Gee Gee said, "Baby, can you wash Mrs. Malone's hair?"

I nodded.

"I'm gonna get you taken care of, Mrs. Malone," Gee Gee told her.

I pursed my lips when she wasn't looking. My aunt looked pretty much the same, sitting in that chair like she was Queen of Sheba and shit. I turned on the water and waited for it to get hot before turning on the cold.

"Now be gentle. My husband is taking me out to the theatre," she yelled. "Gee Gee, make sure you get my hair silky."

"I will, babe." Gee Gee rolled her eyes at my aunt.

If my auntie only knew, I thought as I scrubbed the dandruff out of her hair. I dug my fingers into her scalp like Bev had trained me to do.

"What play you gonna see?" Quida asked.

"Play? Who said anything 'bout a play? I'm going to see the new Tom Cruise movie."

There were a few muffled giggles and a whole lot of coughing and whispers.

My auntie hummed, the same tune she used to hum around the house. I stayed silent and rinsed the shampoo out of her hair before applying conditioner and a cap.

The chatter in the room continued throughout this. Gee Gee was now talking about somebody else's lowdown husband.

My aunt jumped in the conversation. "And it's a damn shame women don't know how to keep their damn husband at home."

I coughed to cover my laughter, as did the other women.

"'Cause my man knows his address. He damn sure knows when to come home and not to be in the streets with these triflin' heiffas with no sense of direction."

Gee Gee's shoulders were shaking with silent laughter.

"Okay, Mrs. Malone, can you please go to the dryers," I said in a professional voice. I had changed, but my voice didn't. Which was exactly why she froze.

I now stood in front of her, my hands behind my back, so when she opened her eyes, she had no choice but to see me.

Her eyes were wide, and all I saw were eye-balls when she focused in on me. She stuttered at first, trying to find the proper words to address me, I guess. When she wasn't able to, I offered her a smile to let her know that I was cool, that I held no grudge, but she didn't smile back at me.

I ignored the look and asked, "How are you, Auntie?"

Surely, after everything, she couldn't hold on to anger for something my sister had done. But when she muttered, "Humph," and only that. No "Fine, and you," or "I missed you," or "Come give your auntie a hug," I realized I was wrong.

Without another glance at me, she stood proudly and walked over to the dryers.

And, yeah, I was a lot more mature than I was before, but not less sensitive, so I ended up slipping away, ignoring the whispers, and crying in the bathroom. I guess that was that.

The shop was still busy, but I took a lunch break to get away from the whole situation, and by the time I came back in the shop, my aunt was gone. But I couldn't shake the sadness of her coming into the shop brought me. I wanted to have some type of relationship with my family, and she was the only tie I had. And she obviously wanted no ties to me.

Chapter 30

The next day business was booming. I was running around like a headless chicken, which was cool with me, because it kept me busy and increased the size of my wallet. I was still, after all, making money on commission.

I was halfway done braiding a chick's hair for a weave when I heard a man say, "Damn, Bev! Who is this?"

I turned around and met the gaze of a fine-ass man. He was tall as hell, buff, and had wide shoulders, and thick, muscled arms. He was a light tone, like his ass was mixed, with a set of silky curls on his head, had smooth, creamy skin, bedroom eyes, and a neat, clipped mustache over some cherry-colored lips. He favored the dude my mom used to be obsessed with, who'd acted in this funny-ass movie I saw on video, *CB4*, and I forgot the other one. He was dressed in a business suit. Yeah, he was fine, but he was a man, and I had no desire for any of them right now, unless they were on a dollar bill. So after I was done checking him out, I dismissed him by rolling my eyes.

"Bev, who is this fine specimen you got here?"

The ladies in the salon giggled.

"Don't worry about it," I snapped and turned back around to continue what the hell I was doing.

"Baby girl, I can't help but not worry, especially when you look as fine as you do."

I sighed and tried to ignore the giggling from the ladies in the salon.

He started singing, "My, my, my, my, my, my, my, you sure look good tonight."

I shook my head at him.

He stepped closer to me and whispered, "Umph, umph, umph!"

That shit was enough. I spun around on his ass.

"You got something to sell, sell it elsewhere, 'cause, *partna*, whatever you got, I damn sure don't want none of. So take your tired, wack-ass game on for the last time, fool." I rolled my neck on the word *fool*.

That got him. I know it did. He was probably not used to being rejected, especially in front of a bunch of women. But, hell, there was damn sure a first time for everything. He looked irritated that I shot his game down. He walked away and straight into Bev's office.

When I finished up my last braid, I asked Gee Gee, 'cause her nosy ass would know, "Gee Gee, who is he anyway?"

"Demarco. He owns the place."

I had dissed the owner, big fucking deal! What was he gonna do—fire my ass? Come to think of it, I kind of wished that his ass had, 'cause every time I turned around, he was always in my grill, coming by the salon when he never came by before. Bev said that was because he was out of town for a long period of time. Whatever. He was annoying the hell out of me.

He stopped by one day and wanted me to wash his hair. What the hell? Bev and the other ladies thought the shit was funny. I didn't.

"Cashmere, you got a paying customer, and his ass is paying double for this wash, and you gonna tip my poo girl twenty, D!" Bev snapped, laughing as she did it.

Everybody in the shop watched me as I approached him.

You know Gee Gee's ass was the first to comment. "He likes her. She need to stop acting so siditty."

I gave her the finger, and the other ladies burst out laughing.

"Oh shit, Cashmere, did I say that out loud?" she said with a guilty smile.

I ignored her.

As Demarco sat back in the bowl, I huffed out an impatient breath and turned on the water. Once it hit his hair, his curls uncoiled and were silky and soft against my fingers. I scrubbed his head gently and admired his handsome face because, regardless of what I said, I know a fine brother when I see one and they were never really around us in juvie. So I guess I should've been a little more enthusiastic about seeing one now. But I was thinking about how much I had grown to hate men since I had been a prostitute. They were nowhere near as good as Daddy was to me. In my eyes no man can ever exceed Daddy's perfection, not even half fucking way. Damn, I missed the hell out of him.

"I'm not a woman. You can scrub it harder," Demarco said in a husky voice. Then he placed his hands over mine to show me how.

Something weird happened when he did that. I felt a sensation sweep through me. I snatched my hands away quickly, afraid that he would feel it as well, but he chuckled and kept his eyes closed.

I went back to my task. If his ass wanted it scrubbed hard, that's what his black-ass was gonna get.

He started making these sounds with his throat.

"Can you please be quiet?"

"Sorry. You just scratched an itch for me."

Gee Gee's ass went, "Whew!"

I rinsed the soap out of his hair quickly, not worrying about wetting and messing up his expensive-looking shirt. Then I turned the water off, placed a hand on my hip, and snapped, "Done. Where's my tip?"

Demarco opened his eyes and smiled at me, biting his bottom lip. "You sound real sexy when you raise your voice at me, lady."

"Boy, please. You got me twisted with that wack-ass shit."

There was laughter. Quida said in her squeaky voice, "She shot him down again."

"Can you style it too?"

I rolled my eyes. "Bev."

Bev jerked her head toward an empty styling chair, a big-ass smile on her face. "Go over there."

He stood. "Ladies first."

I rushed past him and stood behind the chair. "What do you want done?"

He sat down and got comfortable. "Make me look good. I have a date tonight."

Rona, who had been quiet up until now, asked, "Who you got a date with?"

"Well, I was hoping the pretty lady behind me will have dinner with me."

I rolled my eyes to the ceiling.

"Where you gonna take her, D?" Gee Gee asked. "To get some fish and *scrimps*?"

Demarco chuckled and stretched his long legs. "Lobster and *scrimp*." He turned and looked at me as I rubbed some glaze in his hair.

He was serious too. "How 'bout it?"

I once again rolled me eyes and stabbed a comb through his now curly hair. Then, when I was done, I shoved him out of my chair and went to help the next customer.

And you would think the fool got the picture. He didn't. He made another wrong move, showing up at my doorstep.

"How the fuck you know where I stay?" I demanded, eyeing his ass, my hands on my hips.

"I followed you home."

My eyes narrowed. "What?"

He placed both his hands in the air. "Just to make sure that you make it home safely. You always the last one to leave the shop because you spend all that time cleaning and mopping. Then you take a chance and you walk home by yourself, so I always follow you to make sure you get in your house. Cashmere, I don't have to live out here to know that these streets are dangerous, especially for a single woman."

"So now you stalking me, huh?" I hid my smile, 'cause what he was saying wasn't bothering me at all, for some reason.

"Me? No."

I studied him. "Well, it's not night now. What are you doing here now?"

"And I never officially got the chance to welcome you to the shop."

"Every time I turn around you in my face. If that's not a welcome, then I don't know what is."

"If you weren't so damn fine, I wouldn't be in your face. Blame God for not making you ugly."

I laughed softly, my arms loosening from underneath my chest.

Then my laughter faded when I reminded myself that this nigga was no different from the rest. He damn sure wanted something. "Boy, whatchu think you gonna get from me?"

"Dinner, movies, wanna make you smile. You always seem so sad."

"You don't—"

He stepped closer. "No, listen, I know you're pretty busy, and that's good. You got priorities, and you got them straight, but in the midst of your life, you can't stop living. And from what I can see, you doing that."

It felt good to be complimented.

He stepped even closer. "Let me take you out, Cashmere. I'll be a gentleman."

"No."

"Please?"

"Oh God. Then will you leave me the hell alone, boy?"

"Yes. No."

I laughed, despite the situation. "Which one?"

Demarco didn't reply, just tugged on that bottom lip again with his teeth.

"Wait here while I throw something on." As a precaution, I closed and locked the door in his face.

If his ass wanted to take me out, he would have to wait. I wasn't gonna rush for him. So I took a shower, pulled on a summer dress, some flip-flops, and threw my hair back in a bun.

He really must have wanted to take me out because, when I stepped out twenty minutes later, he was twiddling his thumbs as he sat on the steps waiting for me.

"Come on," I said absently, second-guessing going anywhere with him anyhow.

Old boy drove a Cadillac Escalade. I was no fool. I was sure he was getting plenty pussy in that bitch too. Plus, he owned a business. They was probably throwing it at him, gift-wrapping the shit. Which made me a little nervous.

"Where do you live?"

"Carson."

Then I silently asked myself, *What did it matter?* I wasn't trying to make moves with this man. I just needed to get out the house.

Demarco tapped the steering wheel. He was playing some R&B by Maxwell, the dude Mama was in love with, and blasted around the house. It was that song "Whenever, Wherever, Whatever." I laughed when he tried to mirror the crisp, smooth voice of Maxwell with his squeaky, cracking voice.

He sped down the highway and jumped on the freeway. Once we hit this big-ass bridge, I panicked. "What the hell is this?"

"The Vincent Thomas Bridge."

I stared out the window and clutched the cushion on the seat, as we descended and I saw water underneath us, and a port. Then suddenly I remembered I had been over here before with Daddy, when he'd brought me, Desiree, and Mama. A tear slid down my cheek.

"You okay?"

I nodded and closed my eyes for a quick moment. *Damn, I miss you, Daddy.*

Once we exited the bridge, we pulled into a parking structure in a area called Ports O' Call.

The wind was blowing like crazy and raising my dress.

I held it down as we walked on the pier. He grabbed my hand like I was his woman, and I yanked it away, only for him to pull it back.

Demarco pulled me. "Let's go on a quick boat ride."

I had to jog to keep up with his big-ass feet. Once he helped me on the boat, he held onto my hand, and I didn't pull away. *Fuck it! Let him get his thrill.*

The boat moved swiftly through the water, making me nervous. I saw images of me sitting on Daddy's lap, while Desiree looked out the window of the boat, and my Mama dozed off.

"Look at the sea lions, Cashmere."

I stared out in time to see one do a flip in the water and another one come up from under the water.

"They're performing for us."

"Yeah."

Demarco scooted closer to me and wrapped an arm around me. He was getting too close for comfort, and I wasn't stopping him.

After we got off the boat, he asked, "You hungry?"

"Yeah."

He grabbed my hand again, and we walked to this little seafood stand, where there was all this raw seafood, eyeballs and all looking back at me.

"How you feel about grilled seafood, Cashmere?"

I shrugged. "Don't matter to me."

He surprised me by speaking in Spanish to the dude working at the stand. It sounded sexy as hell to me.

The next thing I know, lobster, shrimps, and crab were being dipped in some sauce and thrown on a barbecue grill, making my tummy growl.

Once it was done he carried a huge tray to a table, and we both sat down.

I dug in—fuck being shy—and grabbed a crab leg. "When did you learn Spanish?"

He popped a shrimp in his mouth and chewed. "My Mama is from Honduras."

"Your dad too?"

"No, he's from here. Where he is now, I don't know." His lips twisted bitterly.

I sucked the juice off my fingers and attacked the lobster, but in my head I was thinking, *I'm not the only one with issues. I'm just lucky enough to work mine out.*

He ate another shrimp. "How about yours?"

"My Daddy and Mama are dead." I lied.

"Sorry to hear that." He cracked a crab leg open and chewed on it. "How did you get that name?"

My mouth was stuffed with pieces of the succulent lobster. I placed my hand over my mouth and asked saucily, "What's wrong with my name? How you get yours, Demarco?"

"You are feisty as hell, girl." He smiled. "And I just asked because I think it's a nice name and it suits you." He looked back at the water at the end of that comment then back at me.

"I don't know. Daddy said some shit about my skin being so soft, it reminded him of cashmere."

I popped a shrimp in my mouth. "Your name mean anything?"

He laughed. "Yeah. I'm named after Mama's pimp."

I almost choked on the shrimp.

"Mama was a prostitute in Honduras. That's why I don't know my daddy. She did it for as long as she could before moving out here. She opened a little restaurant, and that's how we survived. When she died, she left it to me. I turned it into a hair salon because I thought it would be more profitable."

I nodded.

"So tell me something about Cashmere. Where you from, girl?"

"I'm from California. I grew up in Compton."

"With who?"

"What do you mean?"

"You said your parents were dead. So who raised you?"

"My aunt, but we don't talk too much anymore." I pulled my bottom lip in, hoping he wouldn't pry any further.

He just studied me.

I made a face. "Boo!"

He smiled at me.

"What, boy? What are you thinking?"

"That your face has a lot of beauty on it."

If you only knew what that beauty did for me—nothing. Not shit. But it still felt good to be complimented.

"Don't worry, I'm not going to go any further into your business. I probably couldn't anyway. You're on the defense. And you probably won't believe this, but I don't want anything from you, Cashmere. But I do like you. And, believe it or not, it's for the right reasons. And I know these are just words, but if you will allow me to, time will show you that I'm sincere and not out to get you." He stared at me intently.

I smiled in return. Then I looked down at the wood planks beneath my feet, saw the water peeking through. Thinking I could have opened up about my past, this was as good as it was gonna get for confessions, but for some odd reason, I didn't.

That wasn't the last time I saw Demarco. He would come by the salon almost every night and take me home, and since I was comfortable with him, I let him.

"When can I see you again?" he asked me one night when he was walking me to my doorsteps.

"You seeing me right now, silly."

"No, I mean, like out on another date."

He slipped behind me and spun me around so I was all up in his arms. If the shit didn't feel good, I would have pulled away.

"When do you wanna see me?"

He reached over and kissed my lips softly, and I returned the kiss.

"Tomorrow." He kissed me again. "The day after that." Another kiss. "And the day after that 'cause I like you, Cashmere." He kissed me again.

I pulled away, still playing the "rude girl" role. "Boy, go home."

I woke up the next morning to find some pink roses sitting on my doorstep, so I definitely gave him a date after that, and another after that.

Chapter 31

I got a pretty big tip from some lady that came into the salon, so I treated myself to a new outfit to wear for my date with Demarco, who took me to the movies. I was looking at some skirts when I heard, "Hey, beautiful."

I smiled, thinking it was probably Demarco, and turned around, only for my smile to be replaced with immediate shock. It was Black. I scanned his face and stood as still as a statue. Black looked the same. He had on some slacks, a button-down shirt, and gator shoes.

"Aren't you gonna give daddy a hug, Cashmere?"

I stayed immobile and shook my head slowly, but he came over and hugged me anyway. "You get out and don't come see me, Cashmere? After—"

"I have a new life now. I'm not hooking no more, Black." *And if you loved me like you said you did, why is it that I don't recall ever getting a letter, a card—not shit—from you?*

"I missed you."

I looked away.

"I thought you would come home."

"I told you. I don't hook anymore, Black."

He chuckled and reached for one of my hands, but I drew back like he was poison.

His smile dropped, and he narrowed his eyes at my coldness. "Well, you know once you get a pimp, you married to the game, right? Ain't no such thing as retiring . . . unless you dead."

That shit made me shiver inwardly. What was he trying to say?

Then some young chick yelled, "Daddy, I'm ready," and gave me an evil-ass look. She had the same look I used to have—young and impressionable.

Bitch, you don't want it with me was the expression on my face. Then the look instantly faded when I realized I wasn't that same temperamental girl who fought her way out of stuff, so I let it slide.

I took the diversion to duck out of the store. Once I did, I ran down the other side of the street, giving myself distance from Black, his ho, and that store. But I knew I was in for some shit now. Like he said, once you a get a pimp, you married to the game.

Instead of a movie, Demarco took me to this nice restaurant. He was spoiling me to the point that I never ate at home anymore. Afterwards he took me to the park, and we walked and fed bread to those greedy-ass ducks, something I had mentioned to him that me and Daddy used to do together when I was a kid. I guess he really did listen to me.

"Here you go again."

"What?" I asked as we walked hand in hand through the park.

"It's like one minute we havin' fun. Then you go and get depressed again." He tapped me on my head. "Why won't you let me in here?"

I shook my head. "I'm cool, Demarco. I just miss my parents." I smoothed the long sleeves on my dress, hoping he didn't catch sight of them scars when the wind blew, 'cause some hadn't faded.

He nodded like he understood. "I just wish you would open up to me more." Then he lightened the conversation. "Are you bipolar?"

I shoved him. "No, fool!"

When he tried to grab me, I playfully pushed him away until he gripped my waist and kissed me quickly. Then he broke the kiss. "Seriously, though, I shared my past with you. You can do the same. I'm only asking 'cause it seems like you have some unresolved issues, baby."

And you'd drop me like a bad-ass habit once I do. I shook my head. "I'm not ready."

To ward off any more questions, I kissed him, not the regular peck, but a tongue-action-filled kiss. His eyes grew wide, and he returned the kiss and slipped closer to me.

Usually I slapped his hands away and said, "Back up, fool," but this time I didn't. I had been pushing him off for some months, so why not let him get a kiss? I slipped him the tongue and said, "Let's go to your crib."

When I got to his lavish-ass house, and after all that damn kissing and rubbing, I freaked the fuck out and couldn't do it, so I told him no. He didn't trip either. Just laid with me and stroked my hair while I cried and went to sleep. But I did hear him mumble, "Why won't this girl trust me enough to let me in?"

I didn't have an answer for him, nor did I have an answer for the question in my head that stopped him from making love to me. That question was: Could I do the shit without feeling dirty?

The next morning, I was in a rush. I shook Demarco awake and reached for my clothes, but he pulled me back down next to him.

"Boy, move," I said in an irritated voice. "I have to go home and change so I can get to school. On time."

"Quit school."

"And do what?"

"Stay here with me."

I looked at him like he was crazy.

"I'm serious. Cashmere, you don't ever have to go. You can stay here, and I'll take care of you. I almost feel like the shit is my duty. To protect you. Make sure no one else does anything to hurt you."

"And what makes you think someone has done something to hurt me?"

"I know someone has. And if I were your man, no one else will ever get the chance to. All you have to do is just be, Cashmere. Believe me when I say I'll take care of the rest. I just want you here with me. I wanna keep you safe. Seems like someone ain't done that for you in a long time."

I blushed at that and damn near shed tears. It was sweet to hear him say that.

And for the first time, I looked down and noticed that the sleeves on one arm of my dress was pushed up to my elbows and his fingertips were running back and forth across my scars as he talked to me.

I waved at Demarco before he drove away. It was still early, so I unlocked my door, stepped inside, set my purse down, and stepped back out to go get my mail. As soon as my feet touched my welcome rug, a bat swung forward and knocked me upside my head. I flew back into the door and gasped at the pain I felt in my head.

Before I could see my attacker, they swung it again at my back. I crouched over then felt pressure in my chest as it connected with it also. I was too weak to move and hoped they were done with their assault. They swung again and hit me on the back side of my head.

I screamed and slumped over. I moved my head an inch to see the person walk away. I got a glimpse of the gator shoes and the back of their profile. It was Black.

I moaned and crawled back into my door. I tried to stand but collapsed on the floor. Then I felt myself slip slowly into unconsciousness. The last thing I remember was all the pain.

The phone was ringing. That's what got me. I touched my swollen head and felt dried blood in my hair. I dragged myself up to my feet and grabbed the phone. I winced at the pain in my chest and all over my body. "Hello?" I clutched the arm of my couch when I felt my legs tremble like they were gonna give out underneath me. My head continued to throb, so I winced again.

It was Bev. "Cashmere, where you been, baby girl? You know we do our shopping for supplies every Monday."

"I—"

"It's not like you to call off. You okay?"

"Yeah."

"Good. Then get your behind up here now. Someone is here to see you. And they said they not leaving the shop until they do."

The visitor was probably my aunt, but nevertheless, I was happy to see her. Maybe she wanted to apologize for what she had done. It was cool. Maybe I could confide in her about what just happened with Black. And she could advise me on what to do.

I also needed to do something about the throbbing in my head. A little more blood was leaking out of it.

"I'll be there, Bev."

I went into the kitchen, dropped two Tylenol down my throat and chased them down with water. Then I held a cold cloth on my head to stop the blood.

I walked into the salon out of breath. I'd paused a couple times during the walk 'cause I was still in a lot of pain. Once I walked further in the salon, nothing could prepare me for who I saw sitting back and staring at me. It was Mama!

I grabbed a hold of one of the salon chairs to steady my balance.

She smiled and stood her arms outstretched. "Hi, baby."

Baby? I stepped away from her and crossed my arms under my chest that was still sore.

Bev was standing there too, but in all of this I didn't notice her. She winked at me and grabbed her purse. "I'll leave you ladies alone. Cash, I gotta get those supplies. I'll see you later, baby."

My eyes jumped back to Mama.

Mama wrung her hands together. She looked the fucking same, maybe even better—no bags under her eyes, no war marks or scars like the ones I had on my wrist and hands.

"You turned out so pretty, Cash."

Anger was pouring from me. I'm surprised I didn't sprout horns. I winced again at the pain I was feeling. I tried to keep my face clear of any emotion, other than anger.

"Would you believe, baby girl, that I had a hard-as-hell time trying to find you? I went to the last place I ever expected to go. Your aunt's." Mama clutched her chest and burst out laughing. "That damn woman is still bitter."

I didn't laugh. In fact, I didn't smile either.

"I see Mama got a lot of making up to do."

Her hands were now shaking, and her eyes watered. Come to think of it, her whole body was much like mine.

"Your aunt told me you worked here. She also told me about the other"—she cleared her throat, and a hand went to her chest again—"I went back to school, Cash. Decided to take up a trade. I do fingerprinting and background checks on criminals. Would you believe Mama works for the police department? And look"—she wiggled her left hand in front of me—"I'm engaged to a commissioner there."

Still I didn't respond.

"Listen, I know you pissed at me. You probably hate me." She stepped closer again and put her hand underneath my chin. "But, baby. I love you *sooo* much. And I'm sorry for what I did. If I hadn't—if I hadn't . . ."

My eyes teared up again, and some tears slid right into the palm of her hand. I snatched my face away. I was breathing hard as well and my cheeks were popped out.

She started sobbing, and her shoulders shook. She tried to touch me again.

I snatched her hands off of me.

She yelled out and continued crying.

"I'm so sorry, Cashmere. About your Daddy and your sister." Then she yanked open her purse. She pulled out a pen and a small notepad. "Here is my number and address. She laid the pad on a workstation and wrote something down, tore the piece off, and reached her hand out to place the paper in mine.

I didn't grab it, so the paper floated to the floor.

I kept my hateful glare as she bent over to retrieve it and attempted to hand it back to me once again. I eyed her up and down, her expensive shoes, pants and top, her flawless makeup, nails, and hair. The old Mama before the accident. The one daddy couldn't get enough of. Smelling good too.

When she saw I wouldn't reach for it, she laid the paper on the counter and reached out to stroke my cheek. "I love you, baby."

I pushed her hand away yet again.

She nodded slowly. "If you need anything or want to talk, call me anytime, baby. I'm in a position where I can help you with pretty much anything, money, a place to stay, the law, anything."

She walked slowly out the salon. When she got to the exit, she paused and looked back at me. "I love you," she whispered.

And for a moment I was gonna let her walk away. Then I thought to myself, *Naw, fuck that!* "You love me, Mama?"

She turned to face me. "Yes, baby."

"You love me?"

"Yes, with all—"

"Hold the fuck up! You love me?"

Mama started sobbing.

"Did you love Daddy?"

"Yes."

"When you left him to take care of himself so you can fuck another nigga in his house? Or did you love me when you left me and Desiree to take care of ourselves, huh? Auntie hate us 'cause of you! So we had to sell fuckin' crack!"

Her face crumbled.

"And strip to take care of ourselves. And her husband wanted to fuck me. He tried to rape me. But Desiree fucked him because she just like you!"

Her shoulders shook.

"Then we got thrown out. The one person that I loved, Desiree, fucked 'cause she just like you! Then she sold both our souls to the devil. A pimp! I was a ho, Mama, 'cause of you. And 'cause Desiree was just like you, she cut the plug on Daddy. And, well, you know the rest. I went to jail for murdering—"

"But, baby, I read the reports. It was an accident."

"Shut the fuck up!"

She nodded as if she was waiting for this moment, like she expected it.

"Now you wanna come back in my life? After all the shit you did to us?" My lips trembled like hers. "Now it's only me. And you wanna come in here flashing a ring, talking about how good you got it. You the reason for all of this, you know that, right?"

She nodded over and over, tears after tears pouring out of her eyes until they were red.

I walked closer to her. "Do you have any idea how much I have suffered in my life?"

She was silent.

I stalked up to her. "Here's how much I have suffered." I pulled the sleeves up on my shirt so she could see the scars crisscrossed up and down my arms and hands.

Her sobbing turned to bawling. She tried to hug me.

I pulled away.

"Get out, Mama!"

"Baby, please."

"Get your ass out!"

She pleaded with her eyes and she continued to call out my name as she exited the salon.

Chapter 32

I didn't bother going to the police for what Black had done to me, and I stood Demarco up for his dinner date by not answering the phone when he called. And after that day, I continued to ignore his calls. He was the best thing that had happened to me, and I didn't want him caught up in no shit on my damn account.

I also told Bev that I had the stomach flu and that I needed some days off at the shop. Those were the magic words.

"Yeah, baby, take a whole week," she advised. "It's no sense in getting all of us sick."

After I came back from the market carrying a bag of groceries, I found Demarco sitting on my steps. I gave him a mean look and tried to walk past him, which was kind of hard, him being so tall and all.

He stood up quickly. "I been calling you."

No reply from me.

"Cashmere."

"Move!"

"Cashmere—"

"Since when did I give you permission to pop up at my crib?" I sat my groceries down. "You seem to forget that I don't belong to you. You ain't my damn man, Demarco."

His jaw twitched as he stared down at me. "I know I'm not your man, but I was worried about you. You been missing from the shop too."

"Bev knows where I am. She the only one who needs to know, not you!"

Why was I being to mean to him? Oh yeah, to push him away, so he wouldn't get hurt. But it was so hard to do. 'Cause I felt like I loved him.

"You need to stop keeping tabs on me."

I went up the steps and unlocked the door, and he followed after me into my house.

"Damn! What?" I turned to face him.

He just stared at me.

"I'll tell you what, Demarco—if I throw some pussy your way, will you leave me the fuck alone? 'Cause that's probably all you want any damn way, right? It's pretty much what all you dirty muthafuckas want." I started throwing my clothes off until I stood in front of him in my underwear and bra, like I was in the old days with my tricks.

But Demarco was nothing like any of my tricks. He was special to me. So special, I was willing to eject him from my life to make sure he never got hurt.

He went from looking surprised to being disgusted as hell with me. That's what his face said. Without another word, he turned his back on me and started walking toward the door.

"Demarco!"

He had his hands on the door handle. I grabbed him from behind and tugged at his arms, so he had no choice but to turn around and face me.

"Here I am falling for you, and you think that's all I want?"

"Falling?"

"If I can't have all of you, I don't want any of you." He started using his hands to wipe the tears off my face. "What's going on in here, Cashmere? Baby, why won't you tell me?"

I wished I could, but I was too ashamed, so instead I kissed him.

That kiss turned into another and another, until we were fully lip-locking, using our tongues to explore the insides of each other's mouth. He had his fingers in my hair, and I had my fingers in his.

Then he lifted me, so my legs were around his waist, and carried me to my bed, where he laid me flat on my back. He placed kisses all over my body. Even all those scars all over my hands and arms. I closed my eyes and moaned softly as his mouth covered one of my nipples, then the other, then both at the same time. He slid two fingers into my pussy, making me squirm.

My head pushed into my pillow because of all the sensations I was feeling, Demarco grabbed up one of my thighs and placed kisses all over it before dipping between both of them to taste my pussy. I moaned louder when I felt his tongue there, swirling then sliding into me and pulling out, taking my juices with him.

My legs started to shake, and cum leaked out, which he also licked up before rolling over and carrying me to my chair. He sat down on it and lifted me onto his lap so that I was riding him.

I did it slowly, sliding down the length of his dick then pulling myself up, but once he started playing with my titties again, I increased the tempo, riding him faster and faster with each second that went by. His hands slid up and down my waist and he pulled my face down for a kiss. Then he kissed all over me again until I started moaning loudly and bucking on him faster and faster. I felt myself cumming just as he exploded into me.

Once I did cum, I collapsed on his chest. He laughed and held me. So now I knew what making love felt like. And I didn't feel dirty with Demarco, like I was a ho.

But that little sweetness I felt vanished quickly when I realized that I had done exactly what I said I wouldn't do. Fuck with him again. 'Cause I didn't want him in no shit, and now he just might be.

Things always had a way of going from really bad, to good, to really, really bad again. Case in point, somebody had vandalized the salon. I stepped around all the glass on the outside, the spray paint on the walls. I walked in a little further into the lobby area. Shit was fucked-up in there too—pictures broke, chairs thrown all over the place, the register thrown in the wall, and the letters BM, Black's initials, the same initials Desiree had got tattooed on her neck spray painted all over the walls, over and over.

I could hear Bev in her office on the phone yelling, probably calling the police. None of the other ladies were there, 'cause it was early.

"Man, I can't believe this shit!" Demarco stalked back into the room and whipped around in a blind circle, throwing his fist in the air.

He didn't see me though, 'cause I'd backed into a corner. Then the moment he turned his back to access another area of the damage, I ran out of the salon and down the street.

The shit was my fault, plain and simple. I was breathing loudly and crying at the same time. I had got the salon caught up in some shit. If I had just stuck to the plan—stop answering Demarco's calls and break it off with him for good—this shit would have never went down. But I felt like I loved him, wanted to be loved back, wanted to be looked at the way he looked at me, wanted my ugly scars to be kissed. He gave me all that and I fucked up.

"Life's gonna be hard as hell on you, baby girl."

Instead of going home. I turned the opposite corner. I walked slowly and cried. No matter what, I couldn't escape my damn past. I cried because I really loved Demarco, and I couldn't be with him. It was just a matter of time before he found out what I used to be.

I cried because I was about to break the promise I'd made to myself and Ms. Hope. I was about to get high. I was about to cop some ecstasy. Inside I was crumbling.

Somebody was yelling, "I got that techno! Techno! That techno!"

The further I walked, the louder his voice got.

"That techno, yo." He turned around and faced me. "What you need, little mama? I got white girl too."

"Give me one," I muttered, gesturing toward what he was shuffling between his fingers. I didn't want cocaine.

"Ten."

I dug into my purse for the money he requested for the ecs, my heart pumping. My wallet was
empty, so I dug deeper at the bottom and at first
only felt change. My fingers scrambled around
until I felt something crumpled up. I yanked it,
and it was a twenty. But a piece of torn paper
covered it. I removed the paper and scanned it.
It was Mama's number. I held it in my hand and
took a deep breath.

"You got the money, boo?"

I stared down at the twenty in my hand then at
the torn piece of paper. I threw the money back
in my purse and said, "Never mind." Then I ran
back the other way until I found a phone booth.

I dug some change out and dialed the number
on the paper. I was shaking and couldn't believe
I was doing this shit. Each time the phone rang,
I took another quick breath. I bit my lip so hard,
I drew blood. Then I couldn't stop fidgeting as it
rang.

Just when I thought she was going to say
hello, I heard, "Hi, you've reached Pearla. Leave
a message, and I'll return it."

I paused, about to hang up the phone. Seconds
flew by before I said quickly, "This is Cashmere.
I'm ready to talk. You can reach me at 562-223-
3222. Or you can stop by. I-I stay at 2343 Bullis

Road, apartment 29." Then I hung up the phone before I changed my mind and erased the message.

I kept on walking. I didn't buy no damn drugs. I went home.

I went up the steps to my apartment and unlocked the door, walked in, and threw my purse down on the table. I switched on the lights in my living room, which was dark as hell, and nearly jumped out of my skin when I saw Black sitting on my living room couch. I shivered and damn near peed in my pants. I couldn't bring myself to move.

He stared at me coolly. "I had enough of this bullshit, Cashmere. When you coming home?"

"I ain't coming back!"

I spun around and made a dash for the door, but Black was on me in seconds. He slapped the fuck out of me, making heat rush to my face and drawing blood from my lip. He pulled on my hair until some strands escaped my scalp. Then he bent my hands behind me so far, I thought my limbs were going to break.

"I'm not handling you with kid gloves no more, Cashmere. You want me to do bad shit to you, huh? Why I can't be nice like I used to be? You force me to do bad stuff. Now I'm gonna have to take out this new dude you been fucking and running around town with, huh?"

I pleaded with my eyes. "No, Black, don't."

I tried to get away again, running for the door, when he loosened his hold, but he kicked me down so I fell on the floor. I banged my nose, and blood flowed from it.

I screamed when he grabbed me by my neck and lifted me to my feet.

Black placed one hand over my face and muffled me. He took the edge of his shirt and wiped away the blood on my face, and as he did, he said, "There's no escaping the game, baby. You married to it. And the only way you leaving it is when your heart stops beating. And, I promise, if you don't leave with me tonight, I will make that happen for you."

When he removed his hand from my face I said, "No, Black. Please . . ."

He started kissing me on my face then telling me to shush. I tried to pull away, but he had a tight grip on me.

That's when Demarco walked in the room.

I tried to pull away, but Black tightened his hold on me and kissed me again, sliding his tongue in my mouth in front of Demarco.

I gagged.

Demarco's jaw twitched, and his eyes narrowed. Maybe he didn't know what to make of this shit.

Black pulled away. "What's up, man? You the one dabbling in my pussy, right?"

Demarco must have seen my swollen lip and bloody nose. He took a step toward Black with his fist balled.

Instantly Black pulled out his gat and pointed it at him. "Easy, dude. You don't want it with me," he said calmly. Then he walked over to the couch and sat back down.

"You lucky you got that gun, muthafucka!"

Black didn't respond to that comment and, instead, beckoned me over with his gun. I hesitated, but when I heard a clicking sound, I obeyed, feeling hot tears run down my face.

Black started running his free hand up and down my body, grabbing ass, titties, thighs, and rubbing the gun up and down my pussy. He was making my skin crawl.

Black smiled calmly, looked over at Demarco, who was rooted in the spot that he was in, his face filled with rage, and started unbuttoning my shirt. "You know Cashmere and me go way back, right?"

I closed my eyes as I felt the shirt being removed from my body. Then my bra.

"She was and still is my favorite girl."

"What the fuck you talking about?" Demarco demanded.

"Cashmere is one of my hoes, and boy, is she a good one."

I sobbed when he unbuttoned my jeans and pulled them from my body.

Demarco nodded his head, his face expressionless now.

Black angled the gun at Demarco and managed to pull down my panties at the same time.

"Black, please," I whispered.

Black split my legs open, so Demarco could get a view of my pussy. "She good at bouncing that ass on some dick." He slapped my bare ass, and the sound rang out in the room.

I closed my eyes in humiliation, afraid to look at Demarco.

Black ran his hands all along my titties, cupping them, rubbing his fingers across my nipples. "But since she been locked up, she probably a little rusty." He stuck a hand in my pussy. "But if she turns you on, man, you got me to thank for that shit. I went through a lot with the girls, meaning Desiree too, Cashmere's older sister, the one she killed."

Too scared to see the shocked look in Demarco's eyes, I didn't look at him.

"I thought all you needed was to know who your loyalties were to, Cashmere. I mean, you needed to understand who was number one in your life, and that was me. Which was why I told your sister to get rid of your pops."

My eyes widened, and I sobbed loudly.

"Sssshh, girl. Wasn't no need for him. And all he did was get in my way, in the way of all my love. 'Cause all your love, Cashmere, belongs to me. And I don't play second fiddle to no man. So with him out the picture I'd get all of that. And here you come along thinking you gonna take what is mine. Nigga, please."

Black pounded his finger into me sharply. "Lie down, ho. I'm gonna show you who's in control here—me, daddy—so you understand, don't no other nigga control this pussy but me."

"No, Black."

When the gun clicked again, I jumped.

"Have a seat, young blood," Black said to Demarco. "Watch the show."

Demarco had no choice but to sit on the couch across from us while I was on all fours naked. Black kneeled behind me and slid a few fingers in my pussy, before plunging his dick into me.

Blinded by my tears, I cried out loudly from the pain and humiliation as Demarco watched Black rape me.

Black moaned and pounded in and out of my pussy, slapping my ass at the same time, his fingers grabbing me everywhere. And he was sucking on my flesh roughly, until I was bruising. Still, he kept on pounding.

I kept on crying, and kept my head down, scared to face Demarco.

That's when Black busted a big-ass nut into my pussy, grumbling loudly and smacking my ass. "You still got some good pussy, Cash."

When Black took his eyes off both of us to pull up his pants, his gun dropped. Demarco rushed him and started throwing punches, catching him off guard. As he fell back into the table, Demarco used his boots to stomp him in the head.

I stood and tried to reach for the gun, which was a few feet away from me, near my shirt. I rushed forward and grabbed it. I'd never used one before, but I would have to now.

As Black rose and threw some blows back at Demarco, knocking him into the wall, I angled the gun, scared as hell that I might hit Demarco.

After Demarco fell to the floor, Black stood him up and knocked him upside his head. But then Demarco reached for Black's neck and started choking him.

"I'm gonna kill you, you dirty muthafucka, for what you did to her! Put your ass in a box where the fuck you belong!"

Black was trying to pull his hands away but couldn't, so he head-butted Demarco, making blood shoot out of his nose. Then he punched him in his mouth, but still Demarco wouldn't break his hold.

I angled the gun again, my heart pumping. *Lord, if I fire this shit, please don't let me hit Demarco.*

Black had managed to break free from Demarco's hold and punched him again and again until his face was bloody. Demarco was weak now and couldn't swing any more punches.

I screamed out when Black pounded his head into the wall and it looked like he weighed nothing. Blood gushed out of Demarco's head. Black threw him to the floor and kicked him in his head. "I told you not to fuck with me."

I angled again. I had a good shot, now that there was no way I would hit Demarco, because he was lying down. I could get Black, if I could just bring my numb fingers to pull the trigger. I sobbed and gripped one hand over the other as Black turned to me, but with my shaking hands and shivering body, I damn near dropped it.

Black left Demarco alone and stepped to me, blinking. "After all I done for you, you gonna pull a gun on me, Cashmere?"

Why the fuck couldn't I pull the damn trigger? I adjusted the gat in my hand and raised it higher, aiming it at his head.

Tears seeped in the corner of his eyes. "I love you, Cashmere. You know that, baby. You were the only girl to get under my skin. Drop the gun, baby."

I shook my head, blinded momentarily by my tears. I glanced over at Demarco quickly. His body was twitching. I knew he wasn't dead, but he couldn't help me right now.

"I just want us to be together like we used to be when you belonged to me and only me, when no trick came between our relationship." Tears ran down his face. "Baby, put the gun down."

I exhaled deeply and felt more tears drop. My hands were getting sore. I had to do this shit, to free myself from him. *Cashmere, this is the only way.*

Suddenly Black leaped toward me and slapped the shit out of me, and easily pulled the gun from my hands. Then he started whipping on me, punching me in my stomach. As I bent over in pain, he punched me in my face and pulled a plug of my hair out of my head. With the gun to my temple, he put me in a chokehold like Demarco had him earlier with his free hand.

"Make a decision, Cashmere. You leaving with me, or I'm taking you out—pick one."

I screamed, "Take me out, muthafucka, 'cause I hate you, and I rather die than be with a piece of gutter trash like you!"

Black tightened his hold on me, cutting off my air supply. My eyes watered, snot started shooting out my nose, and my body was getting weak as hell. I knew he was gonna take me out in that moment. Then he quickly released my neck and drew back. He shoved me on the floor.

As I lay on the floor coughing, he stood over me and looked down at me, cocking his gun and aiming it at me.

I closed my eyes and waited for the hollow tips to pierce my flesh. But before he could fire, the door burst open.

"Police! Drop your weapons!"

I opened my eyes to see a gang of cops running through the door, Mama leading the pack, their guns drawn.

Chapter 33

A month later

"You okay to do this, Cash?" I stared at Mama and gave a nod before entering the courtroom. Entering courtrooms always made me nervous, but not today.

Demarco testified to Black's assault on him and his raping me. Mama was also able to give the district attorney evidence that Black was the one behind vandalizing Demarco's salon.

Black was facing some serious time because that gun had some bodies on it, one of them a 20 year-old former prostitute that had been missing for the past year. It was later discovered that he'd killed her after she tried to run away from him.

I shivered when I found out that tad of info, since I could've just as easily been another body on that gun, had it not been for Mama. I remember closing my eyes and breathing a sigh of relief when they closed the case. One thing I'll never forget was how cold his eyes were while we were in the courtroom. Man, if looks could kill.

Finally after days and days of cameras following us and shit, the judge sentenced Black to forty years to life without the possibility of parole. Now neither, Mama, Demarco, or me would be caught up in any more drama behind Black.

Now that chapter of my life was closed, but I still had some left open. The first was Mama.

Yeah, she had saved me and Demarco. She told me that she'd jotted my address down and was on her way over, and that when she got to the house and heard the scuffling and yelling, she quietly called the cops.

"My honey told me to always carry my gun 'cause you never know what will happen. And, Cashmere, I'm so happy you called me. If you hadn't"—Mama started sobbing, cupping my face in her hands.

I hoped she didn't think we were chummy now.

Before stepping in the courtroom, she'd asked me, "Cashmere, when this is done and over, can we sit down and talk, baby? Really talk?"

I hesitated. I thought, *What would I gain if I continued to hate her?* There was no way my anger or hate could change what had already happened to us, to me, so I gave a slight smile and nodded. "Yeah, Mama, we can talk."

So after court, me and Mama sat outside on an empty bench.

Before she got any words out, she started crying. "I was weak, selfish, and dumb, Cashmere. Oh so dumb. Your daddy, you, and Desiree were the best thing that had ever happened to me, and here I was thinking about myself. Baby, if I could turn back time, I would have never left. I would have stayed and did the best I could, which is what you all deserved. But I ain't got no time machine, so all I can give you is now. Baby, love, time, anything I got, it's yours, Cashmere, if you can say you can forgive me. I just wanna right the wrong any way that I can."

Truthfully, I'd never stopped loving Mama. Instead of giving her that long speech I had in my head all these years of what I was gonna say if I ever saw her again before whipping her ass, I allowed her to take my hands in hers and didn't pull back when she hugged me. Now I'm not saying I was gonna be her best friend, but maybe we could try to rebuild something. After all, her and my aunt were the only real family I had left.

There was one other person I had to make it right with. Truth be told, I hadn't spoken to Demarco all too much since all the court proceedings, and I knew he didn't have much to say to me. But Ms. Hope always told me to make my amends, so that's what I did.

I strolled up to the shop to see him. He was outside, repainting the name of the salon—Studio Six Hair Salon—and was doing a good job at it too. His back was to me, so he didn't see me when I approached.

I asked in a quiet voice, "Did it cost a lot to fix the place back up?"

He paused with the brush for a second. "Insurance covered it." Then he went back to his letters. He had just finished the S in Six, and was now on i.

I felt a lump in my damn throat, but it wasn't gonna prevent me from doing this. So I tried to swallow it on down before I started crying. "I know you don't want me around, and that's cool, but I just wanted to, ah, say, I'm sorry for not being honest with you about my past, Demarco." I laced and unlaced my hands, nervously, and took a deep breath.

He turned around to face me. "Cashmere, do you know how much gossip I hear in this salon? Between Rona, Gee Gee, and Quida, they could start their own gossip column, with the shit I hear."

My eyes widened. *He knew? All this time?*

Demarco stepped closer to me and, to my surprise, pulled me in his arms. "I knew about your past, what you used to do, who you were before, but I didn't care, 'cause I loved you, and that stuff was just that, the past, Cashmere. It's not who you are now. You were a victim of fucked-up circumstances, and instead of you giving up like the people around you, you kept on going. I told you once, and I'll tell you again—I love you, Cashmere."

I sniffed and smiled through my tears. "Then why you ain't came to see me?"

He laughed. "I can't chase you forever. You know where I'm at."

He was right, but still I gave him attitude. "And you know where I'm at too," I lied, since I wasn't staying at my old apartment anymore.

Mama and her fiancé let me stay with them until this stuff blew over—the media was on me like I was a celebrity—and possibly longer, if I wanted.

"Yeah, I know all right. You stay a ways away from here."

My mom stayed in Lancaster, two hours from where I used to stay. "How you know that?"

"'Cause I follow you home from school to make sure you get home safe. I never stopped doing that and never will."

I smiled, but just as soon, my smile dropped, and I took a deep breath. I needed to to say it, confess it, even if he did know. For some dumb-ass reason, I needed confirmation. Don't ask me why. I just did. "Demarco, I used to be a prostitute."

"I know."

"I did drugs."

"I know."

"I've been to jail."

"I know."

"And by accident I killed my sister."

"You don't say."

"Do you still love me?"

"Yes, Cashmere. Always."

I don't think I've ever cried and laughed at the same time, but that's what I did at that moment. Then he lifted me off my feet and kissed me.

Epilogue

Yeah, I said I forgave Mama, but if she thought it was gonna be that easy, she was a damn fool. Now since all wounds were healed, she thought it was all good. Naw! I wanted some answers.

Me and Mama sat down on her couch. She bit her bottom lip. "Now we have managed to become cool, Cashmere, I'd hate for what I'm about to tell you to change the way things are with us."

I shook my head. "Mama, it won't."

We had both been going to therapy to salvage our sanity and relationship, meaning that we were both going crazy. Every time I thought I was cool with Mama, another memory was coming up of the scandalous shit she had done, and I'd find myelf being mad at her again. And she'd find herself crying again, and refusing to eat or leave her house. The therapist said that my mom wasn't being as open as she should be about everything, and that as soon as she opened up, we could put all this bad stuff to rest.

"Desiree wasn't Desmond's daughter, Cash-mere."

My eyes bulged. "But you named her after Daddy!"

"Listen before you judge me, baby. We had an uncle named Douglas. He would come around and give all of us candy and ribbons for our hair, say how pretty we are. Talked about the people made of the good stuff and those made of the bad. Asked us which one we were. I always said, 'I'm made of the good stuff.' And my sister would always find reasons to tell me that I wasn't. Even then your Aunt Ruby was envious of me. We were both beautiful ladies, none prettier than the other. But I had a way of being so animated, I guess, having this presence like you got. Baby, that caused them to want to be around me. I was popular in school, knew how to entertain, and your aunt hated me for this.

"Anyhow . . . our uncle came to visit us all through our childhood. And he liked to visit me in my bed while I was 'sleep, and he did some things to me that I still have a hard time for-getting about, Cash. Touching me and kissing me. Stuff that filled me with shame, baby, real shame. A shame I feel to this very day."

Mama's hands were shaking, and her lips trembled. "I use to go to church with Daddy just to pray that he never came back. And he didn't. He went off to the armed services for a long time, so I didn't have to deal with him sneaking in my room and touching me any damn more. But my sister always reminded me that he did what he did 'cause he knew I was made of the bad stuff and he never did it to her 'cause she was made of the good. And that the only reason that people liked me more than her was because other people knew—even God knew—and everyone pitied me. And I believed her. Those thoughts was still in here, Cash, always fucking with me, so I dealt with it by partying, getting drunk, and smoking weed with my girlfriends. But I never had the urge to have sex. The thought of being with a man sexually made me sick, after what my uncle had done to me all those years." She paused then shuddered.

"I continued that way for years into my teens. Then one night I snuck out to go to this party. Usually your aunt would wait for me at twelve and unlock the back door for me. My payment to her was the allowance our Daddy gave us.

"I waited in the backyard for the longest, and she never came out. Someone was in the back-yard." Mama pulled her lips in. "Our uncle had came back, to my surprise, and was smoking out there. He asked me if I had forgotten all the things he taught me. I said yes and tried to run, but I couldn't do much running in my heels, so he caught me easily and raped me out there. Cash, that bastard raped me on the ground in my parents' backyard." Mama shook her head, her eyes closed, as if she was still reliving the memory.

My eyes widened.

"But that ain't the worse. The worse was looking up in the window and seeing Ruby watching the whole thing while I begged her to help me. She didn't help me. She just watched the whole time with a smirk on her face. And shortly after the rape I found out I was pregnant."

I gasped.

"This made your aunt happy now 'cause I wasn't seen the way I used to be seen. I was now damaged, and she was the one going to get married to a decent man. Now even more she drilled in my head day and night that I was made of the bad, and I believed it. Believed I wasn't shit. Shortly after that incident we had new neighbors, and my sister was twenty and in nursing school now, and ready to get married. She was in love with our neighbor's son, Desmond."

I smiled at the mention of Daddy.

"But as much as she tried bringing him goodies, 'cause your auntie sure could cook, and bragging about going to nursing school, when he laid eyes on me, it was over for her. He went after me viciously, even though I had a baby growing in my stomach. He would take me to the movies, buy gifts for a baby that hadn't even arrived yet, even take me for my hospital visits. And once I hit eighteen he said he was going to take me to the movies, but instead he hit the freeway straight for Vegas and married me, Cash, baby and all. And I was huge as a house. And, Cash, he loved my baby like he himself created her.

"I knew I was young, but Mama had already passed away, and Daddy was getting old, so I thought I needed someone to take care of me 'cause I thought I was too weak to take care of myself, let alone an innocent child.

"When we came back from getting married and your aunt saw my ring, she went crazy. Said she hated me and I was nothing, and that he was a damn fool for marrying me, that I was weak and dumb and could never survive without a man, and that my kids would be cursed. That I was soiled goods because I was carrying another man's baby. And I believed her, Cash. I believed her. As good as your Daddy saw me, I never saw myself the same 'cause I thought I was flawed 'cause of all those years that man molested me then raped me.

"I thought I was weak, ugly, damaged. That's why I was so into buying things for myself to make me feel good, why I was so quick to give my panties to the first man who gave me a compliment, Cash. Why I always had to have a man even when your Daddy wasn't around. The only blessing out of what my uncle did was my precious baby girl, Desiree."

"Anyway she ran out the house, yelling, 'I might as well be a slut too, if it could get me a man like him. That bitch don't deserve him.' Word had it that she went to a bar, partied and was so drunk, she went home with some dude and ended up getting pregnant by him. She figured she wouldn't be lucky like me to land someone she loved with a baby in her stomach, so she gave up and married the fool she got pregnant by. Your uncle. But he made her miserable. He never doted on her the way your Daddy doted on me. He cheated on her, left her alone at night. Then food became her comfort. She has hated me and blamed me for her being miserable ever since, Cashmere."

"Why did she hate me so much, Mama?"

"Because, Cash, even though I told you Desiree was just like me, it wasn't the full truth. You are the most like me. You have something that sets you apart from other women, makes people gravitate toward you. And, most of all, you are the child of the man she was madly in love with. Whenever she looks at you, she sees him and the life she felt she should have had. 'Cause she never fell in love with your uncle and never fell out of love with your Daddy."

I sat back on the couch blown away. Desiree was only my half-sister. She wasn't Daddy's child. *Wow*! That explained so much. Why my aunt was the way she was and why my mom was the way that she was. *Damn*! I wondered if Desiree ever knew.

"But, Cash, there was one part of that saying about 'people with the good stuff versus the bad'—God's favorites are the ones who often have a hard time."

I nodded. Then I held Mama's hand, and she smiled at me. I guess her confession was like weight being lifted off her chest.

I thought about what Ms. Hope often said, *"So the past was now open and like a book. We had no choice but to now close it."* It made more sense now than ever. What else was we gonna do? It wasn't like we could change the stuff that happened. So once you realize you can't, you do the only thing you can. You move on. So, me and Mama, we did.

***

Now I know I wasn't graduating from Harvard, and I wasn't getting a doctorate degree, but when I stood on that stage and accepted my certificate for graduating from cosmetology school, shit, it felt just as good.

And there staring back at me was some amazing shit. The woman I thought I'd never see, or want to see again, Mama, was clapping and screaming out so loud, her voice was cracking. "That's my baby! That's my baby!"

I didn't tell her to shut up though. I just shook my head and laughed.

Then somebody else caught my eye. It was Demarco. After all of this, that man was still by my side. That has to stand for something. It did. My heart. He had it, and I was never going to take it back.

As I stood there and those cameras flashed, and Mama kept saying, "Smile, Cash," I reflected on my life. I had been through the fire, hell, and back, and here I was still standing with a smile on my face.

Man, what I'd give for Ms. Hope and Daddy to be here to see this. Then I remembered they were there, and they'd always be. My heart got enough room for them both.

Allow me to introduce myself. My name is Cashmere. I'm twenty years old. I was a prostitute, I used to do drugs, I've been raped, and through a freak accident, I killed my sister. All this shit I went through, were trials' and tribulations' tests. But I'm also a survivor, and I know I could handle anything that came my way. 'Cause I was made of the good stuff. One of God's favorites.

Coming soon . . .

The People

vs

Cashmere 2

Chapter 1

Cashmere

"Black Mitchell! Wake your motherfucking ass up!" My gun was aimed at his sleeping form.

As soon as I saw a speck of white in his eyes, as his lashes touched the bottom of his brows I wasted no time in pumping those bullets into that sorry motherfucker as his body jerked to and fro. In fact, I emptied the entire clip. I enjoyed seeing all the bullets pierce his flesh as smoke filled the air and blood started to seep from his body. But still, despite the fact that he was no longer breathing and his eyes were wide, I still loaded another clip and emptied it as well, ignoring the terrified screams of Dominique. I smiled at his dead body for a moment, then as my daughter continue screaming, I looked over at her tear soaked face.

I lowered the gun.

She stood to her feet.

"Dominique. No!"

Before I could grab her, she ran towards the bed and threw her body over Black's. She started bawling.

I rushed over to her and grabbed one of her arms. "Get off of him baby!" I started crying.

What had he done to my child?

"How could you, Mom?"

"I had to baby. I"

"You killed my father!"

Chapter 2

Seven months before.
New Years Eve Night. 2011

Cashmere

I covered my ears at the sound of our dresser mirror shattering from Demarco putting his fist through it. I wanted to go to him and help him as he looked down at his bleeding hand. But I knew he wouldn't want me touching him. So I just sat on the bed and cried tears as he wrapped a towel around his hand and looked at me hatefully. Seems like every day I was crying. No wonder I couldn't get pregnant. I was always super stressed at all the arguing between Demarco and I. And I really didn't know where we stood. But one thing I knew for sure and that was that he hated me. My baby hated me. And I loved him. I loved him like I did when I was eighteen. When I was going through all that mess with Black af-

ter I had gotten out of jail. Throughout it all he
had been there for me loving me uncondition-
ally. Even when he found out the truth about my
past . . . That I had been a prostitute, addicted
to drugs that went to juvenile hall for murdering my sister at the age of fifteen. None of that
mattered to him. He stayed by my side and never
left it.

After the trial Black was locked away and no
longer a threat. Demarco and I moved in together. We both bought a house in Inglewood,
the city where he opened up another hair salon.
I worked as a hair stylist there and cared for my
man. Things were perfect. Demarco also opened
a shop in Long Beach and one in Marino Valley.
So he was always busy and business was thriv-
ing. I had a huge rock on my hands and bitches
that worked at the salon were so, so jealous. At
least twice a day I would hear, "What's so special
about her?" And I would chuckle. I had calmed
down a lot and wasn't the hot head I used to be
that was always willing to fight at the drop of a
hat. I think it was Demarco I had to thank for
that. He was always so calm, so happy and smiling. He was my peace. Then a few months into
us living together, I found out I was pregnant.
Now while I was far too young to have a baby, I
was still excited. I gave birth to a little girl named

Dominique. My mother and her commissioner retired from Lancaster Police Department and bought a house down here in Carson to be closer to me and her granddaughter. Now my baby . . . she was absolutely perfect. She had my coloring, my eyes. That was my partner in crime there. Seemed like after I laid eyes on her, everything in my world made sense. It just did. And I was the most doting paranoid mother ever. Without a fact, no one was going to be able to let any type of harm come my baby's way. When I was twenty four and Demarco was twenty nine we got married in Vegas. The thing was, part of me knew he had drifted apart from me. And part of me also questioned whether or not we should have gotten married. And when I asked him he told me, "It's the right thing to do." But it wasn't. Life for us was not good. He drifted further and further away from me. Like he resented me. And what didn't make the situation better was the fact that I couldn't get pregnant again. And Demarco felt like I was doing this on purpose. That I deliberately didn't want to give him a baby.

I thought about how loving he used to be towards me. A tear couldn't drop without him wrapping his arm around me and kissing them away. Now he would see me sobbing and would say. "Good. I'm glad you're hurting, bitch!"

Things between us had changed around the time Dominique turned five. He became more angry and hateful towards me and more distant. But I continued to play the role, pretending that my marriage was good and we were happy. The chicks at the shop thought I was so lucky to have such a fine and successful man in my life. But if they only knew. . . . Despite how much I faked the funk, we were in a miserable marriage. Yet still, I loved Demarco and I was so desperate to save what we had. Because of the resentment he harbored, I sometimes didn't think it was possible.

His yelling snapped me out of my thoughts.

"Get it right, Cashmere! You don't run me. I go as I please. I have always been my own man until I let myself get pussy whipped by you. But those days are over. And truthfully I don't want to be around you, if you want to know the fucking truth, Cashmere! This shit is your fucking fault. Things between us will never be right. And you know why. If you had done one simple thing we wouldn't be like this."

"What was I supposed to do, Demarco?" I demanded.

"What did I ask you to do?" he raged!

When I didn't respond he got all up in my face. I was so hurt at how he was coming at me.

"Answer the fucking question, Cashmere!" He now had his hands gripped around my shoulders and he was shaking me.

I started crying and said, "Get your hands off me, motherfucker!"

"Man, I should slap the fuck out of you." He shoved me away. I lost my balance and fell on the floor.

I just laid on the floor crying. It had no effect on him. It never did anymore. That made me hurt more.

Suddenly, his phone started ringing. He stepped over me and grabbed it off of the dresser top.

"Hello?" he paused. "What's up, Dame?" He looked, over at me in disgust, shook his head and said, "Man, yeah, I can get out. Because this shit right here is for the birds. I got no time for it at all *anymore*." He paused, "Alright I'm heading out now. I'll meet you up there."

He grabbed his wallet, keys and shoved them along with his phone in his pants pocket.

"Where are you going?" I demanded. I got up from the floor.

"Bitch, your reign over me been gone a long time ago. Don't ever ask me what the fuck I do!"

He stepped past me like I was trash on the floor or dirty laundry that he didn't want his legs to touch.

Chapter 3

Dominique

Things between my parents were super weird. I tell you, I just don't get why my daddy hates my mommy so much. But more importantly, I don't get why he acts like he hates me. To tell the truth it seemed like it came from nowhere. When I brought it up to my mom she would tell me I was tripping. "Look at your baby pics and see the love in your father's eyes!" She would always shove a photo album in front of me. With pics of me as a baby with him and her in them. I don't know. . . . That's just one thing I never saw in his eyes . . . love. But love that was something my mother gave me in abundance. I knew my mother deeply loved me. She told me every day that I meant the world to her, although my dad didn't pay me any mind. I might as well had been invisible. Even when I got good grades it meant nothing to him. I could also play the cello so good that my mom would come in my room, lie on my bed and close her eyes and listen to me like she was at an actual concert. But my daddy never showed any interest. He wouldn't come to my concerts (so I stopped playing) at school or to any of my open houses, teacher conferences or when I graduated from elementary or junior high school. Funny thing was I was a real good student. My teachers always said I was a joy to have. I knew my mother felt the same. I just wish my dad did as well, nothing meant more to me than having my father's love. I needed it. I would always remember my mother talking about how much her daddy loved her and how much he treated her like such a princess. I wished my daddy loved me like her daddy loved her. I would do all kinds of stuff to win him over, like baking him cakes to washing his car. When he would nap I would take off his shoes, socks and massage his feet. He would always wake up, look at me, jerk away and snap, "Go play." Then finally, I gave up.

Despite my relationship with my father, our life was pretty decent. We lived in Inglewood, CA, in a nice and organized five bedroom two-story house. My mom did hair for a living and boy was she super good at it. I was amazed at all the hair styles my mom could do. My hair, which was long like my mother's, stayed nice. In fact, we looked a lot alike. I was dark like her with her set of gray eyes. Life was really simple. Our family was a triangle with me at the tip and and my mama and daddy at the base. I went to a private high school where I was pretty quiet. My mom said I was worse than a church mouse. I just wasn't a very social person. Sometimes other girls at school would pick on me or make fun of how quiet I was. I hated it and it made me even more closed off to people. I thought back to the last time a senior girl had shoved me down some stairs. I came home crying. The other two times she had put her hands on me, one time pulling my hair and the other time she smacked me I kept it from my mother. But this time I couldn't. The fall had me limping. My mother, furious, called my grandmother and the next thing I knew we all drove in my mother's Cadillac Escalade to the school. The whole way there my mother drove like a bat out of hell. On the way there my grandmother urged, "Now, Cashmere we are going to go in there and be ladies. No yelling cursing we are going to conduct ourselves with class."

Right.

When we got there, they cursed out the entire school office.

"Why the fuck are you letting little bitches at this school bully my fucking grandchild?" my grandmother demanded. I wondered how her husband would feel about the way she was acting. When the staff in the school office didn't respond. My mother spied the principal's office. "Come on." She pulled me with her and with my grandmother in tow, we walked directly into the principal's office. In a quick motion, my mother swiped all the items off his desk while my grandmother took a fighting stance waiting for the principal to react.

"Mrs. Pena."

"Shut the fuck up! Let me tell you something. My daughter don't bother anyone. So whoever the bitch is that put her hands on my daughter needs to get up in here now and there needs to be some type of corrective action. There are kids killing themselves because of bullies. So guess what principal. If my daughter slits her wrists because she getting picked on I'm going to come in this bitch and slit yours!" she threatened.

His eyes bulged. "I have spoken to—"

"Naw fuck that. Let's be clear you pasty face mother fucker. We're not paying your punk-ass seven hundred dollars a month in tuition for other girls to pick on my child. Come on, Dominique."

***

Needless to say the girl ended up being suspended and she never bothered me again.

When I got out of my shell and would visit my friend Jada's house, I saw how it was so different from my household. She actually had a close relationship with her dad that I wished to God I had with mine. In fact, I spent more time over there than I did at my own home. Jada had revealed to her father that my dad never really treated me with love. So I think that was why he was so nice to me.

I stood on their doorstep and before I could knock, Mrs. Douglas opened the door, prepared to step out but paused when she saw me.

"Hi, Mrs. Douglas."

She gave me a warm smile. Mrs. Douglas was the color of butterscotch. She was a very pretty woman in her forties with a petite frame and a bob that framed her face. My bestie, Jada, had the same haircut. But Jada looked more like her father.

"Hi, sweetness!" she said. I stepped back and lowered my balled left fist that was about to knock on the door, to let her pass. Before she did she planted a kiss on one of my cheeks. Whenever I met adults, teachers family members, and parents of my friends, they always tended to call me this. My mom as well always told me I was the sweetest kid in the world. I wondered if my daddy felt the same way. Probably not. It was crazy because I loved my mom one hundred percent, my mommy seemed to love me one hundred percent and it seemed my daddy loved me zero percent and hated me one hundred percent.

"Jada's inside. You going to have to wake her behind up because I'm sure she fell right back to sleep."

She walked past me down the steps. As she walked towards her Benz she turned back to me and said, "My hubby gave me some shopping money. I was surprised. That's a nice little treat this Saturday." She ended her sentence with a giggle and unlocked and opened her car door.

"I asked Jada if she wanted to go with us but she said she was too tired." She hopped in and closed the driver's door back.

"K," I said with a smile.

She rolled her window down and backed out of the driveway.

"See you later, honey."

I waved at her as she backed out of their driveway. She was such a nice woman and was always sweet to me. Made me feel a little guilty about the secret I was keeping from her and Jada.

I turned and opened the door to their house and stepped inside the living room. I called out my friend's name. "Jada."

When she didn't respond I walked towards her room.

I walked quickly and nervously.

Once I made it to her door, my hand reached out for the knob. But before I could grasp it I felt two hands cup both of my breasts and felt a kiss planted on the side of my neck. I closed my eyes as pleasure and shame filled me.

"She's sleep. Don't wake her until we done," a husky voice said in my ear.

I was silent but I didn't pull away from Jada's father.

"Why didn't you come to my room, baby?" he asked me.

He spun me around and kissed my lips while rubbing one of his hands between my legs. "Has someone?" He gripped between my legs aggressively.

I shook my head.

"Good."

He yanked one of my arms gently and tugged me towards his bedroom.

I protested. "Mr. Douglas I told you. I don't want to do this with you anymore. I feel bad about what I'm doing to your wife. It's wrong."

Still he was stronger and as a result managed to pull me into their bedroom, closed and locked the door. Then I was at his mercy as my body betrayed me. But still I continued to tell him no as he peeled away my clothes.

As he did he said, "Mrs. Douglas don't give a fuck about what I do, pretty baby. She been checked out of this marriage. Now. You know I love you." When he had me naked, he sat down on their bed and sat me on top of his lap.

"This is wrong Mr. Douglas. Please stop making me."

"Be quiet, baby," he told me gently. I gave in again. Despite the promises to make the last time the last time.

If your daddy won't be a real father to you, you know I will," he always said to me.

"You make love to me better than my wife ever could."

So I gave in all the way like I always did knowing I would feel guilty later.